ABOUT THE AUTHOR

Maggie Allder was born and brought up in Gamlingay in
Cambridgeshire, the second daughter of a village police
officer. She studied at King Alfred's College, Winchester
(now the University of Winchester) and later at Reading
university, and taught for 36 years in a comprehensive school.
After exploring and appreciating more orthodox forms of
Christianity, Maggie became a Quaker, and is happy and
settled in the Quaker community in Winchester which
inspired the unnamed community in her first novel, *Courting
Rendition*, and upon which this novel is loosely based.
Maggie volunteers for a not-for-profit organisation, Human
Writes, which aims to provide friendship to prisoners on
death row in the USA.

Living with the Leopard is the second book of a planned trilogy.

LIVING
WITH THE
LEOPARD

MAGGIE ALLDER

Matador
9 Priory Business Park,
Wistow Road, Kibworth Beauchamp,
Leicestershire. LE8 0RX
Tel: 0116 279 2299
Email: books@troubador.co.uk
Web: www.troubador.co.uk/matador
Twitter: @matadorbooks

ISBN 978 1785893 582

British Library Cataloguing in Publication Data.
A catalogue record for this book is available from the British Library.

Printed and bound in the UK by TJ International, Padstow, Cornwall
Typeset in 12pt Bembo by Troubador Publishing Ltd, Leicester, UK

Matador is an imprint of Troubador Publishing Ltd

To Richard who is the brother I never had, to my dear friend and travelling companion Jack, and to all those family members and friends who have given me so much support as I have learnt to live with my own particular leopard.

CHAPTER 1

The year we were married was the year they banned the wearing of white poppies, and carrying a bouquet of white tissue paper poppies, made by young friends from our community as my wedding flowers, was our first act of defiance as a married couple. It was also a little unusual. In our community, which prizes simplicity, it is not normal practice for the bride to carry flowers at all, nor do we dress in white. Even the most serious and elderly of our community turned a blind eye to my flowers, though. White poppies have been important to us for well over a century and we were smarting about this new ban, as about many other regulations.

Tom and I had met in the community. I was brought up by parents who took me to Meetings every Sunday, and to national gatherings every year. My childhood was rich in sleepovers, in night walks to study the stars, in older friends who smiled benignly at my first clumsy attempts at articulating my growing awareness of a Light within and who called me formally 'Charity' instead of the friendly 'Carrie' my parents and peers used. It was a childhood of shared lunches sitting in the Meeting House garden while my parents discussed politics and social issues with the parents of my friends, and we children discussed programmes we had seen on our DeVs, which is what we all called any Wi-Fi devices, and sometimes problems with school. Education was already a bit of a challenge for children from our community by then. We learnt to keep our mouths shut when teachers extolled the virtues of the New Alliance or when members of the ATTF, the Anti-Terrorism Task Force, came in to talk to us about radicalisation. Tom's upbringing was very different, far more conventional even to the extent of going to Summer Camp in Maryland two summers in a row. He started coming to Meeting when he was at university, and when he was received into membership his father especially was horrified. They have never really accepted me.

With the help of my parents and various other people from our community we bought a house at the bottom of town. It was old, in a Victorian terrace backing onto the river, and in need of much repair. Mortgages were pretty much impossible to get at that time without a reference from someone in authority, and there was not a chance of us obtaining such a thing. It was, of course, part of the programme to prevent 'undesirable aliens' from 'colonising' England, but people like us got caught up in it. In response, our community started offering interest-free loans to allow its young people to buy their own homes. Of course, homelessness was a huge problem by then. It still is.

Tom was working in a place in the centre of town, a shop that provided photocopying facilities, but which also printed local magazines and all sorts of documents. His parents thought the job was beneath him and no doubt if he had not belonged to our community he might have done better, but he liked it there: he could walk to his work from our house and his work colleagues were fun. I had trained to teach but as I would not take the Oath Against Extremism I could not be allowed alone in a classroom with vulnerable children. Instead I was a teacher's assistant and that suited me too. It was undoubtedly less stressful than taking full responsibility for thirty or more little individuals, and for the first two years of work I was assigned to the same teacher whom I respected enormously and worked with comfortably. Of course, I knew he was obliged to report on me regularly and I was extremely careful in what I said to the children or in the staff room. Coming up through the school system had taught me to be quiet while discussions took place. People thought my silence was a reflection of the way we worship, which is usually without speaking, but of course it wasn't. You should have heard us younger members of the community discussing things when we were sure we were safe!

The house needed a lot of work, and we were doing improvements piecemeal, as time, money and skills allowed. We extended into the roof early on and the bedroom and bathroom up there were clean and fresh even when the rest of the building seemed like an absolute tip. We planned to get the bulk of the work done before we started a family although Tom said, and my parents agreed, that with a house the age of ours you have never really finished.

Our community does not treat marriage as a rite of passage because we try to avoid anything that tends towards differing status. Each life is to be lived as we are guided to live it, and there is no virtue in being married or single, young or old, educated or not. Even so, when Tom and I married I did feel as if there was a slight change of attitude among those who were at that time in leadership among us. There are no rules about what the Jews call 'marrying out', but I suppose that two people from the community married to each other meant that there would be less stress, fewer difficult choices about allegiances to be made. For example, they would perhaps not have asked Tom if he would like to be involved on the night soup runs if his young wife had not also been a member of the community, especially after all that trouble a year or two earlier. It would have been asking a lot.

As it was, Derek approached Tom only about a month after our marriage. We had gone, as was usual for us, to the earlier Meeting. It was a bright spring morning with buds just appearing on trees and bushes, and crocuses planted in circles glowing their gold, white and purple colours on public land around the city. The Meeting had been quiet, with one simple ministry towards the end. I have no memory of who ministered or of what was said, but I remember the familiar peace that sometimes engulfs such Meetings, a sort of calm joy. Afterwards we went back to the Meeting House for coffee, past the crowd of homeless people who always gather on Sundays for the toasted sandwiches and coffee which the warden and her helpers prepare.

Derek started the conversation. I was never really sure if I liked him, but he worked hard for the Meeting and indeed, he had been one of the ones who had started the soup runs when we heard that the Feeding Station had been closed down.

"There seem to be more people here every week," he commented, as we walked past a row of scruffy-looking men standing around eating their sandwiches.

"Yes…" Tom sighed. "I see kids in doorways in the High Street when I walk to work sometimes, but it isn't really safe for them. I heard that the shopkeepers douse them with water if they find them there, and the police arrest them for vagrancy."

Derek was frowning. "They say the homeless are not being responsible, that they have made bad choices, but I don't know – I mean, what choices do they ever have? If they try to help themselves it always ends up with trouble."

This is a sore point in our community. Derek was probably thinking, as I was, of the events of a few years previously. Homeless people had started to camp on one of the city parks and members of our community had tried to help them. I never knew the whole story – it was not discussed in front of us and in those days I went to the Young People's Meeting for Business rather than the adult group – but I picked up bits and pieces of what happened. I know they started a school and I think it was very radical, so that quite quickly the ATTF got involved and a group of people was arrested and eventually left the area. There were rumours and newspaper reports at the time of deportations and maybe worse, but it is impossible to know the truth about such things. Nor am I quite sure the group which was involved was all from our community. We have never been averse to working with other like-minded organisations, and I did hear that some of those who were arrested came from a completely different religious group. My parents say they fear the worst; they knew several people who were either arrested or who vanished at that time, and they do not think they were dangerous radicals or terrorists.

Anyhow, since then we have had to be even more careful. We have never stopped serving food and coffee to homeless people from the doors of the large Meeting Room across the road from the Meeting House on Sundays, and several churches within the city do the same. For a while, though, that was all we did. Then Derek, who manages one of those cheap stores that sells left-over food and food that has reached its sell by date from the shop's loading bays at the end of the day, reminded the Meeting of the ever-increasing number of people living rough. It is a hidden problem. The authorities bulldoze anything which starts to look like a permanent settlement, on hygiene grounds, so people sleep under bridges and, in the summer, in the new drainage pipes which the council installed to deal with the ever-increasing risk of flood in the middle of the city. Derek didn't make any suggestions about what we might do, he simply brought the matter to the notice of the Meeting, and someone suggested we should start a soup run. Perhaps under the circumstances it is not surprising that they asked Derek to organise the whole thing.

Tom liked Derek better than I did. He warmed at once to Derek's comments that morning as we walked across the road for coffee, and said what members of our community

5

often say when this topic comes up: "It's shameful that in a wealthy country like ours there are people who are homeless and hungry! I'm glad we're doing at least something to help."

"I thought you might feel like that," said Derek. By then we had crossed the road and were about to enter the old Meeting House, but Derek drew us both aside, so that we were standing a little away from the paved path and from other people coming and going. "The thing is, we need more people to help with the soup run, and we wondered whether you," he was looking at Tom, "might be interested?"

Tom looked at me. I had mixed feelings. I really wanted to be involved, if only it were organised by someone else. Derek made me feel uncomfortable. I felt there was a sort of unwholesomeness about him, but if I tried to explain that to Tom I found I could never describe what I meant. There was something about that greasy-looking hair and that green jacket that gave the impression of unsavouriness, but as Tom pointed out, we are the last people on earth who should judge by appearances – we, who know that the true worth of every person lies within.

"I'm interested…" I said hesitantly.

"Give us a week or so," said Tom, "to hold the matter in the Light and to try to find the right way forward."

"You're on!" said Derek, slapping Tom on the back and grinning at me. "We'll talk next week."

★ ★ ★

I talked to Mum and Dad about it. They live further south, near the coast, and go to a different Meeting, but I visit them or they visit us on alternate weeks. Of course there's no way we would talk about anything so sensitive over a DeV.

Mum looked pleased. "I hoped you and Tom would start to get more involved," she said. "When we were your age we

6

were already demonstrating against the New Alliance and the situation in the Caribbean. You feel so much more involved and, well, fulfilled if you're doing more than attending Sunday meetings."

Dad looked more serious. "But you must be prepared to pay the price," he reminded me. "And it can be quite a price. How would you feel if Tom were to be imprisoned? Or even if you were?"

I was a bit blasé. "Well, you and Mum coped," I said. "Isn't it better than doing nothing?"

Dad looked serious. "We did," he agreed. "We still do. But there were times when we didn't know what was going to happen next. There still are. Opposing authority is a little like sharing your life with a wild animal. You never know when it will pounce!"

He wanted me to count the cost and, of course, he was right, but I didn't understand then that nobody can count the cost without knowing what it might be – and I had no concept of the price Tom and I might have to pay for this particular involvement.

Tom talked to Ephraim. Obviously he couldn't talk to his parents, who were still keeping us both at arm's length at that time. Ephraim was a relatively new member of our community, probably in his mid-sixties, with fair hair going elegantly grey, and a comfortable, upright posture so that he looked like a man in authority, even when he was just standing drinking coffee and talking to someone, or sitting silently in Meeting. I had never heard Ephraim minister and I knew very little about him. We are advised to *know each other in the things that are eternal*. I don't know how our community interpreted that in more liberal days, but nowadays it is generally understood as a reminder that we shouldn't pry. It is better not to know things about other people than to be the cause of them getting into some sort of trouble.

7

At that time I thought Tom did know Ephraim in the things that are eternal. Ephraim, still relatively new to Meeting himself, had been one of the people who interviewed Tom when he became a member, and at that time Tom held Ephraim in very high esteem. I would see them sometimes sitting in the Meeting House garden talking. Before Tom and I were engaged I even felt a little jealous. Still, Tom needed to talk the soup run over with someone.

We also sat in silence together at home. At the back of our house is a rickety old conservatory with those plastic windows and doors which are now known to be environmentally unfriendly and which one day we planned to replace with fairtrade wood. We spent a lot of time out there that spring. I remember sitting in an old rocking chair gazing at the river and asking for guidance and, because of Dad's warnings, for safety. All I felt each time I thought about the project was excitement and a sense of moving in the right direction – the way I had felt when Tom and I first started seeing each other, in fact. We knew by Friday that we would say 'Yes.'

* * *

I must admit it was exciting. Derek had suggested we wear dark, waterproof clothes and trainers, so that we would be warm, dry and inconspicuous. It was half-term and I had spent part of the afternoon preparing. We didn't meet at the Meeting House. There was a feeling our community might be being watched although some people wondered whether that was a little paranoid. Instead we met in a pub at the bottom of town in the High Street. I had never been in there before, but I saw at once that it made a good meeting place. It was full of people, mostly around our age and like us casually dressed, and not taking much notice of people outside their own groups. Derek bought us both a beer and we sat at a stained wooden table on upholstered stools and looked around us. It was close to eleven at night and I suppose some people had been drinking all evening. There were sticky patches on the floor where things had been spilt, and the smell of cigarettes brought in on people's clothes.

"I have all the stuff we need in the van," Derek told us. "We follow a different route each night. Today we'll start at the foot of Old Hill, where the motorway which is on the other side of the hill used to run. There are usually people dossing in the copse by the maze on the top, and they leave a lookout at the bottom to tell the others when we arrive. We often find people in the nature reserve too, where the Feeding Station used to be, but the gates are locked so we'll have to go through the park and climb over the fence. There's an old cemetery up at the top of town which will be our last call. We've got food for about thirty people tonight so there's no point in going out to the recycling centre. Anyway, the Salvation Army often take food out there."

A row broke out at the bar. Two men were squaring up to each other and a blonde girl in a sparkling waistcoat started to shout, her language full of words we don't use in our community. This was a very different world from mine. We finished our beers and left. As far as I could tell nobody even glanced at us.

The van was parked beside an ancient Assembly Rooms building, now a headquarters for the ATTF, and I thought that was both very cheeky and rather clever of Derek. Nobody would expect someone to park there if he or she were up to no good! We climbed in, all three of us wedged into the front, and drove off towards Old Hill.

★ ★ ★

Of course, I was ridiculously naive and that night as we drove out of town towards the old sewage works (now a rather elegant private hotel of some sort, I believe) on dark roads with our headlights dipped, it felt pretty much like the sort of thing the young adults used to do a couple of years back, and probably still do. I remember once we had a new member of the community who had come out of the Roman Catholic Church. She is a really lovely person and she told us about a teenage group going up to the top of a hill on Easter Day morning with a young priest, and celebrating communion as the sun rose. We don't celebrate communion but we thought it sounded like a great idea, so we set out early one Sunday morning and drove in a convoy of cars to a hilly, wooded area west of the city where there are public barbecue sites, and Tom and some of the others built a fire. We sat round and had a silence while the sun rose, then cooked sausages over the fire. That was just before Tom and I started seeing each other, and that morning I was very aware of him wherever he went and whatever he said. Now I was wedged between Tom and Derek and it felt fun and adventurous in the same sort of way.

I think Tom had a better grasp of the seriousness of what we were doing. There isn't actually a law against giving food to homeless people – how could there be? On the other hand, a very prominent member of the New Alliance had stated categorically that if people without work are given food it encourages them to depend on others and not to help themselves, so giving out food is considered anti-social. Some of the mainstream churches who were still registered had objected to that, which was why we were all still free to give out food on Sundays – but only on Sundays. Giving away food in an organised way through the whole week has become an 'activity contrary to the common good'.

We parked among some trees at the foot of Old Hill. Years ago there used to be a road here, but it goes round the other side of the hill now. On one side is a branch of the river, and a footpath much beloved of walkers. I have seen groups of

American volunteers there in the summer, escorted by leaders who tell them about the Stone Age settlement which once existed on the top of the hill and about the maze, but I have never seen them actually climb up there to see for themselves.

As soon as we arrived Derek turned his headlights off and as we sat in the darkness he said, "Okay, we need to give them ten minutes or so. They'll check us out before we see them. When they show themselves we don't talk. All the food is in the back of the van. They will give us the urn we brought up here two nights ago and we'll give them the new one. Be careful, it's hot. The sandwiches are in the cardboard box in the other corner of the van, under the blankets. There are big bottles of water. Only give them one box of sandwiches and one pack of water, the rest is for the people at the nature reserve and the cemetery. We don't give them soup because of the difficulties of hiding the urn – they're too close to the centre of the city."

We sat in silence. The water on the right looked dark and still, the trees were almost motionless too, and the shadows were black against navy blue. Nothing seemed to move for a while, until out of the corner of my eye something seemed to flicker, and then three people appeared directly in front of the van.

It was hard to tell in the darkness but I thought there were two men and a child. All three wore woolly, knitted hats and the collars of their coats or jackets were turned up. I didn't think it was a particularly cold night, but I suppose if you live outside it's hard to keep warm even in quite mild weather. Derek raised his hand in greeting and opened the door on the driver's side. Tom opened the other door and we all clambered out. Following Derek's instructions we went at once to the back of the van and without saying anything opened the creaking metal doors. It was exactly as Derek had said. The empty urn of two nights ago was already standing there, and the new urn was still dangerously hot. Tom and one of the men from Old

Hill lifted it down and I found the box of sandwiches and the water. Nobody said anything and we could hardly see the faces of the three people. I suppose they couldn't see ours. Still without speaking we went round to the front of the van and climbed back in. The two adults lifted the urn by the plastic coated handles and more or less disappeared into the trees. The child looked at us, picked up the box of sandwiches and balanced the water on top, said "Thanks, mate", and was gone after them. We sat there for a moment or two, still in silence. It felt almost as if nothing had happened.

Derek sighed. "Okay," he said, "now to the nature reserve. Thanks, guys."

I noticed he didn't turn the headlights on again until we were nearly back at the old sewage works.

★ ★ ★

The city streets were dark. The lighting goes off after midnight on week nights and we saw only a few cars on the roads. There is a one-way system, and our route took us very close to our house on the way to the nature reserve. We parked in the car park next to the reserve, and again sat with our lights off, in silence, for several minutes. There were quite a lot of other cars and vans parked there. I knew, because we lived in that sector of the city, that there is limited street parking. It is the cause of some bad feeling.

Out of the silence Derek said, "This is not so straightforward. We're so close to the centre of the city that at any moment we could be spotted. They won't come here – our friends. We will need to go to them. That's another reason why we don't bring soup." He looked at us again, checking our clothes, although he had already done that once in the pub. "You're both in dark colours. That's good." He paused for a moment thoughtfully, then, "I'm not expecting trouble," he said, "but if trouble comes you need to get out of the way and hide *at once*. There's a lot of cover in the reserve although it's better later in the year. Lie low and move as little as possible. Tom, you'll probably want to look after Carrie and vice versa, but for goodness' sake don't try to look out for me. If anything goes wrong I'll separate myself from you as quickly as possible. Okay?"

I had a lump in my throat now. It didn't feel like a young people's adventure any more.

"Okay," we both agreed, and climbed out of the van.

★ ★ ★

The nature reserve is lovely at night. We walked into the park where there is a footbridge across a strand of the river into the wilderness, carrying nylon bags containing the provisions. The gate was closed and locked but we climbed over it without difficulty, and soon we were walking along the edge of a small, gravelled footpath which followed the line of the stream. We tried to keep off the gravel, because it made a crunching sound under our trainers, but if anyone was listening out for us I was sure they would hear us. Derek seemed to know exactly where we were going. After a while we turned away from that strand of river and followed a wooden boardwalk, rolling our feet on the planks to keep the noise down. We turned again onto an earthen footpath and the sound of a small, rushing stream grew louder. There was a bench under some black trees, and sitting on and around the bench were the darker silhouettes of a group of about seven people.

"Evening, friends," said Derek in a low voice.

"Hi!" came from several different people.

One woman stood and came towards us. Without any greetings she said, "We've got a problem."

"What's up?" Derek seemed unfazed.

"One of the children. She tripped on a root and fell – we think she might have broken her arm. Any suggestions?"

13

Even now that we were used to the darkness I couldn't see the expression on Derek's face. He was quiet for a moment, then said, "Let me see."

The woman went back to the bench and whispered something. Another woman got up and came towards us, leading a small child by the hand.

Derek squatted down and said softly to the little girl, "Hello there. I hear you've had an accident. Does it hurt?"

The little girl nodded, but didn't say anything. The mother said, "It feels sort of lumpy, and when I touch it I can see she's in pain. Of course, she knows to keep quiet."

"Will you let me look at it?" I was amazed at Derek's calm, quiet way with the child. I had never thought he was the sort of man who would know how to talk to little ones.

The girl nodded again.

"Okay, then let's take this jacket off, shall we, so that I can assess the damage."

The mother squatted down next to her daughter and together she and Derek eased the coat off the little girl. "Has anyone got a blanket?" Derek asked. "We don't want her getting cold, on top of the shock."

Someone draped something round the child's shoulders and then, because people gathered around and it was such a black night, I couldn't see what happened next.

There was a muffled cry from the child, and Derek said soothingly, "Good girl! Good girl! We're nearly done." Then, after a pause, "Can someone find a good straight stick? We'll make a splint. I'm not sure it's really necessary but we don't want it mending crooked."

Then, to Tom and me, Derek said, "Can you put the food and water under the tree by the spring? When this is done we'll need to be going."

We picked up the provisions again and looked in the direction in which Derek had nodded. The rushing sound came from a little stream that issued from a spring by some stones. I had been there in the daytime as an ordinary walker, and remembered the spot. The nature reserve is all low land, loamy not rocky, but at some point someone had built a hard surface around the spring. We took the food and water over there.

"This would be a great place," whispered Tom, "under other circumstances."

"Yes," I whispered back. "When I was thinking of moving up here Mum and Dad came with me to look at those lodgings I had by the art college, and we came here for a picnic. Look," I took him past the spring and through a clump of willows and pointed across a bed of reeds, looking black and ominous in their night-time colours. "Over there, there used to be a hide for bird watching."

My only excuse is that we hadn't been married long and we were still in that first, exciting part of our relationship. It was dark and quiet, we could hear the gentle conversation of the people on the other side of the stream and the willows, and it was romantic. I turned to face Tom and reached up to kiss him. He put his hands on my hips and kissed me back, a deep, gentle kiss that promised more to come. We didn't hear the approach of the police.

One minute I was standing in Tom's arms, the next minute there was a voice which sounded as if it were right next to us. "Well now, what have we here?"

The comment wasn't addressed to us. We hadn't been seen in our dark clothes on the other side of the willows. It was the homeless and Derek who were being accosted.

"Duck!" whispered Tom in my ear and we both crouched quickly on the ground. We looked around us. We could hear the police officers – there seemed to be several – talking to the others.

"This reserve is closed at night," announced one deep voice. "There should be nobody here. And what is this?" A pause, then, "Water? Sandwiches? Are you living here?"

For a moment nobody spoke. Then a voice I didn't know, one of the homeless people I was sure, pleaded, "What do you suggest we do? Do you have children? Don't you try to do the best you can for them?"

"This," asserted the deep voice, "is definitely not the best parents can do for their children. I'm sorry, but you will all need to come with us."

A woman's voice spoke. "No! Please! We'll move on. We'll leave the area. We won't cause you any bother! Just let us go, please…"

"Sorry, ma'am." The owner of the voice didn't sound sorry. "Rules are rules. And where did this food come from?"

Nobody spoke. "Well," said the police officer, "living rough in a public space is an offence against public order, but providing this sort of support could be construed as terrorism. Someone here is deliberately working to undermine the values of our society. I need to know who. Tell me that and I will turn a blind eye to the rest of you."

Still nobody spoke. Then the little girl said, "They've gone away."

A new voice, a woman's voice, spoke in a gentler tone. "Who have gone away, sweetheart?" So there was a woman officer there too.

"The people who brought the food. They've gone now." I suppose she was remembering us.

"Which way did they go?" prompted the woman officer.

"Dunno," answered the little girl. "I hurt my arm."

A male officer said, "These people are small fry. We need to catch the ones who are supporting them. Put this lot in the wagon and take them outside the city limits. I'll call in the ATTF."

Then, "All right you lot, this way," and with the sound of feet on the wooden boardwalk and the new noise of a whimpering baby, everyone left.

16

Crouched in the reeds behind the willows I sighed with relief. "Wow," I said, "I thought we'd had it then."

"Carrie," said Tom, "we've got a big problem. The ATTF will be here soon, they'll bring dogs and weapons. I'm not sure what we need to do."

★ ★ ★

There are very few rules in our community, but some very strong traditions. One of those traditions, which we children had objected to loudly and generally without effect, was that watching DeVs was on the whole a bad thing, and viewing anything on a screen was an activity to be restricted. When I was growing up I was allowed to watch for two hours a day, and I had to clear with my parents the programmes I wanted to see. I could listen for a further two hours to the radio and music channels. Tom, on the other hand, grew up with unlimited exposure to almost all forms of entertainment. It stood us in good stead that night.

"They'll bring tracker dogs," said Tom. "They'll start at the spring, I suppose, and pick up our scent in no time…" He was quiet. I was looking round; there were no trees to climb except the willows and I'm not sure they are the sort of tree a person can climb, and anyhow, wouldn't the dogs just track us to the foot of the tree?

"I watched a movie once," said Tom, a little excitement in his voice now. "An escaped convict was running for it, and to kill his scent he waded upstream in a river. There's loads of water here. Come on!"

He grabbed my hand and we both stood. The little stream coming from the spring was probably too small for our purposes and it was a bit of a trek back to the larger channel we had crossed when we first got into the park.

"You said there used to be a hide over there?" asked Tom.

"Ages ago, I don't know what they did with it."

"So is there water there?"

"Oh, yes!" I remembered Mum, Dad and I clustered on the old wooden decking where the hide had once stood, looking for river birds. "There was a pool, and a stream came in from the right as we stood facing the pool."

"Right," said Tom. "So let's head over there and see if we can find it." Again he took my hand and we stepped away from the willows into the reed bed.

It was crazy walking. The ground under our feet was squelchy and soft, the reeds were high – sometimes as tall as Tom, who is nearly six feet tall. It was a very dark night and we were walking almost blind. It was slow progress and all the time I was listening out for whatever sounds the ATTF might make. Sirens? Dogs barking? Would they call out to us?

It was impossible to guess how far we had gone, but I thought we were making good progress. Once a bird flew up out of the reeds right in front of us and I jumped almost out of my skin, and there were rustlings in the reeds around our feet. I was about one step behind Tom, and a little to his right. Then all of a sudden when I put my foot down it met no earth, not even marsh, it just kept descending and the next minute, with a loud splash I was up to my neck in water.

"Carrie!" Tom was there at once, reaching out his hand, pulling me back onto relatively solid ground. "Are you okay? At least we've found our water!"

I was soaked to the skin and at once I was cold. A breeze I hadn't even noticed before started to chill my wet face and hands.

"I'm okay," I assured him. "What do we do now? Wade in the water? Swim?"

"Let me think." Tom was still for a moment. One of the things I loved about Tom was his quiet thoughtfulness, his ability to make decisions mindfully rather than being panicked into activity. "Okay," he said after a few seconds. "Let's see if this is a pool or running water. Running water leads somewhere.

There's no point in hiding in a pool, they'll just track us there and find us. Was the water still or moving?"

"I don't know." It was not the thing most on my mind when I fell in.

"Let me see," said Tom, feeling his way to the edge of the water and kneeling down, so that he could put his hand in it. "Right! Good!" he said. "It's moving. Quite fast. Are you up for wading along it? It will be cold!"

"I'm already wet through," I reminded him. "You're the one who'll get a shock!" I was grinning in the dark. Tom hates swimming in cold water. "Come on."

We held hands again and stepped down into the stream. It was quite deep, up to my waist, and muddy on the bottom. In some places it was only one person wide but we kept our hands linked all the time, even if it was a little clumsy. Tom took the lead, and I realised we were wading upstream, away from the city.

"How do you know where to go?" I whispered.

"I don't," Tom whispered back, "but we don't want to end up in the city. These water meadows might go on for miles this way, we stand a better chance of finding some good cover."

We kept wading. Despite the exercise I was starting to get really cold. When Tom asked me how I was doing my teeth chattered as I answered.

"Just keep going," encouraged Tom. "We must have made quite a distance by now. Don't touch the reeds at the edge if you can help it."

★ ★ ★

We were still in the channel of water, still making our way further and further from the city, when the blackness of the night started to turn a dull grey. At about the same time we heard vehicles some distance away and then the barking of a

19

dog, persistent and ominous. "Now we'll find out if our plan works," said Tom grimly. "Perhaps it's time we found a hiding place."

As the world became gradually lighter we were able to take stock of our situation. I guessed we were out of the official nature reserve by now, in a less managed piece of wild water meadow. To our left it was becoming apparent that there were reed beds and then, maybe a quarter of a mile away, meadowland with cows grazing. On our right was a small copse, and beyond it a narrow scrap of unkempt land and then a hedge.

"Could you climb one of those trees?" Tom asked. His teeth were chattering too. "I suppose I ought to know my wife better than that!"

We both grinned. *Husband* and *wife* were still new and special words with which to describe each other. It felt as if we were playacting.

"I think so," I replied, feeling thankful for all those adventures with other children from our community while I was growing up.

I looked around. It was still early spring and the deciduous trees were only in bud they would provide us with no cover. A little to our right, though, were two tall fir trees.

"Up here," I said, and headed for the shorter, bushier tree at once. It was prickly and uncomfortable to climb, but quite straightforward, and within minutes we were perched in the greenery, hidden from preying eyes and also, mercifully, from the worst of the cold breeze. We could see a narrow country lane on the other side of the hedge and beyond that meadowland.

We grinned at each other. "So I wonder what happens now?" said Tom, and shuffled closer to me. We were like a couple of kids sitting on a branch with our feet dangling and our arms around each other. It was difficult for me to believe anything could go too disastrously wrong with Tom around.

20

★ ★ ★

The wind grew stronger as the light grew brighter. There were dark clouds scudding across the sky and the temperature seemed to be dropping, although it may just have been that we were no longer moving, and we were sitting in wet clothes in the open air. For a few minutes I just nestled into Tom's shoulder, a little uncomfortably because of the knobbly branch on which we were sitting, then Tom said, "Ephraim always says, *when in difficulty, don't pray – listen!*'"

"Listen with my ears, or listen with my heart?" I asked. Children in our community are taught to know the difference from an early age.

Just at that moment we both heard a dog barking again, some distance away. "Perhaps both, under the circumstances!" said Tom.

I closed my eyes and tried to open my heart and my spirit. It was difficult to do while listening with my ears too. I could hear the barking of the dog, and that made my heart beat faster. Was it getting closer? In order to listen with my heart, as I try to do in Meeting, I tend to shut out the noises I pick up with my ears. There seemed to be a conflict within.

Then a strange thing happened. I cannot explain it and I see no reason why it ever should be explained. I could hear the dog barking and it did seem to be getting closer. Then, in my mind I could actually see it. Perhaps it was a pit bull terrier, anyhow it was something full of muscle and aggression, straining at a lead which was held by a man in an ATTF uniform and who was leaning backwards to restrain the dog. The dog was a frightening sight, but in my imagination or my spirit, wherever this picture was happening, I was not frightened. I felt I was standing a little above and to one side of the dog, and as I watched it seemed to me that someone else, some perfectly ordinary elderly lady with a wrinkled smile, walked over to the dog and bent to stroke it. As I watched, the dog opened his mouth, panting with pleasure at the attention, then gave a soft growl and lay down. The picture vanished from my mind, but I thought I could feel in my spirit the contentment of the dog, enjoying the sensation of being stroked by someone who knows and loves animals. I opened my eyes and I listened normally again, with my ears.

The dog, wherever it was, had stopped barking.

I sat in silence, looking out between the fir branches until I felt Tom sigh.

"It's going to be all right," I said.

"Yes."

We were both quiet again.

"I think we ought to head for home now," suggested Tom. "Shall we see where the lane beyond the hedge leads?"

★ ★ ★

My absolute certainty of safety and security evaporated gradually as we walked along the narrow road. We passed a wooden public footpath sign which told us that a track across the fields to our left would lead us, in three quarters of a mile, to a little village which is a well-known beauty spot. We briefly considered going that way but we were filthy, dishevelled and damp. We looked like a couple of vagrants and villages like that tend to be full of people who want anti-social elements such as we appeared to be off their streets. It would be a shame to have escaped the ATTF only to be arrested by a village police officer! So we stayed on the lane.

There was almost no traffic. A tractor drove past pulling a trailer full of steaming manure, and two boys on bicycles pedalled furiously in the other direction shouting to each other in excited American accents. In a way it was a pity we had no sort of device with us, but Derek had insisted we leave our DeV7s at home, and of course he was right. Everyone knows people can be tracked using anything electronic. So we just kept walking.

By that point I was beginning to feel rather unwell. Tom had only got wet up to his waist, although I'm sure that was bad enough. I had been wet all over, and although bits of me were beginning to dry I was chilled to the bone. I felt a bit sick too. I am a person who needs to eat in the morning soon after I wake up, and in fact we hadn't eaten since around six yesterday evening.

After half an hour or so I confessed to Tom, "I'm sorry, I really don't feel good. Do you mind if we sit down for a while?"

Tom looked concerned. "Of course, of course. You need some water but we haven't got any. Would you like…"

At that minute the sickness overtook me. I just had time to lean over and then I was disgorging everything that was left of last night's dinner into a ditch. Afterwards I sat down, my head swimming and my heart pounding.

"Sorry," I said. "I…" then I retched again.

Now Tom was looking really worried. "You can't go on walking like this. I wish… I think we'd better try hitching a lift."

"We could." I was doubtful. "But we need to be careful. How would we answer any questions? We need a story…"

"Oh – we went for a walk yesterday afternoon in the nature reserve," suggested Tom. "We got lost."

"I think that's rather unconvincing," I said. "I mean, the nature reserve is right on the edge of town. Even now that it's been extended it isn't that large. How could anyone get lost?"

"Yes…" Tom thought for a while and I battled another wave of nausea. "How about this. We found ourselves locked in. We tried to find another way out. We've been walking all night…"

It sounded thin to me, suspicious even, but at that minute we heard a vehicle approaching.

"Hold me in the Light!" demanded Tom, and held his thumb out in the age-old gesture of the hitch-hiker, as an old silver-coloured car came round the corner and started to slow down.

I was in no condition to hold anyone in any light; my stomach was churning and I couldn't stop shivering. I just sat on the grass verge and watched as the vehicle slowed down and came to a halt. The driver's side window rolled down.

"Ephraim!" I heard Tom gasp. "What...? Where...? Am I pleased to see you!"

"Hop in," came Ephraim's quiet voice. "You look as if you've both had quite enough for one night!"

★ ★ ★

It's hard to describe the relief of being in the front seat of Ephraim's car, driving quietly through the country lanes, Tom in the middle of the rear seat leaning forward so that he could join in the explanations.

"How did you know where we were?" Tom asked. "How did you find us?"

"It wasn't hard." Ephraim fiddled with something on the dash board and a pulse of warm air blew onto my feet. "Take your trainers off," he suggested, turning to me. "You need to warm up."

Tom said, "Did you hear what happened? Where's Derek?"

"I'm not sure about Derek," replied Ephraim thoughtfully. "We knew something was wrong when Wolly and Madge called at my flat earlier this morning. They live out by the old Primrose Barracks and they always report to us on movements or transports they think might interest us. They said a group of vagrants had been dropped off just outside the outer sector of the city. At first we thought it might have been the folk from the cemetery, but we – someone – checked on them, and they're fine. Then we thought of the nature reserve. We would have checked Old Hill afterwards if we hadn't seen Derek's van parked down at the bottom of town by the old Feeding Station. Then we guessed. Paul and Flo are checking the road out to Mistlethrush Village in case you had gone that way, and I said I'd check round here."

I was amazed. It was suddenly seeming as if we had been part of a whole organised group about which I had known nothing.

"But how did you know we'd escaped?" prompted Tom. "We heard the police say they would call in the ATTF."

"And they've got Derek," I added.

"Perhaps," said Ephraim to me. "I've got a feeling Derek can look after himself. He wasn't with the people shipped out beyond the city, or at least, not the ones Madge and Wolly saw."

"And us?" prompted Tom again. "How did you know we weren't just sitting in a cell somewhere?"

"Cells," corrected Ephraim. "Plural. They would never have let you stay together. We didn't know where you were," he added. "But we hoped – and prayed."

We were not approaching the city by the direct route back. For all our hard work wading upstream for hours, it seemed we had actually only made it a couple of miles outside the city. Ephraim took tiny roads, some no more than tracks, until in the end we arrived in the city from downriver.

"Best not to alert anyone to where you've been," suggested Ephraim as we drove round the one-way system so that he could drop us off at our little house. Then, "Carrie, go to bed – you're ill. A hot bath, some toast and a glass of wine if you've got it would be ideal. You both need to try to act as normally as possible. Tom, were you supposed to be at work today?"

"Yes." Tom sounded worried.

"No problem," encouraged Ephraim. "It's only just after nine. Phone in, say Carrie was ill in the night and you'll be a little late. Shower and go straight up there."

We were parked outside the house now. "What about Derek?" I worried.

"I'll look into that," said Ephraim. "The most useful thing you can do right now is to act normally," then, smiling kindly at me, "and get better!"

★ ★ ★

I slept all morning, curled up in our big double bed in the loft room, with the sounds of wind and rain against the dormer window and the duvet pulled up around my ears. Even after a long hot shower I hadn't been able to stop shivering so Tom had warmed a hot cushion in the microwave and I curled up around it, feeling safe at last. Tom showered after me and put on his usual work gear, then kissed me on the cheek and left.

I woke at midday with a racking cough. One minute I was fast asleep, the next moment I thought I was choking. I sat up in bed quickly but the cough went on and on, I just couldn't stop. When at last it eased my throat was sore and there were shooting pains in all the muscles around my neck and abdomen. I gasped for breath. My head was aching and my face was burning. I turned the pillow over and the cool cotton was pleasant against my burning cheek when I lay down again.

Later in the afternoon I thought I should go and get something to eat, or at least to drink. Tom had left a glass of water by my bed but it was long since gone. It was only a few steps to our bathroom but when I thought about getting out of bed and walking over there it just seemed too much, and I went back to sleep while I was still thinking about it. Twice more, at least, I woke up coughing.

When Tom came home it was a light, grey, spring evening. He brought a pizza and salad from a place in the High Street, and carried it up to our room so that I could eat in bed. He looked well, perhaps a little tired but not desperately so.

"Good day?" I asked, and was surprised at how croaky my voice sounded.

"Oh dear," said Tom. "You do sound rough! Yes, it was fine. We had a whole run of documents to print for the university. I'm sure they would save money if they did it for themselves but they like to outsource. It was interesting stuff on revisionist views about the origins of Stonehenge. We got the whole lot done by the end of the day. Malcolm was pleased – we're ahead of schedule. Oh, and Pat and Feany send their love and hope you're better soon."

I was trying to eat the pizza but my throat was so sore it was almost burning, and I was finding it hard to concentrate.

"Actually," said Tom, putting down his pizza which we were eating with our hands, not knives and forks, "you look pretty rough." He put his hand on my forehead. "Yup!" he announced cheerfully. "You've got a temperature. Have we got any flu stuff in the medicine cabinet?" He went off to have a look.

I drank the fresh water Tom had brought in. By the time he got back with whatever cold cures he had found, I was asleep again.

* * *

I coughed badly all that night. Poor Tom moved down to the front bedroom, which at that time still needed decorating, and slept on the futon passed on to us by my parents. In the morning when Tom brought me breakfast I felt a little better, but when I got out of bed to use the bathroom I was as weak as a kitten. I slept on and off all day, listening to the radio on the little solar-powered DeV1000 we sometimes kept upstairs. I heard bits and pieces of news, which seemed to fade in and out. There had been a bad bomb explosion on one of the Caribbean islands. The Venezuelan prisoners of war were on hunger strike. They were still discussing the final changes to our inheritance tax, to bring our tax laws into line with the rest of the Alliance. The Scots were strengthening their border controls and we, in turn, were to boycott certain products from Scotland. At one point I heard a part of an interview which sounded really interesting, of a young woman who had started making traditional musical instruments of the sort that would have been played in the court of Henry VIII. She was a teacher, and was teaching her students to play these instruments. I was asleep when the interview started and went back to sleep before it ended, so I had no idea where this enterprising young teacher worked. Of course, I could have checked on the DeV but I was too weary to care. Still, the extracts of music which they played were beautiful.

Tom came in just after five in the afternoon, looking happy and well, but when he saw me he frowned.

"Carrie!" he exclaimed. "You look awful!"

"Well, thanks!" I croaked. "Actually I'm feeling a bit better. Have you had a good day?"

"Mm." Tom looked thoughtfully at me. "Ephraim came in just before one and took me to the Black Boy for a pint and a ploughman's. He sends his best wishes."

I started to feel a bit more awake. "I don't really understand how he found us," I said. "Or what went on that night. Is Derek okay? Do we know?"

"It seems like it," said Tom. He had made a pot of tea when he first came home and took a sip or two before going on. "Ephraim said he was at the midweek Meeting for Worship, just as if nothing had happened."

"That's really odd," I said. "Wasn't he arrested with the nature reserve crowd?"

"Yes, well, so it seemed. He was still there when you took me to show me where the hide had been. According to Ephraim, Derek just laughed when he asked him how he got away, and said that there is more than one way to skin a cat."

"I hate that expression," I commented. "I think there's more going on than we realised. Do you think so?"

"Oh yes!" Tom sounded convinced. "Well, I've thought so for a while. In fact, there's bound to be, isn't there? I mean, feeding homeless people is a good stop-gap measure but it won't really change the world for the better! Somebody needs to do something more drastic."

"Tom..." I started to feel worried. Our community is non-violent. My parents and the parents of my friends had all maintained, as we were growing up, that there is Light and goodness in everyone. Our job was not to change things by force, but to live in the Light in such a way that others found it attractive and wanted to live like that too. It sounded as if Tom was talking about revolution.

Perhaps he read my mind. We were still very close in those days and we often seemed to know what the other was thinking. "Oh, I don't mean violence!" Tom exclaimed. "One of the things I love about our community is that we don't force our ideas or opinions on others. You know that! But living in the Light can mean living outside the law. I suppose it's better not to know."

We were both quiet, drinking our tea. I started to think again about our good fortune in being found by Ephraim. He is such a kind man, but somehow a bit mysterious too. With lots of people in our community you can pretty much guess at the way they have lived their lives, but with Ephraim...

"Tom," I asked, "where does Ephraim come from? I mean, he just seemed to turn up a few years ago. What does he do? Has he got a family? I don't really know anything about him."

"I know him a bit," said Tom, "from when he interviewed me for membership. He's retired."

"Retired from what? Do you think he was a school teacher? A head teacher maybe?"

"I don't know. Somehow I don't think so." Tom hesitated. "I'm not sure if I should tell you this," he added, "but I think he only joined the Society a few years ago. I think he changed his name when he joined – you know, like Anna and Daniel did, to mark a new beginning. He lent me a book when I was preparing for membership, an old red booklet, so that I could compare the guidance texts they used at the turn of the century with our wording, and in the front cover it said *To Karl from all in Aylesbury Meeting*. I think he used to be called Karl."

I thought about that. "Could be," I agreed. "But it could just be any old second-hand booklet. It doesn't mean anything."

"No, but…" Tom stopped. "Well, anyhow, he's here now and he saved our bacon, that's for sure! Talking of which, are you up to eating anything? I bought carrot and coriander soup on the way home."

★ ★ ★

For the next few days all I seemed to do was sleep, cough, listen to parts of radio programmes and nibble at meals brought to me by Tom before and after work. On Sunday Tom went off to Second Meeting on his own, having coaxed some porridge into me before he left, and came back with the flowers which had been on the table during the two Meetings and lots of greetings and best wishes from other people. On Monday he phoned the doctor, but she said there was a virus going round, and checked that my flu jabs were up to date. Of course they were, so she told Tom I should stay warm, rest up and drink lots of fluids. Tom asked me if I wanted him to buy some of those American carbonated drinks which are so bad for you.

They are full of sugar and Tom was worried that I wasn't eating enough. I declined. It was only a virus, after all there was no need to start straying from my principles!

On Tuesday Mum and Dad came up. Mum changed the sheets on our bed and on Tom's futon, and cooked us a wonderful roast dinner for when Tom came home from work, which I hardly touched. It was good to see them and I could tell that Tom was relieved to have someone else looking after me for a day. On Wednesday Tom had a day off (he had worked the previous Saturday) and I got up and sat in the rocking chair in the conservatory for an hour with our morning coffee. It was lovely. The sun was shining, the daffodils were just beginning to flower and the grass was long and very bright green. The only trouble was that when I tried to climb the two sets of stairs to get back to our bedroom, I ran out of energy half way up. I sat on the bottom step of the second flight and cried with exhaustion. Tom sat beside me stroking my hair helplessly. The stairs were too narrow for Tom to carry me, but in the end I made it back upstairs and was asleep almost before Tom had pulled the duvet up over me.

I didn't go downstairs again for three weeks after that, and by then I think I knew something more serious was wrong. This was not just a virus.

★ ★ ★

Looking back it seems as if I missed most of that spring. After about ten days the coughing and the occasional nausea eased and for a while the coughing went altogether, but the utter exhaustion remained. Once or twice when I woke up in the morning I felt fine. The first time it happened I thought, *Yes! I'm finally over it!* I jumped out of bed, had a shower, washed and dried my hair, and went downstairs. Tom is very good around the house and my parents had been in a couple of times, but the kitchen still looked a bit disordered, so I did a thorough clean, even washing the slate flooring. Then, suddenly, it all hit me again. I felt sick, my head started to swim and my legs felt wobbly. I almost staggered into the conservatory and collapsed into the rocking chair. I slept there for the rest of the morning, waking up cold and disorientated at lunchtime. I went back to bed.

Tom phoned the doctor that evening and told her what had happened. She didn't seem alarmed. "Yes, it was a nasty virus that went around," she agreed. "It'll take your wife some time to recover fully. She needs to take things slowly."

About a week later I woke feeling well again. The sun was coming and going between huge white fluffy clouds and there were leaves on all the trees, new and young and fresh. I felt optimistic and happy. I remembered the doctor's caution, and took things easy. I sat in the conservatory reading and drinking mint tea, and that day I really thought I was over the worst. It was the first time I was up and dressed when Tom came home, and the first night we made love since I became ill. I went to sleep peacefully, glad to have Tom beside me again. Next day, though, I could hardly lift my head off the pillow, and it seemed I had made no progress at all.

★ ★ ★

Tom, meanwhile, was living quite an exciting life. After a couple of weeks of staying in with me, he had started going out with Derek and the other volunteers (I never knew who they were) taking food and water to the three established locations. It seemed there were people back in the nature reserve. "It's just too good a place for people to avoid," Tom explained. Then, gradually I became aware that perhaps Tom was doing more, not just distributing sandwiches and water, but something more radical.

It came to a head one evening. I had come down for dinner in my trackies, because it seemed a good thing to spend at least some time out of our bedroom every day. We were sitting in our front room, which was still decorated with the plain walls and simple blocks of colour of a generation or more ago. We had an old settee and a chair they had thrown out of the Meeting House, and rugs scattered on the wooden floor. In winter draughts came up from beneath the floorboards but in the summer it was a cool and pretty room, with a charm of its own. Our house looked out directly onto the street. We had no front garden, so people walked just feet away from us as they passed, and often looked in. Other people in the terrace had installed one-way glass, and we intended to do the same eventually, but for now we were content with things as they were.

Someone from Meeting had given Tom a wine box to bring home because red wine is apparently good for us in moderate quantities. We were both checking out the theory, with great enjoyment. I was stretched out on the settee feeling deathly weary, as was usual by that time of day. Tom was lounging in the chair next to the window, looking fit in every sense of the word.

"I'm out again this evening," he said. "I think we'll take longer than usual, so don't worry."

"Are you feeding more people?" I asked. Then, frustrated as we all were, "Can't they see what their benefit cuts have done? Don't they realise what it does to people when they issue permanent benefit sanctions for anti-social behaviour? Do they *want* to make the problem worse?"

We had been here before. The whole community had been here before. We were coming to the conclusion that those in power *did* actually want to make the problem worse. The only way the two countries of the Alliance can compete with the rapidly developing economies of Asia and Africa

33

is to have pools of workers who are so desperate that they will do anything, work in any job, put up with any working conditions, even protect bad employers, rather than be jobless, homeless and hungry. According to international statistics we are now one of the hardest-working nations on the face of the earth, but of course it is not because of our good work ethic, it is simply the economics of desperation. Meanwhile the rich get richer, and those of us on middle incomes wonder what we should do. Europe, of course, has gone in a very different direction, embracing sustainability and quality of life. The Alliance calls it *socialism*. We call it *civilisation*.

"Derek wasn't sure I should tell you," answered Tom. "We're not just feeding people any more."

"What do you mean?" Not for the first time I wished that Tom had been brought up in our community. Was he getting involved in something we wouldn't like? Derek was a comparative newcomer too...

I needn't have worried. "When you were a kid," Tom went on, "did they tell you stories about the Underground Railroad in the United States, during the time of slavery?"

"Oh yes!" We had loved those stories. In fact, one of the games we had played had been of helping slaves to escape north. I had often had to be the slave because of my mixed race, although Dylan was sometimes the escapee because his turban still made him look a bit foreign to our eyes.

"Well," said Tom, "we're doing it again. Only this time it isn't slaves."

"What...? Who...? Tom, are we helping people to get to the border?"

"We are!" Tom looked pleased. "Derek and some of the others have been setting this up for months. There are communities all the way from here to Scotland. We take families who have been given permanent benefit sanctions, and pass them on to friends in the north."

"But…" I was finding this hard to take in. "Tom, I thought the borders were closed. Don't you remember, we watched that documentary about the way the European Union is resisting immigration from the Alliance? They say our people are economic migrants and Rescue International say they are refugees, because the permanent benefit sanctions and the Oath Against Extremism amount to persecution."

"I know," Tom agreed. "But there are people in Scotland who don't see it like that. There are a couple of places where we can get people across the border, even now, and people in Ireland and Scandinavia as well as in Scotland who will take them in." Tom looked at my perplexed face. "It's the right thing to do, you know," he said.

"Yes." I thought about what it must be like to have to live so desperately from hand to mouth, and the way the system seemed to be rigged to stop people from ever climbing out of poverty. I thought of the school in the park which had ended so mysteriously a few years previously, and the people from our Meeting who had vanished. "Yes, you are right." Suddenly I felt so proud of Tom. I had been brought up with these strong notions of social justice and equality, but Tom had been raised believing in a sort of social Darwinism: survival of the fittest. And yet look where he was now! "Oh Tom…" I didn't know how to express myself or even, really, what I wanted to say. I felt a surge of gratitude that I was living with such a man. "Oh Tom, this is great! When I'm better I want to help too."

Tom grinned. "I thought you might!" Then, a little more seriously, "But I'm not going to tell you much. We're playing with fire here. Derek didn't want me even to mention it but I can't keep secrets from you. Will you give me your word you won't tell anyone, not even your parents?"

I would find that hard. My parents would be so pleased if they knew, but of course Tom was right. We don't make promises in our community, our word is always supposed to be our bond. "I give you my word," I said seriously, and he came over to the settee and kissed me.

CHAPTER 2

As spring turned to summer I seemed to regain a little of my energy. A little, but not much. I started to get up and dress every morning and to go to Meeting some Sundays again, but I found it hard to stand and talk over coffee. I couldn't go to work. Friends from Meeting came round to visit me, but after an hour or two of animated conversation I would be bone-weary again. I walked into town, a mere ten minutes' walk, to do the odd errand, but my ankles ached and my head swam by the time I was home again. My cough had come back. It seemed as if my neck was always stiff. I slept in the sun in the conservatory most afternoons, and when I could I cooked simple meals ready for Tom when he came home. The garden, which had been my domain, grew wild although Tom mowed our tiny lawn every weekend. We didn't do any more improvements to the house. My world became small and limited, and Tom and my parents grew worried.

In late May, when I had been ill for nearly three months, Tom phoned the doctor again. They had a long conversation and she said she wanted to see me, to run some tests. Tom was at work that day and I could no longer walk that far, so my mother came up and we went together by taxi (my parents don't own a car). The doctor was kind in a brusque sort of way. She explained that sometimes following some viruses the body takes time to recover and she just needed to check that in my case that was all, that there was nothing nastier lurking. It sounded sensible and I was reassured. She didn't say anything to suggest that I wouldn't recover eventually, in fact quite the opposite. Nor did she, at that stage, suggest that I was malingering. It was even quite interesting. She had one of those wands that are waved over the body and which take readings and send them to a computer for analysis. She would phone me when she had the results.

★ ★ ★

Meanwhile things were going well for Tom. At work they had put him in charge of the print division when Feany took over running the shop and Pat moved to the new premises out by the hypermarket. Malcolm let him make some changes he had been itching to try for months, and productivity rose. They took on a new apprentice, a kid from Meeting who was unable to go to university because they had started to insist that all undergraduates should take the Oath.

Soon after we married we had started going to the general Business Meeting instead of the one convened by and for the young people, and now Tom was asked to help with the practical organisation of Monday evening discussion meetings. He was working with Derek on the soup runs – sometimes now he was even the leader – and at times he was away for most of the night, presumably helping with what we called by then *the Overground*. This was the shorthand we used for our escape route to the north. We first called it *the Underground* because of the old term they used in America: *the Underground Railroad*. Then someone pointed out that the most modern transport in London was the new Overground, and the term stuck. Of course, I was not around to hear any discussions about escape routes or what they might be called. I depended on what Tom told me, and we both knew that Derek disapproved of Tom telling me anything.

I spent most of my time at home, reading and sleeping and

watching daytime TV on our big DeV30. Tom was always kind and caring, but it seemed we had less and less to talk about. He was full of energy and enthusiasm, he moved around the house quickly and went upstairs two steps at a time. When I started to cough at night again he moved back down to the futon as he had when I was first ill, so that now we rarely slept together. I was always so tired. I no longer felt that wonderful magnetic pull towards Tom which had been so magical. It seemed as if all I ever needed to do was sleep. I could feel us drifting apart and a bit of me was too tired to care.

Of course, I should have known that Tom and my parents would not be the only ones to notice that all was not well. Ephraim was in some sort of pastoral leadership at that time (we more or less take it in turns) and he started popping round about teatime when Tom first got in, bringing iced cakes or doughnuts, or once a fresh pineapple. He never stayed long and he was good company – quietly spoken, thoughtful and peaceful. He was a man who often paused before he spoke, and who smiled easily but who rarely laughed out loud. I liked him more and more, and felt safe when he was around. He had a sort of air about him, a feeling that somehow he was in control. He always wanted to know what I had been doing, and seemed to be interested even if I was just reading some light novel from the charity shop at the bottom of town or playing games on my DeV. One day he brought round a pole and some wood, and he and Tom rigged up a bird feeder in the garden. Hummingbirds were still a relatively new addition to England's bird life, and it was lovely for me to watch them.

Perhaps, then, I shouldn't have been surprised when he first made his suggestion, but I was – stunned, in fact. We were sitting in the garden drinking mint tea and eating sweet oat biscuits which Ephraim had brought with him.

"How was your day?" he asked, as he always did, as if he was really interested.

"Quite good," I said. By then my definition of *good* had changed. A day was good if my neck and ankles didn't ache too much, if I wasn't coughing and if weariness was not making me feel low. "I sprayed the roses after my rest with that organic stuff Tom bought from Madge at Meeting. They're lovely this year."

Tom and Ephraim looked at the rose bush concerned and Ephraim said, "They are. Who prunes them?"

"It used to be me," I said. "Mum did it this year."

"I don't know anything about gardening," grinned Tom, taking another biscuit. "Carrie's family are naturals."

"When did you last go out?" asked Ephraim. "I mean, not just out here into the garden, but out of the house altogether?"

I looked at Tom. "Mum and Dad took us out for a pub dinner last week..." I hesitated. "I walked to the charity shop on Monday, I can go there and back. I buy books there, and give them back when I've read them."

"How well do you cope with sitting in a car?" he asked.

Tom and I looked at each other. "You know, we don't own a car," said Tom. "That's why I can't take Carrie out. We used to walk to restaurants or along the River Walk but..."

"No, no!" Ephraim smiled his warm smile at Tom. "I wasn't suggesting you should be doing something you're not! It's just that – well, it seems I need to go on a trip to visit some friends, and I wondered if it might be nice for Carrie to get away for a day or two. It will be quite a long drive, several hours, and we'll have company. We'll stay at the home of my friends. I think you'll like them. And I'll explain about your condition. They won't expect you to be the life and soul of the party!"

Tom frowned. I could see he felt uncomfortable. For all Ephraim's reassuring words, we really had no idea what sort of trip was being proposed. And why just me? Why not Tom too? Of course, Tom had to work, but...

"Think about it," Ephraim suggested. "I'm planning to leave on Friday. The car we'll use is quite comfortable although it's not as classy as the new Overground in London!" and with that he was gone.

"Oh ho!" said Tom, looking relieved. "I told Ephraim you'd said you'd like to help when you were better. It looks as if you might not have to wait until then. Will you go?"

I grinned. "I think so. What do you think?"

Tom reached across and held my hand. For a few minutes it was like the early days of our marriage, before I was ill. "I think you should," he said.

* * *

I saw the doctor again just a couple of days after Ephraim's invitation, and before I knew any details about the trip. She phoned and asked me to come in, and once again Mum came up by bus and we went together, although Mum waited in the waiting room, making notes for an article she was planning on *Religion: An Extremist Activity?* I pretty much knew how it would pan out. Mum would submit the article to the news titles for which she used to write when she was younger, and with various degrees of reluctance one editor after another would turn it down. Finally, she would submit it to the weekly journal of our own Society who would publish it. If we were lucky we would hear later, sometimes months later, that the Scottish and Irish press had picked it up and published it in their mainstream news outlets, and perhaps even that Amnesty International had featured it. Mum had once made a good living as an independent columnist but the New Alliance had put a stop to that.

My surgery is the smallest in the town, and the only one still not run by a multi-national health provider. As a result, it looks a bit worn and shabby: some of the fabric on the chairs in the waiting room is thin and stained, the electronic signing-in DeV is often out of action, and a piece of black tape stretches across the corner by a flight of stairs, because the carpet was damaged by flooding several years ago. Nevertheless, it has a good reputation among many people in the city. It is generally believed that the doctors would earn more and work in better conditions if they would give in to the blandishments of Alliance rhetoric and sign up to work in the dominant privatised sector, as indeed I think some doctors did. My surgery still allows anyone to register with them if there is space on the lists, and over the years more and more of the really poor, the people on Medical Assistance, have gravitated up the hill as obstacles were put in the way of them registering at the larger, smarter clinics. I noticed as we waited for my delayed appointment how shabby many of the other people who were waiting looked, and a child in a dirty pink buggy had bare feet, something we used never to see in this city.

Dr Edwards is a large, clumsy-looking woman who wears bright blue contact lenses and blinks in quite a pronounced way, almost as if her blinking is a tic. Whenever I have seen her she has always been wearing a pair of pale pink dungarees. She must take her wedding ring off when she arrives in her consulting room, because there is a pale line on that finger, and the ring is always in a saucer by the DeV screen.

"Come in," she called as I knocked on the half-open door. "How are you today? Take a seat."

I sat where patients always sit, but she didn't look up from her DeV for a further few seconds. Then at last she turned to me, and smiled.

"How's it going?" she asked.

"Okay – well – no differently, really," I admitted.

"Tell me!" Dr Edwards demanded in that blunt fashion of hers.

"Well... I have these aches, especially in my ankles and my

neck. I am tired all the time, and if I walk any distance at all I feel an urge just to lie down and sleep, or to cry. I cough a lot."

"Um. Do you find you cry a lot?"

"No." I hesitated. "Not a lot, but more than I used to." I could feel the tears welling up even as I spoke. "Somehow it all seems such hard work at the minute."

Dr Edwards looked at the screen again. "How's your sex life?" she asked abruptly.

I felt myself going bright red. "Not... not good," I admitted. "I'm just so tired…"

Dr Edwards was frowning at her DeV. There was a silence as I rummaged in my bag for a tissue.

"Right!" Dr Edwards seemed to sit up straighter, so that the buckle on one shoulder of her dungarees made a sort of clicking noise. "Well, this is the situation. The tests brought up nothing, which of course is good news. I wondered if you might have caught one of the new viruses that have migrated into Europe with the change of weather, but there is no sign of any virus, old or new, in your bloodstream. In fact, on paper you look like an entirely healthy young woman."

She turned and looked me straight in the face. "You look well to me, too," she added. "You have colour in your cheeks, you don't have rings under your eyes, you might even have put on a little weight, though nothing to worry about."

I felt as if we were leading up to something.

"Have you gone back to work?" she asked. "A teacher, aren't you?"

"A teaching assistant," I corrected. "No, I don't… I can't… I don't really do anything any more."

"Right." She frowned back at her DeV screen. "So let me explain – it's Charity, isn't it?"

"Carrie," I corrected.

"Okay, Carrie. So this is the situation. Obviously you have been very ill. The virus which went round this spring was a nasty one and it hit you hard. We all know that this can happen, sometimes it takes a long time to recover from something like that. However," Dr Edwards sighed, "sooner or later, however ill we have been, if the illness has passed we all have to get back on our feet. Society doesn't owe us a living, you know."

I went hot and cold. What was she saying?

"I know, of course, but..." Then the tears came and I couldn't do anything about it. I *couldn't* go back to work. She didn't understand. I was *so* tired.

Dr Edwards reached out and put a fleshy hand on my arm. "Carrie," she said, "let me explain. I think you are suffering from CFS, Chronic Fatigue Syndrome. They used to call it ME. It's a known phenomenon, but it's also a bit of a mystery. The current thinking... I'm sorry, Carrie, but the current thinking is that it is a habit. The health insurance industry has done a lot of research. There really is nothing wrong with people who have CFS – nothing physically wrong. The thinking now is that you have been ill and you have formed a sort of illness habit. Just as you might form the habit of – oh, I don't know – drinking hot chocolate before you go to bed, so that you don't feel quite right if you have to go without sometime. In the same way you have formed the habit of being ill. You expect to be tired, so you are tired. It's in your mind."

I gulped. Was it true? "But..." I thought of how I felt after climbing two flights of stairs to go to bed last night. It did not feel as if it were all in my mind.

"CFS," continued Dr Edwards, "is treated in the same class nowadays as addictions and certain other psychiatric illnesses. The NHS will only support sufferers for a certain time, and then only if they show that they are trying to help themselves. Generally speaking, you will only get cover for nine months after the initial diagnosis, which for you is today."

"Is that what you think?" I couldn't believe it. I wasn't choosing to be ill! I didn't want this.

"I... no." Dr Edwards looked embarrassed. "No, Carrie, if you are asking whether I think you are malingering, then no. I think you are ill." She sighed. "But I have no idea what sort of illness you have." She looked back at her screen, a frown on her face. "But I can tell you this: we may not like the attitude of these big medical insurance companies, but they have the incentives to find what works. We *can* help you, Carrie. We need to teach you how to manage your symptoms. I'll refer you to a specialist clinic and your attendance there will satisfy the National Insurance people that you are taking responsibility for your condition. That will give you nine months of recovery time, and it might work – I have known cases when it did."

"And if it doesn't?" I gulped. The tears had stopped but I felt a bit hollow.

"If it doesn't..." Dr Edwards looked down at her hands. "If it doesn't..." she started again. Then, "Does your husband work?"

"Tom? Yes, he's..."

"Good." Dr Edwards went back to her screen. She was not meeting my eyes. "If after nine months you still feel you cannot work, your benefits will be withdrawn. We will move you onto Medical Assistance which covers you for emergency treatment and infectious diseases. You will need to live on Tom's income..." She turned to me again, and now she looked sad, not embarrassed. "I'm sorry, Carrie," she said. "I wish I could do more. There was a time... But don't give up hope. You'd be surprised at how many people are able to work again at the end of the nine months, even if they have to take a less physical job... And you won't lose your benefits if you work twenty hours. It doesn't have to be full time..."

"Right," I said.

Dr Edwards became calmly efficient again. "Good, so I'll do that referral today and you should hear within two weeks.

They will expect a minimum of eighty per cent attendance… Do come back to me if you find you're struggling. Anything I can do to help…"

She was inputting stuff onto her DeV. The consultation was over. I felt I needed to sleep for a month. My legs felt weak as I stood to leave. If I didn't recover within nine months… I saw the abyss of poverty looming ahead of Tom and me and I felt a deep sense of shame. Now I needed to explain to Mum…

★ ★ ★

Tom and Ephraim arrived together that evening. Mum was still there; she had cleaned the house from top to bottom, cooked a chicken casserole, and was cutting back plants in the garden. There was a fresh vase of our own roses smelling sweetly in the living room. I had stopped crying and we had shared a silence together, Mum and I, after a long and wearing discussion of Dr Edwards' verdict.

Tom came in looking happy and somehow bright. It was a warm day, more like June than May, and he was in shirt sleeves, his face and arms looking brown. As he came in he was talking over his shoulder to Ephraim, who was smiling back at him. They both looked so fit and healthy and I felt like such a weakling, a person only nine months away from being transferred from National Insurance to Medical Assistance. It was the first time it occurred to me that Tom would have been better off if he hadn't married me.

Mum made a pot of tea and we all sat in the conservatory, watching the hummingbirds and the river. It should have been idyllic but I felt utterly exhausted and almost numb.

"How did it go, Carrie?" Tom was looking at me with kind eyes, a gentle smile in his enquiry. He knew Mum or I would have phoned him at work if it had been something terrible, like cancer.

"Not good," I gulped. "She said… she thinks… If I don't get better in nine months, they'll transfer me to Medical Assistance."

"What!" Tom's shock was immense. "Why? What do you mean? Carrie…"

My mum butted in, using her quiet speaking-at-Meeting voice. "Don't panic, Tom. Listen. Dr Edwards says it's Chronic Fatigue and that isn't a medical condition. She says it's a habit which Carrie can break, given the right help… We'll all help her. Carrie is going to get better."

Tom jumped up and sat on the arm of my chair, putting his hand on my shoulder. "This illness isn't a habit!" he exclaimed. "That's ridiculous. Carrie was as well as anyone – as well as me. Then she got that virus. Now she's ill! We need to get a second opinion. She isn't a malingerer!"

Mum looked taken aback. "No, of course not… well… of course she isn't. But the tests all came up negative. She hasn't got anything wrong with her – with her body."

"Well," Tom was really angry now, "she certainly hasn't got anything wrong with her mind!" Then, looking at my mum, "Sheena, you should know your own daughter better than that!"

Mum and Tom had never argued before. I loved Tom for springing to my defence like that, but I wanted him to stop. It was Ephraim who restored peace.

"Hey Friends!" he said, very quietly. "Friends!"

Mum took a deep breath. Tom sagged a little, his hand heavier on my shoulder. "Mum, I'm not malingering," I said. "I really don't think I am. I'm just so tired…"

Ephraim said, "Did Dr Edwards think you were malingering, Carrie?"

"I… no, I don't think so." I remembered her unfinished comment, *I wish I could do more. There was a time…* "I think her hands are tied. That's the impression I got."

"Quite." Ephraim was quiet for a moment, then, "It's how these things work. The big health care conglomerates and the insurers are in it together to make money. People with psychiatric illnesses or addictions, or with long-term illnesses, cost the insurers a mint. They do what they need to do to get rid of that expense." He looked directly at Mum. "If they can convince the public that people are responsible for their own ailments it lets them off the hook. If they can convince the sufferers and those closest to them that it is their fault, then all the better. Then everyone can resort to the mantras of our day: *responsibility* and *choice* and we are all free to go our own way without helping."

He turned to me. "Carrie, we are not going to do that to you. We know you. We don't understand your illness, but we *know* you. You will go to that clinic and we will support you. We'll do everything we can to get you well, but if we can't… if in nine months you still can't work, we'll find a solution. You and Tom are *not* going to suffer for something which isn't your fault!"

Tom sat up straight again. "That's right!" he said.

"Thank you, Ephraim," my mother said quietly. "Thank you."

"And now," said Ephraim, "let's eat!"

★ ★ ★

It was after dinner, the same day, that Ephraim told Tom and me about our proposed trip. Mum had gone to catch her bus, and we were back in the conservatory. I was feeling strange, a bit hollow and a bit exhilerated at the same time.

"Are you still up for it?" Ephraim asked of the expedition.

"Yes, as long as Tom doesn't mind." I looked at Tom, who was staring out across the river.

"I think it's a good idea," said Tom.

"I think you'll enjoy it," said Ephraim, "and it'll be a help to me. I want to navigate without using the DeV, which means having a map reader. Can you do that, Carrie?"

"As long as I can stay awake!"

"Then we go this weekend – the day after tomorrow. There'll be four of us. The story is that we are going to visit relatives. We will be going east, a bit northerly too, but not enough to raise suspicion, and nowhere near the coast. We'll stay for the weekend, two nights, and you and I will come back on Sunday afternoon. Is that okay with you, Tom?"

"That's fine." Tom smiled at me. "Actually, it works rather well. Derek asked me if I'd help him with something on Saturday evening."

Ephraim gave Tom a sharp look, but then said, "Good, that's settled then." To me he said, "Bring clothes suitable for wearing to church, won't you?"

"*Church!*" We almost never went into conventional churches, especially not those registered under the new Charity Commission and Extremism law, and those whose young people at school used to try to evangelise us, although of course we tried to remember that each church member has that of God in her or him, like everyone else. So, "Right," I agreed, and Ephraim left.

* * *

I was ready by three in the afternoon that Friday. It was difficult to rest knowing that Ephraim was going to pick me up mid-afternoon, so I felt weary as well as excited. I didn't realise it was him when the car first pulled up outside the house, although I was in the sitting room waiting. Instead of his silver ten-year-old hybrid, Ephraim was driving a rather smart electric blue hatchback. When I went to the back of the car with my case I saw that he had one of those bumper stickers with our new flag and the stars and stripes merging into each other, and the words 'out of the strong, something sweet', the motto of the pro-Alliance party.

There were two people sitting in the back of the car. Ephraim introduced us, first names only. They were a very ordinary-looking couple. Naomi had dark hair, badly cut, with a fringe that was too long to be fashionable. She was wearing one of those tent-like embroidered pregnancy tunics. Josh had a thin face and mousy hair. They both wore glasses. We all said 'hi' rather warily to each other as I settled in the front seat next to Ephraim and he opened an old road atlas to show me the route. We didn't speak again until we were out of the city.

"Ephraim says you've been ill," offered Josh. He was young, an adult, but with a voice that still sounded adolescent.

"Yes. Well, in a way," I agreed.

"Tough," said Naomi. "There was someone where we've been living who was diabetic, type two. They put her on Medical Assistance because they said she brought it on herself. Bad diet."

"We all had bad diets where we were living," added Josh.

"That's why we're getting out," said Naomi. "Well, not just our diets. We don't want our baby to grow up the way we did."

"Careful," warned Ephraim. "The less you know about each other the better. Carrie, can you look in the glove compartment for the toll sticker? We don't want to have to stop each time we reach a booth."

★ ★ ★

It was an interesting and a comfortable journey, though perhaps less so for Naomi who, I discovered, was seven months pregnant. We avoided the I roads (the motorways) so it was not the shortest route, but the map reading was easy. We also

avoided Oxford and Milton Keynes. Ephraim explained that
there are heavy volumes of military and ATTF traffic there,
the result of some large US bases and various ATTF and Royal
English Army camps. We stopped several times. Poor Naomi
kept moving around on the back seat and she needed the loo
quite often, but we didn't use service stations. Instead Ephraim
took us off the main roads into small towns and villages. We
had tea and muffins at the first stop, but just used the loo and
bought a chocolate cake at the second – to keep the tea shop
owner happy, Ephraim explained, and to give to our hosts. I
wasn't called on to do much map reading. Ephraim seemed to
know the way, but every now and again he would just check a
detail with me. "If we turn left towards Oxford will we reach
Appleford? Good, there's a little café there I think you'll like",
or "Is that road to Wallington Barracks marked on our map,
Carrie? Okay, we'd better not go that way."

The countryside was pleasant. June is a pretty month and
it was a sunny and cloudy day, with cloud shadows making
patterns on the hillsides, and grass verges thick with flowers
whenever we left the main roads. Unlike Naomi, I was really
comfortable in the car. The seat was padded with memory
foam and the headrest was just in the right place, so that my
neck ached less than usual. I think I dozed a little when we
first started out, but after that I felt quite bright.

Long car journeys were not part of my childhood. My
parents, like most people at our Meeting, didn't own a car
for environmental reasons, so our journeys always involved
public transport: usually trains, sometimes coaches. From
what I had read and heard at Meeting I expected that we
would be stopped and our papers checked quite often. In
fact, it only happened twice, and then the checks were pretty
cursory. Of course, I am mixed race, but not black – I don't
think I stand out too much and the other three were as white
as a Republican president! Ephraim was very relaxed about

the whole thing, smiling courteously at the police officers and asking whether they wanted us to get out of the car. Would they like us to open the boot? He casually referred to Naomi and me as his nieces and asked one constable whether there was any news of the American hostages in the Caribbean. I realised that our bumper sticker served a really useful purpose.

Towards the end of the journey, at about four in the afternoon, the land flattened out. We looked through the windows at huge skies with towering cumulus clouds drifting across them. The bright yellow rape was already harvested but fields of wheat and barley were turning gold. We passed a large wind farm on our right, the arms of the generators gliding through the air in lazy arcs. They axed subsidies for renewables years ago in favour of nuclear, so it must have been quite old, but I thought how beautiful it was, and how interesting that with almost no money spent on upkeep, every tower seemed to be working still. Ephraim said, "Okay, Carrie, we leave the main road now. We're nearly there. Look out for the signs."

We wound through narrow lanes with ditches instead of hedges on either side of us. We could see for miles: an old water tower, church spires among trees, slight rises and falls in the landscape, a sign to a ford. We went through one village with yellow brick houses squatting right up against the road and a village square with some sort of municipal building in the middle, then out, up a hill, with views across the countryside again, over a bridge which seemed to span nothing in particular, and into the village of our destination.

"We're almost there," said Ephraim. "Three minutes."

All three of us peered out of the windows. I had grown up in a large southern conurbation, and the villages in Hampshire are pretty in a thatched cottage sort of way. You can almost smell the money. This village was different. The road was narrow with old hybrids and a few modern cars parked on both sides. Most of the cottages and houses had no front gardens;

those that did were beautifully planted but a bit dusty looking. There were humps in the road to slow down the traffic. We passed a bakery on our right and one of those all-purpose twenty-four hour stores on our left, then came to a crossroads.

"It looks really old," said Josh, looking back the way we had come.

"Not all of it." Naomi was looking at a row of terraced houses at the junction where we had stopped, waiting to turn right while a tractor passed. "I grew up in a house like that." She was right, I thought. I had seen houses like that in the poor end of our city: narrow, with ugly windows and bad proportions.

"Why would they build those here?" I wondered aloud.

"This is an interesting area," Ephraim said. "A bit like Yorkshire in a way. The people round here are very independent. They always have been."

We turned right into another village street, a little wider this time. There were more yellow brick cottages, some kind of restaurant with a gravel car park at the front, small shops at intervals as the road sloped gradually down, alms houses on the right, and the sight of an old village church. Ephraim indicated again and we turned right into an area of twentieth century red brick houses and a fire station, then, "Here we are!" announced Ephraim and we pulled into a drive just before the fire station, past a sign that said *St Mary's Vicarage*.

A woman came out to greet us almost at once. She was wearing jeans and a t-shirt with a message printed on it, *Wise men still seek Him*, with flip-flops on her feet, and a cross made out of some coloured beads around her neck. "Hi," she said, and gave Ephraim a hug. "It's good to see you. And these two will be the nieces? And Josh – welcome. Come on in. Good journey?"

Ephraim was taking bags and overnight cases out of the

boot. "Great," he said. "Better than expected, in fact. How are you two? Is Will around?"

"Gone to see a parishioner." The woman led us into a long, sunny living room with pale green settees and a DeV50 on the wall. There were French windows at the far end of the room, open to let in the early evening breeze, and a view of flowers and a rich green lawn. "Sit down, sit down!" she said. "I'm Mia – or would you rather sit outside? I've got mint tea if you're interested. Or would you like to see your rooms? Or do you want to freshen up?"

Ephraim was smiling – no, grinning – as he carried in his bag on his shoulder, my bag in one hand and the third bag in the other. "Rooms, freshen up, mint tea in the garden in that order, please!" he requested. "You're looking well, Mia. How are the twins?"

"Oh, they're great," answered Mia, and looked at us three, gathered shyly at the foot of the stairs. "Charlie and Harry – Charlie's the girl. On summer camp in Virginia. Episcopalian Youth Action. They've been going for years but they're counsellors this year." She smiled at Ephraim and started to climb the stairs. "They'll come home as brown as berries and with faint southern accents that will last about one day once they get back to school." Then, almost without pausing, "Naomi and Josh, you're in the front room, here. You've got your own bathroom but the water temperature is a bit unreliable in the shower. Carrie, yours is this little room. It was Charlie's for a while so forgive the overwhelming pinkness! Ephraim, you've got Harry's room, the same as last time. I hope you don't mind the basketball posters? Just put the bags on the floor, will you, Ephraim. Come down when you're settled." She started to go back downstairs but said over her shoulder, "Tea in the garden when you're ready."

We all looked at each other. Naomi said, "I've never had a room with an en-suite."

Ephraim said cheerfully, "Well, make the most of it!" To me he added, "There's a bathroom at the end here, Mia and Will don't use it. Their room is over the garage with their own bathroom and Will's study. Carrie, will you fetch the cake from the car when you come down, I didn't have any spare hands to bring it in." He paused, "Oh, and if you can remember, Naomi and Carrie, you ought to call Mia and Will *auntie* and *uncle*. Josh, you can stick with first names. See you soon!" He picked up his bag, dumped it in Harry's room, and went downstairs whistling.

★ ★ ★

Will was not what I expected. He arrived back on his bike while we were sitting in the garden drinking mint tea and eating big slabs of the chocolate cake I had brought in from the car. It was very good. Mia was chattering away nineteen to the dozen, talking about her salad crop (lettuce, spring onions and tomatoes which were just beginning to ripen. We would have them for dinner later) and Naomi was very quiet, sipping cautiously at her mint tea and exchanging glances with Josh. It was strange calling Mia *auntie*, but rather nice, and she responded really naturally with "Yes, dear?" when I asked her if there was any sugar. I thought Naomi might find her tea more palatable if it was sweetened.

Will was a round sort of man. He was wearing cargo three quarter length shorts and a black, short-sleeved shirt with a dog collar. He was slightly bald, his face was moist from the exercise of cycling, no doubt, and he looked deeply cheerful, as if nothing would ever unbalance his good mood. He came into the garden from the garage, put a Bible and some papers on the garden wall, kissed his wife and said, "Greetings! Greetings! So you got here safely! Everyone okay? Chocolate cake I see? Which one of my kind nieces made that for me?"

Naomi giggled. It was the first time I had heard her laugh, and it was infectious. "Not me, I can't cook to save my life!" she announced.

"Me neither," I added. Then, pretending shame, "It's shop bought."

"Oh dear, oh dear!" bewailed Will. "A shop-bought cake gracing our humble table!" Then, taking a second slice, "Mind you, it's pretty good. Not some ordinary shop, me thinks!"

"How are the Willerbies?" asked Mia. "Are they coping?"

"Mm." Will looked thoughtful, then brightened up. "They're worried of course, but so far, so good." He looked at us. "Benefits withdrawn," he explained. "Feckless living. Five children and another on the way." He turned back to Mia. "Paul's parents live over towards Sandy and grow quite a lot on their smallholding, and the Pearsons are being wonderful, as always. I spoke to Pete on the way back. The free school meals will have to stop and that's a blow, but even here there's the risk of someone reporting the school. It's only just come out of Special Measures over that business with the Ukrainian children, and none of us wants the school closed and the kids bused to another village."

"Even here?" I queried. Will had said *even here there's the risk of someone reporting the school*.

Will and Ephraim looked at each other. Mia said, "We'll eat at seven thirty if that suits you. Is there anything any of you don't eat? Okay, well make yourselves at home. I think you might need a rest, Carrie? I can put a lounger down at the bottom of the garden by the pond. Do you need a rest too, Naomi? I still remember being pregnant with the twins… it's not twins, is it? No, well, good… although of course I love Charlie and Harry to death, but they were hard work!"

I got up while Mia was still talking. Will winked at me. "Have a good rest," he said, as I headed inside.

★ ★ ★

It was still light when we sat down to eat but Mia had put a candle in the middle of the table and there were cloth table napkins. Naomi's eyes grew round behind her glasses, and she hesitated before she sat down.

"Be seated! Be seated!" proclaimed Will. "We don't stand on ceremony here. Especially," he winked at us, "with family."

Naomi said, "It's like something off a DeV!"

Mia had just put the salad bowl down in the middle of the table. She looked sharply at Naomi. "What is, love?" she asked.

"All this…" Naomi indicated the table, the candle, the wooden salad bowl and the matching salad servers, the wine glasses.

"Ah yes…" Mia sighed. "I suppose it is – like something off a DeV, I mean." She patted Naomi's hand. "You have as much right as anyone to the good things in life. More, in a way. The future belongs to you." She paused. "Will, will you give thanks?"

We ate salad and tinned mackerel, then chicken kebabs with some sort of sweet and sour sauce, and Eton mess to finish. Mia, Will, Ephraim and I drank wine but Naomi wasn't drinking because of the baby and Josh said he had never developed a taste for wine. Will got him a beer, which seemed to go down well. As soon as the table was cleared Naomi and Josh said they'd go to their room. There was a DeV in there and quite soon we heard the sounds of a popular game show coming from upstairs. Will closed the French windows and we took our coffee to the two long settees. It was still light outside but there were shadows in the room, and Mia turned on two table lamps which made a gentle glow. Although their taste in furnishings was very different from that of my parents, there was something about the room which felt like my childhood home. I had slept before dinner and woken feeling thick-headed and groggy, but now I felt good, relaxed and almost without any aches. I was enjoying myself.

"Is it all right to talk?" asked Mia, looking at me and at the same time moving to place a large, floppy cushion over the DeV to block the sound unit.

"Oh yes, within reason," Ephraim assured her. "Carrie here has been involved in food distribution back home. She had quite an adventure, in fact. She and Tom are in the same community as me."

"Great! Good! Excellent!" Will smiled approvingly at me. "No full names or addresses, though. Agreed?"

"Agreed," we all echoed.

"So what's the plan?" asked Ephraim.

"The Birtles will take them from here," said Will. "Via Birmingham and the agricultural show at Warwick."

"Right," said Ephraim. "Travellers again?"

"Uh-huh," Will confirmed. "There's a special place reserved for them in heaven, if you ask me. As if they didn't have enough to put up with on their own account!"

"There have always been travellers round here," Ephraim said to me. "Half the locals have traveller genes although they'd hate to admit it. Isn't that so, Will?"

"Yes and no." Will scratched his balding head. "There are two sorts of locals here. Some families go back generations – centuries, I dare say. In the second half of the last century the village saw an influx of newcomers. They were generally middle class, professionals. You know, teachers, computer experts, a couple of accountants. That's when this house was built. I'm surprised they stayed, but mostly they did, and since... well, recently, there's been a sort of blending of the two parts of the village. We're independent. We stick together."

"It intrigues me," said Ephraim. "It's not a new phenomenon. Weren't there lots of Lollards here, way back at the time of the Reformation?"

"There were," agreed Will. "But not your lot! I don't know what happened to your people here in the east."

"There's a community in Cambridge," I pointed out. "I had friends at yearly gatherings who came from the Cambridge Meeting."

"True, true," reflected Will. "They never took root in the countryside, though. Which is a good thing! Because you do attract suspicion and we could do without that in our line of work!"

"I've got their papers," said Mia. "We'll need to spend some time coaching them tomorrow. And Carrie, you'll all have to come to church on Sunday. We've told people you are our nieces, cousins to each other. They will expect you to know your way around a Church of England service, so we'll need to coach you too."

"It'll be good for her!" announced Will. "Part of her national heritage. Everyone ought to know their way around a C of E service!" He grinned cheerfully at me. "Never know when it might come in useful!"

★ ★ ★

Saturday was fun. I called Tom on my DeV after breakfast, and mindful of the possibility that our conversations might be overheard, I talked about *Auntie Mia* and *Uncle Will*, and about how good it was to see them again. Tom said he missed me and he'd been to the pub with Derek while I was eating home cooked kebabs, and eaten stale fish and chips with too much grease on them. We both said we loved each other, but when I clicked off I thought how separate our lives were becoming.

After a lazy breakfast during which, to my surprise Will and Mia watched *A Fox in the East* for the news, Mia took Naomi upstairs to see whether some clothes she had lying around would work for her. Then Mia, Naomi and I went into the village to pick up a prescription for Will ("Asthma", Mia explained) and just to look around. Mia was very concerned about me walking too far, but I had slept well in Charlie's pink room, waking only once with a coughing fit, and I felt comparatively good. Mia introduced us to several people: the pharmacist, an elderly lady who was walking a dog down the road, and a young mum with a pram and an easy smile. "My nieces," said Mia, with such pride that you couldn't doubt that was who we really were. "Just up for the weekend. From Hampshire."

I slept after lunch while Mia coached the others in the ways of travellers, and when I woke up we all had a rather hilarious session with Will about how to conduct ourselves in a Church of England service and about taking communion, which we don't do. I found myself quite looking forward to it. Then we had a dinner of more salad, spaghetti carbonara and fruit salad, and I slept like a log, without dreaming at all, and without coughing.

★ ★ ★

I must admit, at this point, that despite my upbringing I was prejudiced and rather judgemental, perhaps *arrogant* is the right word, and I really didn't realise it until I went to that church service. Will had gone down early – we didn't even see him at breakfast – so we walked to the church with Mia. Ephraim wore a tie and a jacket, Naomi was dressed in a pretty blue smock which I think Mia had given her and Josh was wearing one of those waistcoats which used to be trendy a few years ago, and have now become more or less normal wear for formal occasions. I don't own Sunday clothes but compared with Naomi and Josh everything I had with me was quite tidy, and Mia said that my New Tex jeans would be the envy of any teenagers who might turn up.

The church bells were ringing as we walked down the street, and two old men were sitting outside a pub by the church with beer glasses in their hands. We all exchanged cheerful *"Morning!"*s, then our feet were crunching on the gravel as we approached the stone, arched doorway.

I am used to those who greet newcomers being outside the building. Since I had heard that conventional churches were rather unwelcoming I expected that there would be no greeters, but when we entered the church, there was a man with grey hair and a huge paunch smiling and ready to shake our hands and give us books.

"My nieces, Carrie and Naomi." Mia introduced us. "Naomi's husband, Josh. Girls, Josh, this is our good friend Michael."

"Very nice to meet you," said Michael. "I heard you were coming. It looks as if we'll be having a christening soon."

Mia sighed, "Yes, but not here. They've got to go back. The demands of work, you know. We don't see anything like enough of them."

I noticed she didn't introduce Ephraim who was standing a little behind us. He took the initiative and at the same time avoided giving away any personal details, asking, "It sounds as if you have eight bells. Is that right?"

"Yes," Michael agreed, "and quite a healthy band of ringers. People come from all over the eastern counties to ring here."

"Very good," murmured Ephraim, took his books and followed us down the aisle to a pew on the left.

The church was old. I mean really old, and large. The seating was what you expect in those sorts of buildings: dark wooden pews which seated about four people each. Ephraim sat with me, and Mia was in front with the other two. There were embroidered cushions on the floor, like foot rests. For a moment I couldn't think why, but Ephraim positioned his and then knelt down, and I remembered my lesson of the previous afternoon and did the same. In front of us Mia was also kneeling but Naomi and Josh stayed seated, looking uncomfortable.

Ephraim gave it a couple of minutes, then sat again. He looked entirely at home. I waited a minute or two more, not wanting to copy his every move, then I sat back as well, and looked around me.

There were more people than I had expected to see. Until we entered the New Alliance we used to hear a lot about the decline of the Church of England and the growth of American-style churches. I had formed the impression that the established church was on its last legs, racked with divisions and scandals. In the last few years there had been less of such talk, and now I wondered, seeing lots of elderly people but also quite a smattering of people my age and just a bit older, whether it had ever been as bad as the press implied. After all, the media made us sound like a bunch of well-meaning but unrealistic extremists. Why did I think they would treat any other faith groups more fairly?

The church was cool and comfortable. From where I was sitting I could see a sort of wooden screen, some shallow steps, an area for the choir and the altar with a white cloth and gold candlesticks with an ornate gold cross between them. As I watched, a girl, about twelve years old I would guess, walked to the altar from some sort of entrance on the left, and lit the two candles with a taper. She was wearing a white robe with a sort of ruff round her neck, but the ceremonial impression was a little diminished by the band holding her ponytail in place, which was one of those that flashes with ever-changing colours according to how she moved her head. Then the tune being played on the organ changed to a hymn tune, and we all stood as Will and the choir walked down the aisle from the back, a small boy holding a huge cross at the front of the procession.

Our worship is very simple. We use no obvious symbols and once, when another church donated a cross to us as an act of friendship, we had to have a long and rather fruitless Business Meeting to decide what to do with it. Us young people favoured putting it in the small Meeting Room, but we didn't get our way. I think I heard that the warden had it in her flat, but I'm not sure.

Anyhow, I was expecting all the ceremonial and I knew I would see a cross somewhere, but I really was not prepared to see it *everywhere*. There was the cross on the altar, a cross was carried at the head of the procession, there was a cross on the screen, our prayer and hymn books had crosses on them, and when the choir had filed into their seats Will approached the altar and made the sign of the cross. Everything in my upbringing led me to think I was witnessing something akin to superstition, but to be honest it didn't look like superstition. Somehow it was too calm, almost too natural. It looked like reverence.

All the words that we were to say or sing were written in the leaflet entitled *Holy Communion. Order One.* Thanks to Will's lesson of the day before it was quite easy to follow, and Ephraim seemed to know in advance when to sit, stand and kneel. We sang a hymn with quite a bouncy tune, and I just did what everyone else did. It felt fine, but at that point it didn't feel like worship. It was too much like play acting.

The change started when we sang a repetitive chant, the congregation echoing the priest, asking the Lord, and then Christ, and again the Lord, to have mercy upon us. The words we sang repeated Will's words absolutely, but the tune was different, so that I felt as if I were answering him, not copying him.

It was a short prayer but as I joined in I thought suddenly of the people on the nature reserve, of them being taken outside the city limits and dumped there, of the little girl with the broken arm. Not many people had mercy on people like that and they really needed mercy. I found I really meant those words.

After that it did feel like worship. Will asked God to make

us strong in doing good, although I cannot remember his exact words, and I really hungered for God to do that in me. When we sang about how holy and great is God, and how powerful, I was thinking about the ATTF and I had a rush of confidence, a sort of assurance that they couldn't win, that we were doing good things and it would work out. I didn't join in with the creed, when everyone recited their beliefs, because I really don't know how much of that stuff is true, but it didn't bother me that the people around me believed it. I didn't feel separate from them, the way I felt separate from the kids at school who kept warning us about hell. When we all shook hands and said to each other, *The peace of the Lord be with you*, it was like shaking hands at the end of Meeting for Worship at home, a sort of confirmation that we were one community.

Then we got to the part where we prayed for other people. At this stage we all knelt down, which was a strange feeling as in our community we don't kneel. Still, thinking about the Spirit being the Holy One, the Lord and the Most High, it didn't seem so much like an *outward form* to kneel, as a natural response. Will was at the front, saying the prayers, his tone quiet and reflective with gaps between each prayer. It felt like ministry, the way it sometimes feels when, out of a deep silence, a member of our community stands and shares something that touches all our hearts. We prayed for those in authority over us and I remembered that even our politicians, even the CEOs of multi-national companies, have that of God within them. We prayed for those who suffer, and I felt a sort of unity in our world: we all of us – the sufferers and those causing the suffering – need the Light. We prayed for the people of the Caribbean and for the American hostages. We prayed for some village people by name, and although of course I didn't know them, the prayers still felt like ministry and I held them in the Light and wished them well. I felt that sort of calm, integrated feeling I sometimes experience after a really gathered Meeting at home. I seemed to float along on the music and the words of the prayer book and Will's calm voice.

When it came to the part where the congregation go up to the front for the bread and wine, I knew I needed to go too, although I really didn't want to. Naomi and Josh had no problem with this. It seemed that somewhere, maybe at school, they had done this before, but it was a huge matter of conscience for me. I just don't believe that eating some bread and taking a sip of wine can possibly bring you nearer to a God who is a mysterious Spirit. I had tried to explain to Will the afternoon before and he had been sympathetic.

"So what brings you closer to God, Carrie?" he had asked, with a note of honest enquiry in his voice.

I had thought carefully. "Obedience to the Truth," I answered at last.

"What does that mean, in real life?"

"I suppose…" I thought for a moment. "I suppose it means doing the things you are supposed to do."

Will was thoughtful. Then, "Do you think you were supposed to come here, on this trip with Ephraim?"

"Oh yes!"

"Even though you are deliberately deceiving people? Your DeV call to Tom yesterday morning…"

"Yes, even so." Actually it had never occurred to me that deceit over a DeV to fool anonymous authorities who might be monitoring my calls could possibly be wrong.

"Well, for what it's worth, so do I. But now you're here, we have to maintain your cover. And that means taking a proper part in the service. If you stay in your seat eyebrows are bound to be raised."

I felt trapped. It was one thing to pretend to be something I was not, quite another to compromise on one of the most essential Truths of my life: that the Spirit needs no mediator, not man, nor book, nor ceremony.

"Suppose you come and kneel at the altar so that it looks as if you are taking part, but I just bless you? We do that quite often, for all sorts of reasons. Could you do that?"

A sense of relief had washed over me. "Oh yes, I could do that."

★ ★ ★

So I stood when the others stood, and queued up to kneel at the altar rail, doing what Mia, Naomi and Josh were doing beside me. Will came along, murmuring quiet words to each person. When he reached me he put one hand gently on my head.

"May the love of the Almighty Father keep you safe, and the example of Jesus inspire you, and the Spirit live within you and give you light." He had chosen words which I could say *amen* to, and I did.

I suppose Will had also known what he was doing when he chose the last hymn. *Dear Lord and Father of Mankind* which started as a poem written by a member of our Society. As the service came to a close I knew I had worshipped.

The whole service took about an hour, the same time as a Meeting for Worship at home, and I felt clean, whole even. How could I ever have judged these people, thinking we knew better than them? The Truths I had been brought up with were more true than I had ever realised. There really *is* that of God in everyone.

★ ★ ★

Sam Birtle arrived just after a huge roast lunch, to collect Naomi and Josh. He looked rough and spoke in a strange manner. He didn't shake hands with any of us, but nodded to us as if he were agreeing with something. Mia gave him a bottle of beer and I saw that his fingernails were clean and manicured, like those of a professional man, and his smile was kind, exposing gaps in his teeth and a twinkle in his eyes. He seemed to call Will *Rashi* and he looked especially kindly at Naomi, and called her *Chavi* which sounded impolite to me, but was obviously a term of endearment. I thought Josh looked more comfortable with Sam than with Will and Mia, and I realised what good cover the travellers must provide for some people.

We all hugged each other while Sam stood aside, and the others climbed into Sam's van and were gone. I went upstairs to rest and left Ephraim and Mia talking over the washing up. I thought I would hold Naomi and Josh, and the travellers who were looking after them, in the Light, but I was suddenly utterly exhausted and my neck started to ache. The cotton pillow case was cool to my hot face and I slept almost at once.

CHAPTER 3

I was worn out when we arrived back. I had slept a good part of the way and we had only stopped once at a pub, where we sat at a picnic table and I drank tea, and Ephraim drank black coffee. It was odd without the other two there. I felt as if I were travelling with an uncle. Ephraim was kind and considerate but he didn't talk much and I had the feeling his mind was elsewhere.

I let myself in, calling "Tom!" expecting him to be in the conservatory with the doors open to the garden, but the house felt warm and close. He was not there. I put my bag at the foot of the stairs and wandered through to the kitchen. There was a cereal bowl on the drainer alongside a mug and a spoon, but no other sign of Tom. The conservatory was all closed up. There were three hummingbirds around the feeder.

I went back to the living room. There is a pad by the integrated DeV where we write messages if we take each other's calls. There was a note from Tom:

Hi Carrie. Hope the weekend went well. Out with Derek and co. Back later. Don't wait up.

I felt absurdly let down. What I really wanted to do was to sit with Tom on the settee with a glass of wine, and tell him everything that had happened. I wanted to ask him whether, before he joined our community, he had ever been to a service like the one we went to. I wanted to exchange ideas about travellers. Instead I pottered around, boiled a couple of eggs and made some toast, and drank tea looking out of the opened conservatory windows at the birds. I was deeply weary and almost overwhelmed by a feeling of anti-climax. I intended to climb those daunting stairs and go to bed, but when I had finished eating I curled up on the settee and fell fast asleep, the sound of the river and some new, squawking bird in the background.

I woke when Tom came in. It was dark and the conservatory doors were still open. I was dreaming about swimming in a deep, cold sea. In my dream I kept swallowing mouthfuls of water as the waves washed over me, I was coughing and spluttering to clear my lungs and then I felt someone gently shaking my shoulder.

"Carrie! Carrie!" I opened my eyes. The kitchen light was on, making shadows and odd beams of light through the conservatory and out onto the lawn. "Carrie, are you all right?"

I sat up and another fit of coughing seized me. Tom went back into the kitchen and fetched me a glass of water. He closed the conservatory doors and put the settee throw round my shoulders. "You're frozen," he said. "What happened?"

My head felt muzzy and I was only half awake. "I'm fine," I lied. "I meant to go to bed. I just fell asleep…" Another fit of coughing started.

"Hold on," said Tom, and went back into the house, bounding up the steep stairs to the medicine cabinet in the first-floor bathroom. He was back in no time with the cough mixture – we always had some in the house by this time – and dosed me with two big teaspoonfuls.

When the coughing subsided he said, "Have you been ill like this all weekend, Carrie?" He looked worried.

"I… no. I was tired of course, but really I was fine." I had woken up properly by now. "It was probably just going to sleep by the open doors. Sorry."

"No," said Tom, a touch of weariness in his voice too.

"Don't be sorry. I should have been here when you got back. It's just that…"

Tom was sitting next to me by then, his arm around my shoulders, and what with the throw, the doors being closed and the warmth of Tom, I was beginning to warm up. "What were you doing?" I asked.

"Oh Carrie! Derek thinks I shouldn't tell anyone. Not even you."

I felt stung. We always told each other things. "But…"

"I know." Tom squeezed my shoulder. "And you've been having quite an interesting time too, I suppose?"

We were both quiet. Then I said, "Tom, we always said *no secrets.*"

"Yes." There was another silence. Then he said, "I owe you far more loyalty than I owe Derek." Then he told me about his weekend and I told him about mine.

He described going into the print shop late on Friday evening and copying false documents by the light of a torch. He told me about Derek standing guard in the front upstairs window where the laser printers are kept, and everything having to stop, twice, when ATTF patrols passed down the High Street. He told me about creeping out the back way into the alley, and Derek going one way with the forged documents, while Tom crept home the other way with the torch and the print shop keys. I told him about Mia and Will, and about going to Holy Communion. We talked for hours. At some point Tom got up and turned off the lights, and we held hands and watched the river in the light of the street lamp on the other bank, by the row of little Victorian cottages. Every now and then I had another fit of coughing, but I felt happy, closer to Tom than I had felt for weeks. We only realised how late it was when the street lights went off.

"Goodness," said Tom. "Midnight! And I've got to be at work by 8.30 tomorrow for the big university Archaeological Society print run! Come on, let's make a move."

I went upstairs ahead of Tom. As I started the second flight, holding the bannisters to give myself leverage because I was so weary, Tom turned off into the spare room.

"Tom?" I asked.

He sighed. "Carrie, I can't sleep with you tonight. You're coughing like – oh, I don't know. And I'm tired, and I have to be at work early." He came back and stood at the foot of the stairs, taking my hand and kissing it in an oddly old-fashioned way. "You sleep well and have a long lie in. It'll do you good. I'll bring dinner back with me. Love you!" Then he turned his back on me and switched on the light in the spare room.

I spent the night crying, coughing and dreaming. This was not how I had anticipated marriage to Tom.

★ ★ ★

I really couldn't blame Tom for the way things developed in the weeks that followed. I seemed to be overcome with weariness and Tom was well and busy, involved with his work and his commitments within our community. He came and went from the house, whistling tunes, bringing us takeaway meals and choosing movies he thought I might like for us to watch together, but which I usually slept through. I tried to go to Meeting on Sundays but it is a ten or fifteen minute walk each way and my ankles hurt, then it was difficult to cope with the conversations and the noise over coffee afterwards. I began to lose touch with what was happening there. One Sunday I counted seven people in Meeting who I could not name, and one of them asked me in a strong accent that sounded vaguely Russian if it were my first time at such a Meeting. I thought about the weekend Tom spent with Derek while I was with Ephraim, and then decided I just didn't have the energy to go there. The new term started and my contract as assistant formally ended. I was drawing benefits which helped us to cope, but Tom was not well paid and we had planned with the idea that we would have two proper incomes for at least the first year of our marriage.

Mum and Dad came up quite often, Mum at least once a week. She cleaned, cooked and ironed, fussed over me and kept silence with me, asking for recovery. Dad helped Tom move the futon into the other first-floor bedroom and they lent us a proper bed for Tom, and new curtains for that room. It nearly broke my heart.

I tried hard to maintain some sort of normality for Tom. When he came in from work or from some activity with Derek I tried to be bright and to ask about his day, his evening or his night. He was always kind, he answered cautiously but I guessed he was not telling me everything he was up to, and in a way that was a relief to me. I was too tired to worry about the ATTF and hungry outcasts being fed at night and I didn't want to think about what he and Derek had done the weekend I went away with Ephraim, Naomi and Josh.

People from Meeting started to visit me. Ephraim came now and again although Tom said he seemed to be away quite a lot. It took me several weeks before I realised that the overseers must have organised a rota. I was grateful, but also a little shocked. I felt I had become a case, a problem on a list.

The first person to visit was Job. Now, I don't know what it is about our communities, but people seem to live to a great old age. Job, at ninety, still pottered around town, attended Meetings, even demonstrated against benefit cuts and the introduction of the Medical Assistance scheme. He lived with a granddaughter and her family in a little cottage overlooking the gardens in the centre of town, and often brought his great-grandchildren to the children's meeting.

He turned up one Tuesday, about eleven in the morning, carrying a bunch of yellow roses from their garden. Job said he wasn't planning to stay but I was up and dressed and quite pleased to see him, so he came in and made tea while I sat in the conservatory and talked to him.

Job was quite a special person. He had been widowed for years and years but he had a huge family, almost a tribe, spread around England and parts of Europe, and virtually all members of communities like ours. I am a bit hazy about what Job's paid employment had been. Older members of the community still reminisced about big Sunday afternoon tea parties in his garden on Mariner's Hill, so the family must have been quite wealthy, but other than that I always heard tales about when he was warden of our Meeting, or he and his wife were Friends in Residence at our conference centre in the Peak District.

Like a lot of people in our community it would be, I think, impossible to pin down Job's beliefs in terms of theology, although easy to recognise in terms of actions. Bringing me roses was quite typical. So was the way he chatted about the hummingbirds rather than asking me how I was. It was also just like Job that I only realised after he had gone what he had really been saying to me.

We were drinking tea and watching the birds. "Do you know," he said, "I didn't ever see a hummingbird until I was in my twenties. Liz and I went to Brazil to visit a small community in Rio, and we saw some in a tea garden outside the city. I find them absolutely fascinating."

"Me too," I agreed. "I think there is more than one sort. When Tom first put up the feeder there were just those yellow and brown ones but... look! See that little red bird with the blue flashes on his wings? His beak seems even longer and the yellow birds keep out of his way."

"I see what you mean." Job seemed fascinated. "It's strange, isn't it, that we can do such harm to our environment and something as good as hummingbirds arriving in England is a consequence. It restores your faith in goodness, doesn't it?"

"Not just hummingbirds," I said. "Mum and Dad are

growing figs and peaches, and we have crocuses all winter now." I thought for a bit. "But there are new illnesses too."

Job looked at me thoughtfully. "Yes, of course there are," he agreed. "But isn't it better to think about the hummingbirds than the sickness?"

After he had left I realised that in his gentle, patient way Job had been suggesting I not dwell too much on my health.

The following week Zofia dropped in. She phoned first, saying she would be in town and had something to tell me, and would I be home? Of course, I was always home.

Zofia arrived with her parents in the early part of the century, at a time when there was a significant influx of people from Eastern Europe. I don't know how her family came to be linked with our community, although I imagine we gave some help to newcomers with housing, and language. Anyhow, Zofia is just a couple of years younger than me and we grew up together doing all those things young people do in our community. We were not that close – two years is a big gap when you are a teenager – but Zofia had not moved away as so many of us did, and she married Freddy whose real name is Wilfred just a few months before Tom and I married.

It must have been the very end of September and the leaves were beginning to turn. Zofia came in smelling of fresh air and autumn wind, with her face pink and her eyes shining. She had long dark hair which she sometimes wore in plaits, but which she was wearing under a red sparkly scarf in a very fashionable style that morning. She had a hemp bag filled with groceries, which she dropped by the armchair in the sitting room, and then she followed me into the kitchen while I put the kettle on.

"So how's it going?" she asked, looking at a poster Tom had made at work and put up with Green Fix on the wall by the mugs. It showed huge waves crashing onto a beach with words which we had found in the little red book Ephraim had given Tom when he became a member, about treasuring our experiences of God, however they come to us.

"Okay," I said. "Well, sort of."

"Poor you," sympathised Zofia. "Freddy was telling me last Sunday that you just can't shake this thing off. I'm so sorry."

"Yes, well. My doctor has referred me to a clinic. I should hear any time now. It might help."

"Mm." Zofia sounded doubtful. "Worth a try, anyhow!"

I wanted to change the subject. "You said you had some news?"

"Ah, yes! I have! Well, we have. Me and Freddy. Well, Freddy and I. Freddy and me? Which is it?"

"Freddy and me," I answered. "Well, actually, Freddy and you!"

"Yes, absolutely. I'm pregnant, Carrie. It's due in March. We're so excited!"

"Oh Zofia, congratulations!" She would not be the first of my gang to have a baby, but she would be the first who had stayed around. "Do you know if it's a boy or a girl?"

"Not yet. Anyhow, we don't mind. Any healthy baby will do! Freddy's over the moon, and my parents have started choosing names. Polish names, of course!"

I felt genuinely happy for Zofia and Freddy, but sad too. Tom and I never slept together any more, it was more as if we were friends than husband and wife. Each time I went a few days without coughing I hoped he would move back upstairs but my peaceful nights never lasted. We had planned to start a family later that year, so that my pregnancy leave could begin the following summer, but obviously that wouldn't happen now.

I cried a bit when Zofia left, then slept, and woke coughing. There were no hummingbirds on the feeder.

★ ★ ★

I was beginning to wonder whether the referral to the clinic had gone through. It was June when I was diagnosed and already it was the middle of September. I had until March to recover or at least to start working again, and then I went onto Medical Assistance. Once on it, I would have to work for twelve months before I could go back onto National Insurance. Twelve months when I absolutely mustn't catch flu, or take time off work for a stomach upset, and under no circumstances must I become pregnant. Becoming pregnant would count as feckless behaviour and that label is pretty much impossible to live down completely. It was an intimidating thought, and there seemed to be no sign of any recovery at all so far.

The letter, when it came, was kind, phrased more as an invitation than a demand, nevertheless it was very clear from the smallprint on the back that if I did not attend I would be putting my opportunities for any support from the Health Service in the future in jeopardy. I was to attend at the local hospital, in the outpatients' wing, for six consecutive Friday mornings from ten thirty until one o'clock, and I was to bring a list of my current medications with me on the first day.

Mum, Tom and I discussed the logistics of the thing. Our hospital is at the top of a hill. There is a regular bus service, but of course I would need to walk to the bus stop, and then walk from the place where the bus dropped me off to the clinic at the hospital end. I could manage all that, but I would be weary, and would then need to rest. After that I would be expected to take part in a two and a half hour seminar and then make my way home. "I can't do it!" I said, and tears came into my eyes. I so hated being this feeble.

"Two and a half hours is a long time," agreed Tom, looking worried.

"It's ridiculous," fumed Mum. "If the clinic is for people with Chronic Fatigue, you'd think they would know that this was asking too much!"

"There will be people coming further than me," I pointed out. "At least we live here. What if I had to come in from one of the villages?"

Mum said, "I think you'll need to go by taxi, at least to begin with. I can't see any option."

"Sheena..." Tom looked worried. "I don't think... you know, Carrie's benefit is quite a lot less than her pay when she was working, and mortgage interest rates have gone up. I don't think... I would like Carrie to be able to have a taxi but..."

"Oh Tom! I'm sorry!" Mum looked a little embarrassed. "Of course, we'll pay! She's your wife, but she's still our daughter. And you're our son! It will be a pleasure." Tom looked relieved and ashamed at the same time, if such a thing is possible.

★ ★ ★

The way they talk about people who have long-term illnesses, it always sounds as if we are a bunch of losers. It was arrogant of me, but I thought I would be the odd one out: educated, clean living and reasonably well spoken. When I walked into the room, therefore, and saw an elderly lady with beautifully coiffured white hair and wearing a pale blue trouser and waistcoat suit I assumed she was a doctor, or therapist, or some other leader of the group.

"Um, where should I sit?" I asked tentatively, looking at the circle of chairs facing an interactive DeV and a table with leaflets, pens and paper on it.

"I don't know," smiled the woman. "Anywhere, I suppose. The man at Reception just told me to come up here. This is the Chronic Fatigue seminar, isn't it?"

"I hope so," and I smiled back.

"How long have you been ill?" asked the woman. We sat down next to each other on the window side of the room.

"I was only diagnosed last week. I can't quite believe it. I've worked for twenty years for the same company, since the kids grew up, then I miss four weeks of work and they refer me to the Employment Health Tribunal!"

"I was diagnosed in June. I've been waiting for these seminars all summer. I've got to get better!" I could feel panic growing inside me.

The door opened again and a young man came in. He was using crutches to help him walk, and he looked pale and tired. He was followed in quick succession by a collection of other people: several middle-aged women; a bearded man with round spectacles who looked like an old-fashioned university professor, and a girl who looked like a teenager, with greasy hair, bitten fingernails, and a stain on her cream blouse. I suppose in all there were about twenty-five people. At first the only way I could tell the leaders apart from the rest of us, when they arrived, was that they went to the front, turned on the DeV and then closed the blinds to make it easier to see. They were young women in fashionable multi-coloured skirts and those silky-looking tunic tops. When they called the group to order I saw that the other way we could tell that they were the Guidance Therapists were their name badges.

The tone was all very upbeat. It started just the way seminars always start. The leaders introduced themselves (they were called Cora and Paisley) and we went round the circle saying our first names and one interesting thing about ourselves. Not all the interesting details were actually all that interesting. Shawn said he knew all the words to all the Beatles songs. Nell said it was her wedding anniversary. Mo said they had bought a car which parked itself so well that her husband allowed her to drive it, the first time she had driven the family car for fourteen years. They started at the other end of the semi-circle, so I had time to think, and I decided the most interesting thing about me is the community to which I belong, so when it was my turn that is what I told them. Cora and Paisley frowned and moved quickly on to Sylvia, sitting next to me, although several people in the circle smiled at me and Ed gave me the thumbs up. Sylvia's interesting detail really was interesting: her husband had written a novel about the first Board School in the city in the nineteenth century, and it was going to be made into a television series.

Then followed various other ice-breaking activities. I began to feel tired. We kept having to move our chairs, to make a pair, then a foursome, then a group of eight. We made lists of our symptoms on the DeV and highlighted in red the ones the group as a whole found hardest to live with. My neck started to ache. Cora and Paisley talked about medication, how it was dangerous to become dependent, how we needed to learn to manage our symptoms without chemical interventions. Then, as we were about to break for coffee, our two leaders exchanged glances and Paisley said in her usual upbeat, almost jolly way, with lots of strange emphasis on some of her words, "There is just *one more* thing we need to say to you, before we break."

People had started to head for the door, but we all sat down again and Shawn sighed audibly.

"Yes, I know," sympathised Paisley. "It's been a long first half. But this is *important*. At the beginning of the session one of us mentioned her religious affiliation." She smiled at me with, I felt, a thoroughly false sweetness. "Now, this is *of course* a free country and we will, all of us, have beliefs and convictions, even if they are not religious. We just want to say this. There is a growing body of evidence to show that *extremist* views can unbalance us in *all sorts* of ways. Our approach here in this clinic is *holistic*. We are not just bodies and minds, operating separately, we are *integrated* individuals: body, mind and spirit. If one part of us, say our minds, becomes *deluded* or fixed on *unhealthy* thoughts, we will slow down our own *physical* recovery too. So let's agree a set of behaviours here. We will not discuss *unhealthy* or *extremist* views within these four walls, and uncomfortable though it might be, we will *all* be prepared to examine our own thought patterns, to aid our return to *successful* social functioning. Is that agreed? Of course I don't need to point out that if you feel you can't *cooperate* there is really no point in you coming here. No point at all. But I'm sure you all *want* to do your best! So is that agreed? Good. Then there is half an hour for coffee and we'll be back in here, *refreshed* and ready to go by a quarter past twelve."

"That's telling you," murmured Sylvia with a smile.

Ed came over. "Extremist, my foot," he said. "You stick to your guns, girl!"

★ ★ ★

It took me a couple of weeks to understand where the course was taking us. A lot of what we did seemed sensible, if a bit obvious sometimes. Each Friday they gave us homework, things to do or think about for the following week. That first week we had to list all our regular activities and decide whether they were green (ctivities we could manage easily), amber (activities which left us quite tired), or red (activities which exhausted us thoroughly). I listed going up stairs as a red activity, along with walking for longer than fifteen minutes, changing the duvet cover on the double bed (although in reality Mum usually did that by then), and any sort of gardening. I also put *Chronic Fatigue seminars* on my list of red activities, but when Mum saw what I had done she persuaded me to delete it. I had told Mum and Ephraim, on one of his intermittent visits, about Paisley's pep talk concerning extremism and we had all agreed that I needed to be careful.

The aim of the colour coding became obvious in the second week, and that week I spotted a real danger too. We were all doing our homework on our DeVs and sending it in on Thursday mornings at the latest. Our homework for week two was to fill in an activity diary – an hour by hour account of the way we had spent our time highlighted in green, amber and red, or left blank if we were resting with our eyes closed. It happened that for once I had been to Meeting that Sunday, so when I came to fill in the table which had appeared on my DeV on the previous Friday, I needed to say something about that hour. For once Tom was home when I spotted the difficulty, and we discussed various options.

"Can't you just be honest, and put *Meeting for Worship*?" Tom suggested.

"I don't think so. We are an extremist organisation, you know."

"Well, how about *church*? It's not exactly a lie and there must be loads of people who go to church. It's a growing spectator sport!"

"Oh Tom, I can't, can I? I already told them where I worship."

Tom sighed, exasperated. I thought he was less patient with me, or anyhow with my illness, nowadays. "True," he agreed, and went back to his DeV.

I sat looking at my screen. How was I going to account for that hour? Then I had an inspiration. We had stayed for coffee afterwards, so I filled in a full hour and a half with *friends – coffee*. It was true without being incriminating, and I shaded the whole thing amber, as a compromise between the true green of the worship and the red of the socialising which followed. What was more, I could use the same ploy again.

When we talked about our charts that Friday Paisley was very complimentary. Two people hadn't turned up. Cora said in her gentle voice that Ed had an appointment at the pain clinic and would be with us the following week. Did any of us know where Sue was? None of us did. Then Paisley said, emphasising lots of words as she usually did, "But *you are* all here and you all submitted your homework. *Thank you!* So this week you'll see where we're *going* with this. Let's look at the background *research* before we go any further. Lights! Action!" And she turned off the overhead lights and closed the blinds, so that we could see the DeV more easily.

They showed us an interview. A beautiful girl with blonde hair and the whitest teeth imaginable was being questioned about her progress. They were fairly leading questions, like "So, Mary-Ann, how would you describe your situation when you first came to the Sibyl Housner Chronic Fatigue and Fibromyalgia Recovery Centre here at Bethel?" to which Mary-Ann dutifully replied, "I would say I was desperate. I had dropped out of school. I had lost all direction in my life. I had given up, really."

"You had given up, you say. Does that mean that you were no longer trying to get on top of your condition?"

"Yes, I would say that. I thought there was no hope for me."

"And would you say you were a contributing member of society at that time, Mary-Ann?"

"No," she said, with a sad and regretful look on her face. "I cannot say that I was contributing at that time."

"Now, Mary-Ann, I know that something changed this around in your life. Would you like to tell our viewers about that?"

Then came the story of how her school counsellor had encouraged her to attend the clinic, of how she had quickly learnt that she did not need to despair, that there were things she could do to help herself. She monitored her own activities, but even more, she monitored her negative thought patterns and she took on board the hints of her therapist, and her life changed.

At the close of the interview Mary-Ann was asked, "And so what are your plans now, Mary-Ann? What do you hope to be doing this fall?"

Mary-Ann smiled happily like the good girl she was. "I have enrolled in school again. I am going to study pre-school. I want to be a teacher."

"And so, Mary-Ann, would you say you are a contributing member of society now?"

"Yes, sir!" affirmed the virtuous Mary-Ann, and the picture faded out.

Under her breath Sylvia, sitting next to me, murmured, "If you want your life changed, just come and kneel at the altar now!"

When the blinds were open again Paisley said, "Well, of course, that interview is all very *American* but we follow much the same programme as they use at Bethel. In fact, Cora *studied* there, didn't you, Cora? So you *see* if you follow the programme with *enthusiasm* there is no reason why you shouldn't be *almost* back to normal in a few months. Any *questions*?"

The group was rather subdued, I thought. Sylvia was twisting her wedding ring round and round on her finger. Shawn was looking thoughtfully at one of the ceiling lights.

"It's very... encouraging," ventured Mo, nervously.

"Oh yes! It is! *Very!*" enthused Paisley.

The group was quiet again. I just had to ask, "So, are you saying that this illness, this Chronic Fatigue, is all in our minds?"

Paisley almost jumped on me. "Oh Charity!" she exclaimed. "It isn't an *illness*. Do you remember, we explained that on the first week? It's a *syndrome*. None of you have any medical symptoms."

"Okay," I wasn't going to be deflected. "So is this syndrome all in our minds?"

Paisley turned to Cora. "Perhaps you'd like to *take* this one, Cora? After all, you're our resident *expert*."

I liked Cora a little better than Paisley, and for a moment I hoped I was going to get a straight answer.

"The thing is, Charity," she started, "no illness is as straightforward as that. As we said, we take a holistic approach here, as they do at Bethel. Our thought patterns have so much to do with our overall health. You'd be surprised."

To my relief Shawn joined in. "Yes, but it wasn't my thought patterns which made me ill," he said. "I had atypical pneumonia, that's what my GP said, and this Chronic Fatigue came afterwards. It was the pneumonia what made me ill."

"Now, Shawn," Paisley said, her voice oozing condescension and superior knowledge, "you *think* the pneumonia gave you fatigue, *if* it even was pneumonia, but what if that is the *excuse* your mind has adopted? We all need to be prepared to *think*, to consider the *possibility* that our subconscious selves have *taken over*. You saw, on this interview, how Mary-Ann's life was *changed*. Well, we believe yours can be too, *if* you are ready to give it a *go*."

So then I knew. As far as Paisley and Cora were concerned, as far as the whole health establishment was concerned, we were self-indulgent and self-deluded.

★ ★ ★

Those six weeks were the toughest of my illness so far. The toughest of our marriage, too. Even with a taxi taking me to and from the hospital, I was so exhausted by the time I got home that I couldn't possibly climb the stairs. After the second week I even used the loo at the hospital before I picked up my taxi, because our bathroom is on the first floor and on one occasion I found myself literally crawling upstairs. I used to drop my bag on the living room floor and curl up on the conservatory settee, and sleep for hours.

A week wasn't long enough to recover before it was time to repeat the process. I couldn't sleep at night and I was desperate to sleep in the daytime, which they said at the clinic was to be avoided at all costs. I faithfully kept my activity diary and submitted it each Thursday morning, and several times Cora took me aside to 'give me a gentle hint' about sleeping in the afternoons. I started to feel really depressed. One morning I was listening to a programme on the little kitchen DeV when they played an old song from the previous century, *Bridge Over Troubled Water*. I started to cry, and I just couldn't stop. I was still crying when Mum arrived an hour later and she hugged me and kept silence until I stopped and then slept. Despite our commitment to honesty Mum suggested that I enter *time with my mother* rather than sleep on my DeV to send to the clinic. "Well, it's true!" said Mum, slightly defensively.

The seminars were emotionally demanding, not just because I found them so challenging, but because of the strong undercurrents that swirled around in the room. The message was clear: we are all responsible for our own health. We make choices and we have to live with the consequences. We may not have realised it, but we have all chosen, at some level, to opt out of various commitments and obligations. However, there was a way back. We needed to challenge our own behaviour and our own thought patterns. We had a session showing how we could find a base level, the most we could do without being tired, and then gradually build back up to normal life.

"How gradually is *gradually*?" Ed asked.

"Well," Paisley was anxious to explain, "if you can walk for *ten* minutes without tiring, then the next week you should aim for *eleven* minutes, the week after, *twelve* minutes, until you can walk for an hour or more. It just takes *discipline*!"

"But I worked in construction," Shawn butted in. "Before I was ill – before I caught this syndrome – I did physical work for eight hours a day, more if there was a rush on. At that rate it would take me years and years before I could work again, and I've only got four months left before I go onto Medical Assistance! And I've got two boys at home…"

Paisley was patronisingly patient. "Shawn, you didn't *catch* this syndrome. I can't *emphasise* that enough. Don't you *remember* that bit of film about the *physiology* of the syndrome? There is nothing *medically* wrong with you. Your body and your mind have formed habits, that is all, and we need to *break* those *habits*! After all," and at this point she looked at us with wide eyes, triumph and hope etched on her features, "we all *want* to be well, don't we? That's why we're here!"

"I thought it was to try to avoid Medical Assistance," murmured Sylvia under her breath.

After the first week Sue didn't return and Paisley and Cora didn't mention her again. Mo did, though, over coffee when a group of us were talking about the seminars.

"Where do you think Sue went, then?" asked Ed.

"Oh, I know Sue a bit," said Mo. "She lives up on New Manor Farm near me. I saw her last week and asked her. She said she thought it was all a load of nonsense. Her husband's health insurance is paying for her to go to a place in London. Anyhow," Mo looked a bit peevish, "she doesn't have to worry about Medical Assistance. They're made of money, that family."

One of the group of middle-aged housewives dropped out too, although her leaving was rather more dramatic. We were learning about our brains, about how some parts come from Neolithic times and other parts, in evolutionary terms, developed more recently, and these areas of our brains function differently. I was making a mental note to ask Tom or my Dad about this. I wasn't sure whether it was junk science or properly recognised theories. Anyhow, this one woman, Fiona, who always sat with the same group and hardly ever said anything, suddenly burst out, "I'm sorry, but I can't accept that!"

Paisley, who was leading the session, looked quite taken aback. "What's the *problem*, Fiona?" she wanted to know.

Fiona's face had gone very red. "All this stuff about evolution. I'm a Christian, and we don't believe in evolution. I believe that God made me the way I am, I am not descended from apes!" and with that she pushed back her chair, grabbed the papers from the floor at her feet, and rushed out of the room. She had tears in her eyes.

Paisley and Cora exchanged looks. "Does anyone else feel like that?" Paisley asked, glancing at me. If I had felt like that I doubt if I would have admitted it, but in fact we have never had a problem with evolution. We are pretty much the opposite to fundamentalists.

Cora left the room and Paisley continued her talk. I can't remember the details although they must have downloaded the outline onto our DeVs for us to review later. This happened round about week four and I was so tired by then I hardly took anything in.

After a few minutes Cora came back in, followed by Fiona, who took her seat again, her head down.

After that session we didn't see Fiona again. I hope she had a rich husband too.

★ ★ ★

At first, Tom seemed quite interested in the seminars. One evening we sat on the settee in the sitting room – it was the first evening when it was too cool to sit in the conservatory – and looked through all the stuff I had accumulated on my DeV. He looked a bit perplexed. "So don't they think you're ill? I mean, if this is a known syndrome, don't they think there must be a cause? Isn't anyone doing any research into it?"

"I don't think so." I had looked on my DeV one morning, and had found organisations offering almost miraculous cures for huge sums of money, and a campaigning blog which I considered signing up to, but never did. I found an apparently very reputable group in London too, and hoped it was the clinic Sue had gone to, but they were a private organisation and consultations were expensive. More to the point, I couldn't imagine having the energy even if I had the money to go up to London.

"Derek thinks it might all be related to air pollution," Tom said. "You grew up quite close to a busy road, didn't you?"

"There's a guy on the internet who thinks it's damage to the central nervous system," I said. I didn't add that he thought that, as with polio, sufferers might never fully recover. In fact, the general consensus on the internet was that a person might get a bit better, but that once you had contracted Chronic Fatigue you would never be the same again.

The trouble was that there really wasn't anything to say about me being ill. There was nothing Tom could do about it. He had started working extra hours to boost our income because even with help from my parents we were struggling to pay our mortgage. When he wasn't working he was often busy doing things with Derek and his crew. They were feeding people on Old Hill and in the nature reserve, and also just outside the city limits in the wood by Punchbowl Farm, where the crop circles used to be when I was a child and was taken up to the Science Park on school trips. Tom and I had more or less stuck to our no secrets agreement although Tom never went into any detail, but that had a downside to it. I had thought about the girl with the Russian accent and Tom's and Derek's activities, and realised that for some reason our Meeting was sheltering someone who probably had no legal right to be here.

I was worried about Tom, but I was worried about our relationship too. It came to a head on the last week of the seminars. Mum was at our house when Tom came in from work, around six thirty in the evening.

When he hadn't arrived at the usual time Mum had said, "Tom's late, Carrie."

"He's working 'til six," I explained. "They've got all this extra work from the university, and we need the money."

Then when Tom did come in, he looked distracted. "Hi Carrie," he said, kissing the top of my head. "Hi Sheena. Something smells good!"

"Shepherd's pie," said Mum. "It'll be ready any minute."

"Oh, I can't stay," said Tom, his foot on the bottom stair. "I need to be at the Meeting House in five minutes! I'll grab some chips later. Carrie, it's another late night. Don't worry, I'll stay at Derek's. I should be a bit earlier tomorrow evening." He ran upstairs and into the spare room – his room – then into the bathroom. The flush went and Tom raced downstairs. Wearing a hoodie and trainers now, he said, "Enjoy your meal!" and was gone.

Mum stood looking at the closed door. "Does that happen often?" she asked, her voice a little tight.

Tears welled up in my eyes and I couldn't talk. I just nodded.

"Carrie, love…" Mum stopped. Then, "I'm so sorry," she added and sighed. "So sorry."

★ ★ ★

That all happened the Wednesday before the raids. On Thursday, the night of the first two raids, Tom was home. He came in earlier, maybe about five thirty, looking cheerful and carrying bags with a Chinese takeaway in them. I think he must have been sorry about the night before, because he had ordered a movie to be uploaded onto our big DeV and had obviously planned an evening in together. I was tired out, and dreading the last of the seminars the following morning. I was in that sort of state where I desperately wanted to sleep, but I knew that if I went to bed I would just lie awake.

The food was good and the film was fun. It was historical,

taking place at the sort of time that Dickens was writing, the storyline was based on two women who took children from workhouses in England to Canada. In the film one family, who had been separated on entry into the Liverpool workhouse, were determined to stay together, so the boys had somehow to escape the activities of Maria Rye and Annie MacPhearson, which they managed through many colourful adventures until, at the end of the film, the family were reunited and lived happily ever after.

Tom and I watched it sitting together on the settee, Tom with his arm round my shoulders, me resting my head against him. At one point I nearly went to sleep but Tom nudged me awake again, and I was glad. The story was fiction but the background was true.

"Things haven't changed so much, have they?" Tom said, when it was finished.

At bedtime Tom followed me up the second flight of stairs. "Do you mind?" he asked. I was very weary, and I suppose I must have hesitated. "I'd like just to sleep next to you," said Tom.

We lasted half the night. I dreamt my drowning dream again and woke up coughing. Tom had gone back to the spare room. I suppose I had kept him awake.

The following morning my little DeV, which was on the bedside table, woke me up with its flashing lights, and I could hear another one chiming downstairs. Then I heard Tom's voice, sounding surprised and angry, and he bounded upstairs.

"Carrie," he asked as he burst into the room, "have you got a message from your mum?"

"I... Let me look." Then, "It's from Dad," I said. "Oh Tom!"

The message was blunt and factual: *Police raid early this morning. Mum arrested.*

Tom sat on the bed. "Oh Carrie... Why?"

"I bet it's that article," I said. As we had expected Mum's submission of *Religion: An Extremist Activity* had been turned down by all the national papers and had ended up, not in our journal, but in an even smaller publication called *Alternatives to Capitalism* which was published on the continent but circulated in England and Wales.

"I'll phone Dad," I said and clicked on his number.

Dad looked tired and drawn, as far as I could tell on my small screen. "It happened about five this morning," he said, sounding shaken. "The police were armed! Why would anyone think they needed to be armed to arrest your mother? She didn't even raise her voice to them!"

Tom looked over my shoulder so that he could see Dad too. "Where did they take her, do you know?"

"The local police station? I don't have a clue, and I forgot to ask. They were searching the house. You should see the state of your mum's office! They took her DeV."

Tom frowned, then, "Do you have anyone from your Meeting there? Do you want us to come down?"

"You can't, can you?" Dad answered. "Carrie's got to go to the clinic and isn't this a working day for you, Tom? It's really important you two go on as normal." Then he seemed to pull himself together. "I'll phone the clerk of our Meeting soon, and let you know what we can find out."

We had just clicked off when the DeVs started to flash and ring again. Tom was still sitting on my bed, so he answered. I thought it would be Dad again, but when the picture cleared I saw it was Johnny from our Meeting.

"Hey Johnny," said Tom, obviously surprised.

Johnny was looking serious. "Hey," he answered. "Tom, have you and Carrie heard?"

"About Carrie's mum? Yes. Her dad just rang."

"Carrie's mum? What about Carrie's mum? Is she ill?"

"Arrested," I said. "Early this morning."

"Oh!" Johnny was looking very grave. "Oh, that's bad. I was phoning to tell you that the Meeting House was raided late last night. They took away the Russian girl, Alexis. You know – and the warden too."

★ ★ ★

It was really hard to concentrate on that last seminar, harder even than usual. For once I did not feel sleepy or weary, the adrenalin was coursing through my veins and I felt buzzy, and my stomach was churning. Of course, this was not the first time Mum had been arrested. She was one of a group of women who protested when they moved the nuclear deterrent from Scotland to our home town when I was still living at home, but that was different. The police had been unarmed in those days and some seemed quite sympathetic. They didn't mind policing our protests because we were always non-violent and didn't treat them like the enemy, unlike the Nationalists with their anti-immigration demonstrations. Mum and all the other women had been put in one large cell and Mum told us afterwards that they sang protest songs. The custody sergeant and another officer had come along the corridor and asked if they would do requests, and later the officers had gone out and bought everyone pie and chips. All Mum's crowd had been released without charge the following morning. I was pretty sure times had changed since then.

Paisley was in especially good humour that morning, although I didn't notice us attenders being particularly happy.

"Well done, *everyone!*" she said as we settled in our places. "*You* are the ones who have *stuck it out*. With attitudes like yours, I'm sure you'll all be back at work in no time! I'm *particularly* pleased because I'm quite *experienced* with these groups. Well, *Cora* and I are quite experienced. I really didn't *expect* so many of *you* to make it." I felt, rather than saw her, glancing at me.

"Nor I," agreed Sylvia under her breath.

"I am *happy* to say that I can *sign* the certificates for *all* of you, to say that you *not only* attended each *session* but that you worked *hard* and *contributed* well. Of *course*, some of you are *quieter* than others and some *seemed* to have certain *issues* at the beginning, but you have *faced* some hard *truths* within *yourselves* and believe me, you have *grown!* You may not be able to *see* it, but I can! *We can*, can't we, Cora?

"So *today* we plan to spend a bit of *time* with each of you *individually*. Then we'll send our *reports* back to your GPs. From *now on* your GPs are your first *port of call*, or the Employment Tribunal *counsellors* if you came by that *route*, but of course, we're *always* here if you want to *contact* us. At twelve thirty we've got a little treat – cake and drinks – to *celebrate* your success."

Ed came over when Paisley and Cora took their chairs to the far corner of the room, ready for our individual interviews, which were obviously not going to be very private. They had called the teenager with the bitten nails first. I had never heard her say anything and I couldn't remember her name. It was something lots of teenagers are called. Brittany? Charlotte? Lane?

"So what have you learnt?" asked Ed.

"Nothing, in point of fact," asserted Sylvia. "Have you learnt anything?"

"I have learnt," said Ed, glancing towards our leaders, in a huddle with the teenager, "that I don't have an illness, I have a syndrome. I don't know how I got it, but it is definitely all my fault. I don't know how to get rid of it, but it is my choice whether or not I hold on to it. Come on, Sylvia, you must have learnt something!"

Sylvia said, "Okay, well, I have learnt that despite working for twenty years with hardly a day off work for sickness, I have deep-rooted anti-social, work-shy tendencies which should not be indulged by responsible tax payers. Carrie?"

"The same," I said.

"Oh no!" said Ed, quite loudly.

"Sh!" hissed Sylvia and I, together.

More quietly Ed continued. "You have learnt that belonging to a peace-loving organisation concerned with justice and equality is really psychologically very dangerous, and might in fact be the very cause and origin of your illness – whoops! I mean syndrome!"

"Oh, I knew that already!" I said, and we all laughed.

When it came to my turn to go into the corner the room was almost empty. Several people had decided not to wait for the cake and drinks, and one group had gone down to the hospital canteen to swap email addresses.

Paisley said, "Well *done*, Charity. What would you say is the *biggest* change brought about by this course, in your *life*?"

I tried to think. "I'm much more aware of the different levels of activity," I said. "You know – red, amber and green."

"Good, good. And are you *using* that knowledge? Are you *doing* more than before?"

Was I? Probably not. "Not yet," I admitted. "Because these seminars have made me so tired. I can't seem to establish my base level in order to increase my activity gently." I felt it was a good move to use the jargon they had taught us.

"Ah yes, that is a problem," agreed Cora, to my surprise. "At Bethel we only expected our clients to attend forty minutes a week, which they could manage more easily."

Paisley was defensive. "But of *course*, this is all at the *tax payer's* expense. You can't expect to be *coddled* if you're not *contributing* anything!"

Cora asked, "Do you feel you know how to establish a base line now? And how to build up gradually?"

I thought I needed to show a bit of enthusiasm. All this was going into an official report, after all. "Oh yes!" I tried to sound really enthusiastic.

"Good. Excellent. Now," said Paisley, a concerned frown on her face, "about those *negative thoughts* you had when you first came – your tendency to *extremism*. Do you feel you've been able to *tackle* those?"

It was a tricky question. On the one hand I don't believe my thoughts are particularly extreme, on the other hand the seminars and Tom's activities had certainly made me think more about my opinions. "I think so," I said.

"She didn't link up with Fiona," Cora reminded Paisley. "It would have been a natural connection if she was still indulging those sorts of ideas."

Much you know about it! I thought. *Fiona would definitely believe I am deluded and led astray!* But all I said was, "I gained the impression that Fiona was a bit troubled."

"Good!" Paisley smiled her biggest, most insincere smile. "I think you are right. Well, Charity, I can see no *reason* why you should not go on to live a *full* and *satisfying* life as a *contributing* member of society. Don't you agree, Cora?"

"I do," said Cora, smiling at me, but I thought, *I bet you don't! I bet you know that getting better is going to be a much more hit and miss business than that!*

Then they gave me my certificate and I went home, without my cake and drink, to see whether there was any news about Mum, Alexis or the warden.

CHAPTER 4

When something happens in our community my DeV is usually buzzing with messages. We often don't phone for fear of intruding, and the messages can be quite oblique, like the time when we were planning a peace demonstration in the centre of the city, and thought the New Patriots might hold an opposing rally. It was, therefore, odd to get home and for there to be no messages at all on any of our devices. I phoned Dad. He looked tired but not frazzled, and I could see that there were people in the kitchen, so I guessed that members of his Meeting were rallying round.

"We know where your mother is," said Dad, reassuringly. "She's still at the local police station, and Ash has gone there to provide legal representation."

I knew about Ash. He was a lawyer, a member of the local Sikh community and very involved in human rights. "Ash thinks she will be out before the day is over. She certainly hasn't broken any laws! You know your mother."

It was comforting hearing Dad talk. They have, both of them, been arrested several times before, mostly as a result of peace demonstrations and sit-ins to do with basing our nuclear deterrent in their home town. The process seems to hold no fear for them, although when I was growing up I used to feel very anxious if they were arrested together.

Dad didn't ask about news from our end, although I'm sure they must have heard about Alexis and the warden by then. We chatted a little, and Saul Goldsmith came on the line too, reassuring me and promising that they were all holding Dad and Mum in the Light.

When the call was over I wandered round the house wondering what to do. It was lunchtime but I didn't feel like eating. It was time I had a rest, but I didn't feel like resting either even though my knees felt like jelly and my head was beginning to feel fuzzy. I wished Tom could come home from work, but of course I knew he couldn't. He certainly couldn't explain to them that his mother-in-law had been arrested.

Then a horrible thought occurred to me. What if they had arrested Tom too? It was perfectly possible, given all that Tom and Derek had been doing. I started to think about Alexis. How much did our Meeting know about her? Would she remain quiet when they questioned her? Could she be trusted? And I thought about our warden. She has grandchildren. Would they threaten her through them, suggest that her activities could damage their futures? I went hot and cold, frightened and alone. I jumped almost out of my skin when someone knocked on my door.

Job was carrying a small pot of blackberries. "I picked these on my way here," he said, handing them over. "You probably ought to wash them, they were growing right by the road." He came in, shrugging off his overcoat and dumping it on the settee. "Shall I make us a cup of tea?" he asked.

I could have hugged him. Everything about Job seemed so absolutely normal. He followed me into the kitchen and put the kettle on. "You sit down," he commanded. "Is this the tea you use?"

We sat in the conservatory drinking our tea and watching the river. The hummingbirds seemed to have gone but there was a robin pecking around in the flower bed under the roses. For a few minutes neither of us said anything, then Job remarked,

"There are times, I have found, when the easiest thing is to expect the worst. In my experience the worst seldom happens."

"But you can't know it won't," I pointed out. "Sometimes the worst does happen. What about the school in the park?"

"Yes…" Job sounded pensive. "It did seem as if, perhaps, the worst happened then. But really, I'm not so sure. Of course, what happened was not good, but still…"

"People vanished, didn't they?" I asked. "I mean, what if people vanish now?" Then, gulping, expressing my worst fears, "What if Tom vanished?"

"Ah…" Again, Job was quiet, watching the river. Two swans floated gracefully downstream. "Yes, you are bound to think about that." He sipped his tea again and crossed then uncrossed his ankles. "I imagine Tom is safely at work."

"But…" I couldn't tell Job what Tom had started doing with Derek, beyond feeding the homeless.

"I know," said Job, although I wasn't sure what he knew. He lifted his mug again, looked surprised that his tea had gone, and stood up to pour himself some more. He waved the teapot in the air to ask if I wanted more too. Then, as he sat, he said, "Why not just phone? You can phone Tom at work, can't you?"

"Yes, well… no. Not really," I said. "In an emergency. That's all."

"Yes, I see." Job looked thoughtful. "And of course they mustn't know anything like an emergency is going on. Is that right?"

"That's right." I watched the robin and wondered vaguely if the pickings were good under the roses. "If I just knew Tom was all right."

"Well then," Job sounded purposeful, "where's my DeV? It's a bothersome thing. My granddaughter insists I carry it around, but I don't like it at all. It buzzes in my pocket and they say people can listen in on any conversation. I liked my old mobile phone. I could switch it off properly!"

He rooted out a little dark green DeV37, the sort with a larger keyboard, designed for older people. "What's Tom's number?"

I gave him the number. He typed it in and clicked *vis* so he'd get a picture too. The phone rang three times and was picked up. It was Feany, with a blue sparkly headscarf, very fashionable, but looking a bit hazy because of Job's device. "Good afternoon," she said politely, obviously not recognising Job.

"Good afternoon." Job was putting on a very old-man sort of voice, sounding slightly confused. "Does Tom work there?"

"We do have a Tom here," said Feany, patient as always with strange potential customers. "Tom Walker. Would you like to talk to him?"

"I would," said Job. "That's exactly what I would like to do."

"Well, hold on," said Feany kindly. "He's on another line talking to a customer. He will be with you shortly."

"Thank you."

"You're welcome," said Feany, and left the device. We could see her jumper as she stood up to move away, then we could see a strange view of the office, with Tom sideways on, talking on another DeV with a large screen, moving his finger around on the VDU, presumably to demonstrate something to a customer.

Job hung up. "There you are," he said to me. "Tom is safe and well!"

I felt a sort of relief wash through me. "Oh, thank you, Job!" I was nearly crying.

"No problem," said Job. "Now I need to be getting back for my lunch, or my granddaughter will be buzzing me on this infernal device. And I think you ought to rest." He stood up slowly and carefully and walked through to the sitting room. "I'll let myself out," he said as he shuffled into his coat again, and then the door banged as he left. I lay down on the settee in the conservatory, pulled the throw over me, and was asleep almost instantly.

★ ★ ★

That evening when Tom came in we both knew we needed to talk. There was still no more news, either about Mum or about Alexis or the warden. A message had gone round that there was to be a special Meeting for Worship at seven in the large Meeting Room. We left our DeVs at home, and discussed the situation as we walked along the river path by the flood defences.

"It's obviously part of the same crackdown. It isn't hard to see how they knew about your mother," said Tom. "That article was pretty provocative, after all. But how could they have found out about Alexis?"

"Well, who knew?" That seemed the obvious place to start, for me.

"Hardly anyone." Tom was looking thoughtful. "Obviously the warden. It was only fair for her to know. Of course Derek and I. You knew. I think Ephraim knew – well, actually I'm sure he did."

"I can't believe any of those people would leak information about her status," I said. "But surely lots of people will have seen her at Meeting. Anyone could have guessed." Then I added, "Although I don't quite trust Derek."

"Don't be daft!" Tom actually laughed out loud. "Derek's up to his neck in this! He's got more to lose than any of us." Then, looking a bit worried, "We don't know much about Ephraim, though, do we? Derek is quite wary of him."

I felt uncomfortable. Ephraim was indeed a bit of a mystery but there was something about him that led me to trust him, whereas Derek...

★ ★ ★

The Meeting for Worship was strained. There were about twenty-five people there and it was clear at once that most of them had no idea what was going on. The Clerk introduced the topic.

"Friends," she said, "some of you will know that last night – well, actually at three o'clock this morning – our warden and one of our residents, Alexis, were arrested. They are still in custody. And our Friend Sheena from another Meeting was also arrested at the same time. We have no news of her except that she is still at her local police station, in one of the cells. All three should be charged or released within twenty-four hours, unless… well, unless this is a terrorism issue."

"So it's not to do with money, then?" I supposed Marcus was thinking about a Meeting a few months ago where a warden had run off to Europe with the local Meeting funds.

"No, not money!" said the clerk.

"Then what?" asked Pru, looking perplexed. "What's going on?"

The clerk and assistant clerk exchanged glances. "We haven't been told," said the clerk.

The assistant clerk added, "It all happened in the early hours of the morning. All the residents were in their rooms, asleep we assume. Beatrice, whose room is next to Alexis' room, woke up, and she thought the uniforms were ATTF, definitely not police."

"Have we been harbouring terrorists?" Pru sounded peevish. "I thought we had agreed to be very careful about our residents?"

The clerk answered that one. "I think we can be absolutely certain that neither our warden nor Alexis are terrorists," she said. Then, looking at Tom and me, "And I am sure all of us know that Sheena is not a terrorist either!"

A gentle laugh went round the room. Although my parents belong to a different meeting all the older or more established members of our Meeting would have known Mum, and the thought of her involved in terrorist activities was indeed ludicrous.

"So, Friends, let us follow the example of early Friends and hold these people in the Light, in the knowledge and certainty that Truth is more powerful than deceit." And so we had an hour of deep, silent worship.

★ ★ ★

Mum and the warden were released four days later on Monday, with cautions. I spoke to Mum and Dad on our DeV. They were being very careful, and Mum talked only about the food in the police station (which was good) and the coffee (which was awful) and asked me to hold in the Light a young man who had been in the cell next door, and with whom she had had some conversation. He was in for a knife crime, and was likely to go into some sort of juvenile detention facility, since it was not his first offence. Mum had spoken to him about the Light that is within him, and it seemed he had been quite impressed. I didn't see Mum in real life until the following Saturday and by then she was more or less back to normal.

I saw the warden the day she came out, though, and that was rather shocking. I was trying to do some sort of physical exercise every day, within my limits, and was recording it on my daily timetable. This I would need if I had to go to a Medical Assistance tribunal at the end of my nine months. Job and a few others play their recorders at the Meeting House sometimes. They had formed a little club with the motto, *Make a cheerful noise to the Lord* and Job said *noise* was the right word for it. He suggested I might like to come and listen, and he would walk back with me afterwards.

The recorder players were just setting up music stands, with much banter about the musical abilities of one of the descant recorder players, when the large Meeting Room door opened and the warden was standing there.

She looked dreadful. Our warden is one of those women whose age is difficult to guess. She has salt-and-pepper hair which is cut straight and hangs like a curtain to about ear lobe level. She wears hand-knitted jumpers which she makes from bits and pieces of old wool, so that they are multi-coloured and often vaguely discordant. Her jeans always have creases down the front like a businessman's suit, and she wears those plastic shoes from America which have been popular with her generation for decades.

When she stood there at the door, though, everything about her looked wrong. He hair looked lank. She had tucked it behind her ears, and there was a bruise very evident on one cheek. She had dark rings under her eyes. Her jeans looked dirty, her shoes were scuffed, and she was swaying slightly.

"Liz!" several people sprang forward simultaneously. "Here, sit down!"

"Would you like a cup of tea?"

"Are you all right?"

"What happened?"

There was a cacophony of voices all at once. The warden just sank into the nearest chair and closed her eyes. Job went through into the kitchen.

"Give her some space!"

"Here, let me take your coat."

"Are you hurt?"

Everyone was surrounding her. The warden just sat with her eyes closed, breathing deeply.

Job came back with a mug of something hot. He took the warden's hand and closed her fingers around the handle. "Here, Friend," he said gently. "You'll feel better soon." He kept his hand over hers as she rather shakily raised the mug to her lips.

She opened her eyes and smiled at Job. "Thank you," she said, "this is just what I needed."

Job looked around at us. He didn't say anything, but the message was clear: "Be quiet! Give her some space!"

"Shall I make tea for everyone?" I asked, and there were nods and smiles of approval.

When she had recovered a bit the warden told us a little about what had happened.

"They thought I had been people smuggling," she said. "Someone had phoned Crime Stoppers and reported me. They needed to check it out."

"Who would do that?"

"People smuggling? You?"

"How ridiculous!"

Again, that surge of indignant voices.

"They have to check these things," said the warden. "People smugglers do a lot of harm."

Molly was looking at Liz's face. "Did they hit you?" she asked.

"Oh, no. No, no!" asserted the warden. "No, I fell. In my cell. Against the door frame." She touched the bruise lightly. "I'll be better soon."

"You will," agreed Job. "But not with all of us around you, asking questions. Why don't you go and have a hot shower and a rest? Someone will bring you some lunch in about an hour. In the meantime," looking at the assembled recorder players, "we have a rehearsal scheduled. Come on, everyone, ready to make a joyful noise?"

The warden smiled a grateful smile at Job, and limped towards the stairs to her flat. "It's good to be home," she said over her shoulder.

"It's good to have you back," we chorused.

On the way back to my house I said to Job, "You don't think the warden fell against the door frame, do you?"

"No, of course not," said Job, and put a hand on my arm. "But there are some stories it's best not to challenge. For all sorts of reasons."

★ ★ ★

Tom seemed a bit strange when he came home that evening.

"Liz is out," I told him. "And I've spoken to Mum. Any news about Alexis?"

"No." Tom seemed to look at me a little oddly. "Well, not at lunchtime. I had a sandwich with Derek. He hadn't heard anything."

"What do you think has happened to her?"

Again, there was that strange look from Tom. "I don't know," he said. "But to be honest, Carrie, even if I did it would be better not to tell you."

I felt stung. "Why...? What about our *no secrets* rule?"

Tom sighed. "Look, Carrie," he said, but in fact he wasn't looking at me. We were in the kitchen and he was looking over my shoulder into the darker part of the house. "The only people who knew about Alexis' status were me and Derek, and I told you, and Derek told the warden. The clerk knew a little but asked us not to tell her any detail, and she told the merest outline to the assistant clerk. That was it. And somehow the ATTF found out – well that's what it looks like. So who told them?"

"Tom!" I was angry and shocked. "You're not suggesting I told the ATTF? You must be mad!"

"No, of course not!" Then Tom shrugged. "But did you tell Ephraim? Someone told somebody and somehow Ephraim always seems to know what is going on. Haven't you noticed? People trust him and tell him things. Did you tell him about the way I helped Alexis, about the stuff Derek and I are doing?"

"No, I did not!" I was really angry now. "You should know me better than that! And anyhow, if it comes to trusting people, I would trust Ephraim a whole lot sooner than I'd trust Derek!"

"Quite," said Tom. "You see what I mean? Anyhow, I'm going out. Don't save me dinner, I'll grab something somewhere."

He went upstairs to change, bounded back down the stairs, and slammed the front door on his way out.

★ ★ ★

I had a whole evening stretching ahead. For a few minutes I just stood in the kitchen where Tom had left me, stunned and a bit breathless. I felt like crying, but I knew it would be self-indulgent. I started to think about what my mother would do in similar circumstances. I couldn't imagine Dad talking to Mum like that, or not trusting Mum, but of course there had been times when I was growing up that they had disagreed about things. I remember once some really sharp words between them about something quite small – whether Dad would drive some of us in the Young People's group to the New Forest, on an evening Mum and Dad had set aside for just the two of them. I remembered Dad leaving the room, and Mum just picking up a tea towel to finish drying some crockery, then, when the job was done, sitting on a stool by the breakfast bar and closing her eyes for five minutes or so of silence.

I went through to the conservatory. The little bush down by the river had a few bright red autumn leaves which seemed to shine like foil. I didn't close my eyes. I lifted my heart to the Light and waited for the peace to steal over me. Gradually my heart beat slowed. I thought about the river, flowing past. There has been a river there since Roman times. Well, before, presumably. The river just kept on flowing. Grandpa used to have a CD, in the days of CDs, of a black singer with a deep old voice, singing, *Old man river, that old man river...* I thought that all sorts of things had happened on the banks of our river over the centuries. Compared to some of them – religious wars, tragic deaths, epidemics, family disasters – this disagreement with Tom was really nothing. Then I thought that in fact Tom was right. I don't mean that he was right not to trust Ephraim. To be honest, I didn't know one way or the other about that. Yet he was right that someone must, somehow, have informed the ATTF. Tom had told me what he and Derek had been doing the weekend I went to Cambridgeshire. It was dangerous stuff. He was probably right that it was better if I didn't know, in the future, what they were up to.

I was still awake when Tom came in. It was late, the street lights were out so it was after midnight. He must have taken off his shoes downstairs; I could hear him tiptoeing upstairs in his stockinged feet, and he closed his bedroom door softly. Did he always close that door? I didn't think so. Did my coughing disturb him even one floor down from me? For how long could we go on sleeping apart and still be married? I could not imagine where we might go from here.

★ ★ ★

Usually if Ephraim came round it was at the end of the day, with Tom, but his visits had been fewer and further between recently. I wondered if Tom and Ephraim had disagreed about something, or whether Ephraim had realised that Tom did not trust him. Ephraim hardly ever came round during the day. In fact, I really had no idea what he did do during the day. Anyhow, it was quite a surprise when he turned up at coffee time the next morning.

I had slept late after a rough night, worrying about my

relationship with Tom, and about whether I would ever get better. I was trying, rather unsuccessfully, to read a journal produced by our Society. There was an article about our communities in Kenya, and the place of music in their worship, but it all seemed a long way away and rather irrelevant, considering all that was going on here. When the door knocker sounded I hoped it would be Job, but it was a pleasant surprise seeing Ephraim standing there, casually dressed as always but somehow looking sophisticated, not like a member of our community at all.

"I've come to take you out," he announced. "Your chariot awaits!"

"I – oh!" I wasn't sure what to think.

"We're celebrating," Ephraim added. "The first of the month, and a sunny day. Come on, you need to be outside!"

"But Ephraim…" I was weary; I was worried about Tom; I was unhappy. I didn't want to go out. I rather wanted to go back to sleep.

Ephraim put down his car keys. He looked very directly at me. "Carrie," he said, "you're having a really rough time; I know you are. These are hard times. But we need to do all that we can to help you recover from this illness. It can't be doing you any good, staying in like this all day. Come on, Carrie. We'll go to the coast. Text Tom and tell him. It really will do you good."

I thought of the seaside, of sand and waves and sea air. I thought Ephraim was right. "Okay," I agreed. "Give me ten minutes."

★ ★ ★

The drive to the coast takes about forty minutes through the New Forest unless the traffic is bad. It was a lovely morning. We were in Ephraim's old silver-coloured hybrid, not the smart car we had taken to Cambridgeshire. Inside the car seemed worn but homely; the dashboard was ridiculously complicated, dating from before they simplified everything, but Ephraim drove almost casually as if all those dials and digits weren't there, below and around the steering wheel. We didn't talk much for ages. I sat with my head back against the headrest, easing my aching neck, and watched the scenery as it passed. The trees were turning, each in its own time and manner, so that some were gold, others red, and some were still shades of green. There was bright red Virginia Creeper growing on walls, and orange flowers blooming in gardens. In the New Forest the ponies were grazing in small groups away from the road, and we saw a few horseboxes in a layby, with women in jodhpurs standing around.

Ephraim stopped at a café just the other side of the forest. We had coffee and shortcake. It was only then that we had our real conversation of the day.

"You're looking tired," commented Ephraim. "It must have been hard on you, your mother being arrested like that."

"Yes – well, actually, no, not really," I answered. "It happened on and off all through my childhood. Well, I don't mean regularly, every week or anything. But you know, whenever they had peace demos or sit-ins there was always the risk of arrest."

"I suppose so." Ephraim looked thoughtful. "Did it have a big impact on you, when you were a child?"

I thought back. Had it? "I'm not sure it did, really," I said. "I mean, Mum and Dad were never away for long, and my friends' mums and dads were the same. It was just part of life. We weren't frightened of the police in those days – you know, they were there to help. But we just knew we mustn't mention it at school."

"You weren't frightened of the police in those days?" It was a question.

"They were just the local police," I explained. "Nobody

vanished. Nobody back then was arrested and was never seen again."

"Oh yes, I see." Ephraim looked thoughtful. "It isn't like that now. So weren't you worried that your mother might not come home this time?"

"No, not really." I thought about it. Then I don't know why I added the next bit: "I was more worried about Tom."

"Tom!" Ephraim raised his eyebrows. His eyes looked kind, enquiring.

"I thought they might arrest him. At work," I added.

"Tom!" said Ephraim again, then, slowly, "Oh yes, I see. Yes. That would be a very frightening prospect. But nothing happened."

"No," I agreed. "Not this time, anyhow."

Ephraim damped his finger and picked up the remaining crumbs from his plate. "Carrie," he said, "I know it's hard – really hard – but try not to foresee disaster round every corner. Half the time it doesn't happen."

"It's the half that does which worries me," I said, but I felt comforted all the same.

★ ★ ★

We parked right by the sea, on a sort of small clifftop car park, and walked down the hill to the pier. There were billboards beside the footpath, large so that they would catch the eye of passing motorists, displaying two posters with similar designs: *Free to Bear Arms* proclaimed one. *Free to Work!* announced the other. I didn't think anything of them. "Lunch first," announced Ephraim, and took me into a fish and chip restaurant, where we ate on a first-floor terrace looking out towards the sea. Afterwards we walked down to the beach and Ephraim spread out a blanket on the sand. "You rest," he suggested. "I'll be back in about an hour," and he was gone.

I lay on the soft sand, my bag under my head as a pillow, looking up at the sky. White, fluffy clouds were drifting gently overhead, and there was a slight breeze stroking my skin. I was wearing my New Tex jeans and I had taken my shoes off. The sand felt good where my feet stretched out beyond the blanket. I texted Tom: *Sunny day. On the beach. See you later xxxx*. I rolled onto my side, and made a hollow in the soft sand for my hip. A few feet away two elderly people were sitting on deck chairs, talking about the celebrities in the magazine which one of them was reading. Their conversation was desultory, relaxed, totally unimportant, and as I listened I fell asleep.

I woke when Ephraim sat down beside me. "Time for ice creams," he said, and I saw that he was holding out a rather luxurious chocolate confection.

I sat up. I had been deeply asleep and now I felt good. "You've caught the sun!" exclaimed Ephraim. "It suits you."

"Thank you." I tucked into my ice cream, looking out at the sea. "That was a good rest," I said.

Just then two young men approached us. "Afternoon," said one. "Would you like one of these?" and he thrust a leaflet into my hand before moving on.

I looked at it. It was a smallish leaflet, with the words in large red letters, the same design as the posters I had seen earlier, *Free to Flourish*. It seemed like a strange motto, and I looked further, expecting it to be something religious. It wasn't. The smaller black print said, *Get rid of National Insurance! Leave us free to make our own way in the world!* Then, in even smaller black print, *The New Patriots. Meeting tonight. 7.00pm. The International Conference Centre.*

I turned to Ephraim. "I really don't like those guys," I said, although it was obvious. The New Patriots are as different as it is possible to be from our community.

"It's strange," said Ephraim. "I dare say they want the

same as you, more or less. They just want to go about it by a different route."

"What do you mean?" I really didn't think I could have much in common with a New Patriot!

"Well," Ephraim was also staring out to sea, "freedom. Isn't it what we all want?"

I thought about that. "Perhaps not," I said. "I think I want other things more. Justice. Equality."

"Why do you want those?" asked Ephraim.

"Well – well." I thought about it. "Without justice and equality there are always some people who can get what they want by treading on others. There are always people who will do that."

"You're right, of course," said Ephraim. "But maybe the New Patriots feel as if the government is treading on them? Maybe they feel they would have greater freedom, as they say, with less government?"

"Yes… well, no!" I could see his point. "But it has to be freedom for everyone. Look," I pointed to the smallprint on the flyer. "They want to get rid of National Insurance. That would mean some people having no health cover, no unemployment benefits…"

Ephraim was quiet, thinking, I suppose. Then he said, "You know, Carrie, I think I'm freer now than I've ever been."

It was a surprisingly personal thing for Ephraim to say. I was almost embarrassed. Ephraim is my mum's age. I thought of him as a sort of uncle, the way I thought of a lot of the older men in our community. I didn't expect personal confidences.

"You mean, because you've retired?" I asked.

"Well, yes, in a way." He continued to look out at the sea. A cloud passed over the sun and its shadow darkened the sea as it passed. "I used to know someone," he said, "a while ago. She was just an ordinary woman. Well, no, not ordinary at all, as it turned out. She was truly free. She did what she thought was right, and they couldn't touch her. They just couldn't touch her."

I didn't think Ephraim was talking to me. He was talking aloud, about something that was not my business.

I thought about how easily I had been frightened for Tom. "I wish I were like that," I said.

Ephraim sighed. "Yes, me too," he agreed. "Me too."

★ ★ ★

The drive back was fun. Ephraim's car wasn't fitted with a DeV but his old car radio still picked up some sort of panel game, with people trying to talk for a minute without repetition, deviation or hesitation. The topics they were given to talk about were crazy, and we found ourselves laughing out loud. When the programme finished Ephraim turned the radio to a classical music station and we listened to something haunting played on a flute – a Celtic-sounding tune. I felt good. My neck had stopped aching during my sleep on the beach and I could feel the effects of the sun on my face. I felt a lot more optimistic. We didn't talk a whole lot, but when we did it was about light-hearted things. We passed a woman walking a dog, and the dog had a sort of parasol attached to its collar, which was so ludicrous; we speculated about the origins of place names – not the historical origins, but fictitious ones, for places like Willow Bottom and Upper Clapton End. I arrived home at the same time as Tom. He and Ephraim waved to each other and I climbed out of the car and followed Tom into the house, determined to build bridges.

"Good day?" asked Tom, sounding a little strained, I thought.

"Great! Thank you. You?"

"Not really." Tom sank into the armchair in the sitting room. "To be honest, Carrie, I'm not very happy."

I felt a sort of surge of panic. I sat on the settee. "Why not?" I asked. "I mean, what's the matter?"

Tom was staring out of the window at people walking past just a few feet away. I saw how worn and tired his face looked. He was quiet for a minute or two. Then, "Carrie," he said, looking directly at me at last, "do you think we've taken a wrong turn?"

My neck suddenly felt stiff – not stiff with illness, but so that it was hard to keep on looking at Tom. "In what way, a wrong turn?" My voice sounded a bit strangled.

He paused again, and swallowed. "Do you think… would you say… Is our marriage working out as you expected?" he asked.

"Well, no!" I answered, indignant and a bit confused. "No, it isn't. I didn't think I'd get ill, for one thing!"

"Do you think you really are ill?" Tom asked. "I mean, physically ill?"

"Tom!" Just a few months ago, when I told Tom, Mum and Ephraim about the diagnosis and the Medical Assistance tribunal, Tom had stood up for me one hundred percent. "You know I'm ill! You see me every day!"

Tom sighed. He was quiet again, frowning. Then, "Well, I know you *think* you are ill," he said. "I know you have these symptoms, and that you seem to sleep a lot. But I've looked on the internet. There's no evidence of actual physical illness, is there?"

"Tom!" I was stunned.

"Anyhow," said Tom, "it's not just that."

"Well, what?" I felt as if I were floundering around in deep water. It seemed difficult to breathe. "What else?"

"It's just…" Tom sighed. "Carrie, I just don't feel we're together at all. We don't sleep together, we don't do anything together because of all your symptoms, you talk to Job and Ephraim more than you talk to me." He was looking directly at me. I suddenly felt he was saying words he had prepared in his head, in advance. "I don't feel I can trust you, to tell you what I'm doing, because I don't know who you might tell, or what you might give away." He gulped. "And the worst thing of all, Carrie – I just don't think you want to be married to me."

A sort of coldness spread through me. I heard my own voice, very far away and quiet, as if I were watching the scene from a distance. "Tom," I said, "I love you!"

"Yes," Tom sighed again, "I know you *think* you do. Well, perhaps you really do, in your own way, in your mind. But I think your body knows better."

"What do you mean?" My voice came out as a whisper.

"Oh, Carrie…" Tom reached out across the gap between the armchair and the settee, and held my hand. "Haven't you noticed? You start to recover, you cheer up, you look good, and then I come back to our bed and at once that coughing starts. Sometimes I haven't heard you coughing for days, but if I try to sleep with you, even if I don't touch you, you start to cough. You drive me out, Carrie. I think, I really think, there's something deep inside you that just doesn't want me there."

I felt a long way away, as if I were hearing Tom talk from the other end of a dark tunnel. I didn't know what to say. Then, "Sleep with me tonight, Tom, please! Let's try again. I do love you. I do want to be married to you! Tom, please!"

He sighed, but went on as if I hadn't spoken. "It's got to the point that even if I'm sleeping downstairs I still listen for that cough. I try to ignore it but I can't. Even if I close that bedroom door I can still hear you coughing, or not coughing. I lie awake at night, trying to think what to do. I think I've got to the end of the road."

"What do you mean?" I asked, but really I knew already.

"I'm moving out for a bit," said Tom. "It will be better for us both. And we need to get some help." He saw the tears in my eyes. Again he reached out and briefly held my hand. "I'm sorry, Carrie, I really am. But you know as well as I do that this isn't working."

★ ★ ★

I stayed up all night. Tom took a few things – clothes and books, his journal and the DeV he kept in the spare bedroom – and left quickly.

"Where will you go?" I asked, standing by the front door, seeing him off as if he were a visitor.

"To Derek's," he said. "I've slept in his attic several times, and it's an easy walk to work." He kissed my cheek as he left – as a brother might.

I sat for a long time in the conservatory. It was getting dark earlier by then, but I didn't turn on any lights. Then I wandered from room to room, remembering things about Tom. Tom putting up pictures when we first moved in. Tom and me laughing at a movie in the sitting room. Tom making love to me in the daytime, in the sitting room, with the curtains closed and conversations of people walking past, so close to us. I didn't cry. I wondered about phoning Mum, but I didn't. I thought of Job, but it was late; his granddaughter and the children would be asleep. I thought of phoning Ephraim but I knew I wouldn't.

I went upstairs, turned on the light in the spare room, and sat on the bed – Tom's bed. Tom had folded the sheet, pillow case and duvet cover, leaving them in a neat pile at the foot of the bed. The bedside table was empty. There was nothing left to tell me that this had been Tom's room. Well, there was one thing. Under the battered table, brought here from my parents' house and placed under the window, was a small red book. I went over and picked it up. It was the old red booklet Tom had mentioned. I looked in the inside cover: *To Karl, from all in Aylesbury Meeting.* I flicked through it. Some passages had been underlined. By Tom, I wondered? By Ephraim? By the original owner, this Karl? I dropped the booklet on the bed. I didn't really care.

I looked around the room. We had been married under a year. Could it really be over already? I found myself looking at a framed quotation on the wall. A friend had given it to us on the day of our marriage. They were old-fashioned words, hand written in a beautiful italic script and decorated with watercolour depictions of flowers. The words told me to remember the value of prayer, perseverance and a sense of humour in times of trouble. I really could not see anything funny about this situation.

I climbed the last set of steps wearily, holding onto the bannisters to give myself a bit of leverage. I took off my jeans and socks, and the green fluffy waistcoat, and climbed under the bedclothes in my underwear and T-shirt. Somehow the night passed. Whether I was asleep or awake, the words Tom had spoken echoed in my head: *You know as well as I do, this isn't working.* I texted Mum from my bed early in the morning: *Tom has left me.*

★ ★ ★

I will say this about our community: when we are at our best we are not prone to panic. Mum and Dad arrived at my house by ten in the morning and they were calm and kind, more the way you might expect people to behave in the case of illness, where recovery was expected but in the meantime the situation had to be managed. Neither asked me questions, although Dad's hug was longer and closer than usual. Mum asked, almost as if I were a stranger, or a fellow member of the community but not her daughter, "Would it help to tell us what happened?" So I told them, even the stuff I was supposed not to mention to anyone, about the Overground and the forged papers. When I had finished Mum said almost nothing but Dad said, "Poor Tom. Poor you, too." Then, after a thoughtful pause he added, "I'm not entirely happy about all these secrets. I have always thought it is hard for the Light to shine if there are things hidden in our hearts."

★ ★ ★

I look back on that October as a sort of on-going nightmare. I started to sleep late in the mornings, waking up to programmes on my DeV which didn't start until ten o'clock. Job called round a few times. I'm sure he knew Tom had left but he didn't mention it; instead he regaled me with stories about his youth, and about his great-grandchildren. He made me cups of tea and arranged displays of autumn leaves and conkers on the conservatory windowsills. Dad visited as often as Mum, which was unusual but rather comforting. We held silences and I picked at the food Mum prepared. One afternoon Dad and I sat with my CFS activity diary on my DeV. He said I had to be prepared for the tribunal in March, and that I mustn't let things slip. We more or less concocted an hour-by-hour 'record' of my activities, based as closely as possible on the truth, without suggesting that I was an extremist.

It was not difficult, actually. I went to the second Meeting for Worship the Sunday after Tom left, assuming Tom would have gone to First Meeting as usual. He must have thought the same thing about me, or maybe he just didn't care, because just after I had sat down he walked in, saw me, hesitated and turned a little pink, then sat down some distance from me. Almost at once Derek came in and sat beside Tom, and they both closed their eyes. The next Sunday I stayed at home.

Of course I was struggling. At the heart of our beliefs is the idea that each one of us can receive guidance from the Spirit, ourselves, in our inner selves, without doctrines or rules, priests or leaders to tell us what we should do. Both Tom and I had believed we had heard that we should marry. Those around us, holding us in the Light, seemed to have discerned the same thing. Less than a year had passed and already our marriage had crashed. So had we really heard what the Spirit was saying? Could people really know the Truth, simply by holding situations in the Light? Were we kidding ourselves?

I was facing another issue too. On the afternoon when Dad and I sat down and caught up with my record of activity, Dad had said, encouragingly, "Still, Carrie love, despite everything you do seem to be getting better."

"Do I?" I was surprised. To be honest, at that point I don't think I cared whether I got better or not.

"You do." He smiled at me, his eyes crinkling up in the corners. "I haven't heard you coughing at all today. Does your cough bother you at night any more?"

Then I realised that it didn't. I no longer woke myself up in the dark early mornings, hacking away, dreaming I was drowning. The cough medicine by my bed had remained unopened for more than a week. I thought of Tom, of his theory that somehow, subconsciously, I was fending him off with my symptoms. Now he had gone, the symptoms could go too. I felt sick and frightened. I didn't tell Dad.

★ ★ ★

Perhaps it was that conversation which started me out on reviewing all my CFS notes from the classes at the hospital. At the time I really hadn't believed what Cora and the obnoxious Paisley were telling us. Back then I knew I was ill. I went to the sessions because I had to. That October, though, I started to wonder. What if, after all, there was some truth in their ideas? I remembered the film extract of the pretty young American girl who was going back to college. What if there was more to all this than mere propaganda? What if I really was avoiding taking responsibility for my own life? Tom seemed to think so, after all.

One morning I read right through my notes about *Dealing with Symptoms*. The part I really noticed was about muscle and joint pains. Ever since I had become ill I had suffered from pains in my ankles. At their worst I felt as if I could not walk at all, at other times I was just vaguely aware, all the time, of discomfort. We had been sent a document which I had dutifully saved (they could tell if you deleted stuff from your DeV because of the way we had been told to register for the course) but which I think I hadn't read. It was an extract from a book by an American physician, *Light at the End of the Tunnel: Coping with Chronic Fatigue*. In the extract the doctor wrote about exactly my symptoms. He said that in the inner life of the Chronic Fatigue sufferer there is a battle between the wilful body and the determined mind. He argued that our wilful bodies throw up excuse after excuse why we should not do things. He said that ankle pains were typical of Chronic Fatigue sufferers, because they provided such an excellent all-encompassing excuse for not doing things: not working, not walking anywhere, not standing up, and so on. He pointed out, and I knew from my own doctor that this was true, that a medical examination of the Chronic Fatigue sufferer would find nothing physically wrong. The American doctor suggested that our wilful bodies were making excuses to let us avoid things we didn't want to do. We needed to ignore our wilful bodies as a parent would ignore the tantrums of a two-year-old. We needed to enlist the support of our determined minds. We needed to act as if we had no such pains.

Job came round while I was sitting thinking about this. In fact, when he knocked on the door my ankles were aching particularly painfully, and I was tempted not to get up to let my visitor in, but following the advice I had just read, I staggered to my feet and limped to the door. As I opened it a spasm of pain shot over the top of my foot and I winced.

"Goodness," said Job, coming in. "Am I such a bad sight?"

"Sorry." I sank into the nearest chair. "My foot hurts…"

Job closed the door behind him, shrugged off his jacket with some difficulty, and folded it onto the settee. He was walking with a stick nowadays, which he leaned carefully against a small oak table – a table Tom and I had chosen together from the market.

"Let me make you a cup of tea," suggested Job, as he always did. "Is this a bad day for you?"

"Yes – well, no. Well…" I wanted to be honest with Job; my body seemed to be full of aches and weariness, but I didn't want to indulge my wilful body. "I'm trying to ignore the aches," I explained.

Job had started to walk through to the kitchen. His movements were slow but steady, but when I said that he turned and came back into the sitting room.

"Why would you want to do that?" he asked. "Ignore the aches, I mean?"

"Well…" How could I explain? "What if it's all in my mind?" I asked.

Job sat down. "Whatever has given you that idea?" He sounded rather indignant.

So I told him about the American doctor and the wilful body versus the determined mind. And then, because Job is such a good listener, I told him about Tom's theory that by my coughing I was deliberately pushing him away. Then I cried.

"Hmm!" said Job, when I had finished, and at last went to make the tea.

When we were sitting again, drinking tea and eating rock cakes made by his great-granddaughter, Job said, "It's junk science, you know."

"What is?" The rock cakes tasted vaguely of ginger, and were really good.

"All this stuff you've been reading. I used to know a bit about the mind, you know, once upon a time."

Job had been retired all the while I had known him. I had heard various tales of his pre-retirement life from Job himself and from others in our community – he is something of a living legend – but I had no idea if he had professional qualifications for anything.

"It does make sense, though, in a way," I suggested.

"That's always the problem with junk science," said Job. "It seems to make sense. It's easy to grasp. It provides false hope."

"So do you think I really do have these aches?" I asked.

"Of course you do!" exclaimed Job. "You should have seen your face when you answered the door!"

"But now that Tom has gone, I have stopped coughing. What if he was right?"

Job drank some more tea thoughtfully, put the mug down on the table, then picked it up again, pulled a coaster towards him and put the mug down again, on the coaster.

"How did you feel when Tom left?" Job asked.

I recalled that awful night. "Desperate," I said.

"Not relieved? Not at all?"

"No, not relieved." A picture came into my mind of Tom bringing me food when he came in from work, when I was first ill. "Abandoned," I said.

"And now?" Job prompted.

"Now…" I thought about it. "Now I just feel lost. What is the point of anything? I can't trust the Spirit, because both Tom and I truly thought it was right to marry, and obviously it was not. I can't trust the symptoms because they might just be my wilful body. I can't trust my friends because someone betrayed us, Alexis and the warden. I can't work, I can't do anything useful with my life, I'm a burden Mum and Dad shouldn't have to carry." I didn't feel like crying as I said all this, but each word seemed crystal clear and true as I said them. I felt desolate.

"I don't want you to read any more of those notes!" demanded Job with a forcefulness I did not expect from him. "You're in altogether too vulnerable a place! The fact is, you love Tom and Tom loves you. Perhaps we are at fault, in the Meeting. We've allowed you to take on too much responsibility too soon. You are ill, Carrie, and it may be that it is partly our fault. But you know, there *will* be a way through this. There really will!"

When Job left I felt completely empty, but somewhere – it is hard to describe, almost like something hiding in a secret corner of my heart or my mind – was a tiny glow of hope. I could not see it or understand it, but I knew it was there. It was flickering like a tiny flame around Job's words, *there will be a way through this.*

★ ★ ★

By that point in October I was into a steady routine of sleeping after lunch. The advice in the CFS clinic had been not to do this. How would we ever be fit for work, to be contributing members of society, if we needed to sleep in the middle of the day? This was not Spain, after all, where siestas are acceptable! Nevertheless by lunchtime, even if I hadn't woken up until ten in the morning, my body craved sleep. I compromised by curling up under a throw somewhere downstairs, in the conservatory or the sitting room, depending on the weather.

When I woke up that afternoon the sun had come out. It was almost the end of October and some of the trees were nearly bare, while others shimmered with shades of green or vibrant oranges, reds and golden browns. I was on the settee in the sitting room and the sun, already low in the sky, was flickering into the room between the leaves. Sometimes I woke slowly feeling muzzy, but that afternoon, I remember, I had woken suddenly, and I lay there feeling fully conscious. I felt good. I watched the trees, the leaves moving in a breeze and some leaves falling, drifting sideways in the wind, and rustling on the ground.

I thought about the morning, and the things Job had said to me. He had been very assertive. In our community it is rare for one person to give another any direct advice. Even if people feel very strongly that someone should or should not do something, they tend to couch their thoughts as suggestions. 'Perhaps you might consider...', or 'Have you thought of...' or 'It occurs to me that maybe...' are the sorts of phrases you hear. Job, though, had been uncharacteristically direct. *I don't want you to read any more of those notes*, he had said, referring to the documents from the CFS clinic. His words had carried real authority. I wondered whether that was because I was so unused to such direct instructions. Then I realised that no, it was not that. Job had spoken as if he were ministering, passing on the words of the Spirit as a person might during Meeting for Worship.

I sat up. He was right. All my life I had trusted the Spirit. I was surrounded by others who did the same. I thought of my parents, of Job, of Ephraim and of some of the adults who had helped us to organise our Young People's activities. Their lives were anchored in this trust. Tom and I had trusted the Spirit when we decided to marry. Those around us had agreed. Who was I, now, to question the wisdom of so many good people?

Then, out of nowhere, came some words Dad had said: *but you must be prepared to pay the price, and it can be quite a price.* When had he said that? Like a page turning in my mind I remembered. It was when I talked to them about Derek's suggestion that we might help him in feeding homeless people.

I saw a cartoon for children once on my DeV when I was a child, watching more than I was really allowed, hiding under the bedclothes with my headphones on so that Mum and Dad wouldn't hear. It was about a robot. Whenever the robot had a decision to make the cartoon zoomed into its head and we saw old-fashioned clockwork wheels revolving round and clicking until the answer came. It seemed now as if exactly the same thing was happening to me. I thought of my illness. I thought of Tom's friendship with Derek, which suddenly seemed to me to get in the way of my relationship with Tom. I thought of Tom leaving. Suddenly it was crystal clear to me that none of these things would have happened if we had not agreed to help with the project. I wouldn't have fallen in the water, I wouldn't have got ill, Tom wouldn't have been involved in forging papers, he wouldn't have stopped trusting me. From that one decision sprang all our problems.

If we had said *no* or *not yet*, then probably I would just now be chatting over the day's work with the classroom teacher, whoever I was assigned to this year. We would be deciding on programmes for individual children, choosing stories to read to them at the end of the day, changing displays on the classroom walls, checking guidelines from the Department for Education. Tom and I would be planning my first pregnancy. I should have felt sad but I didn't. Instead, I felt a sort of clarity. We had thought it was right to help Derek. There was no point now in revisiting that. As Dad had said, there was a price to pay. I had thought of unpleasant confrontations with the police, even of prison, but I had not thought of the sorts of problems Tom and I were facing.

I remembered the other thing Dad had said, looking back over his times of protest with my Mum. "Opposing authority is a little like sharing your life with a wild animal. You never know when it will pounce." In my mind I realised that was not all. You never know *how* it will pounce either. So, I wondered, was

I willing to pay the price? The sunlight flickered in the room. The leaves rustled. The wind sighed in our old chimneys. I thought of those early members of our community, centuries ago, separated for months and for years from those they loved. I thought of the conscientious objectors of World War One, imprisoned in the prison right here, in the city where I lived, some of them never able to work again after the war because they were so scorned. These people paid the price for Truth. Now, I felt, in a small way, it was my turn to do the same.

My neck and my ankles ached, and my throat was sore, but as I sat there, and as the sun sank behind the buildings on the main road and the sitting room turned cool and dim, I felt strong. No, I would not read any more of those documents, but I would wait in the Light. I would wait in the Light as I had never done before, and I would trust the Spirit.

★ ★ ★

At school the Born Again Christians put everything down to the direct intervention of God. If their family found a parking space when they tried to park in town for their Sunday services, it was God's personal blessing on them. If they hadn't done their homework and the teacher forgot to ask for it, that was God's kindness. The atheists put everything down to coincidence. I talked to Mum and Dad about it, once, over dinner, when I was about twelve or thirteen.

Of course they didn't give me a direct answer. They liked me to think things through for myself, but they asked me questions. Did I believe in God? I did, although of course that was not true of everyone in our community. Did I believe that there were laws governing our universe, scientific laws for want of better words? I did. Did I think we, the human race, had yet grasped all those laws? Definitely not! Who or what, if anything, did I think had created those laws, or was behind those laws? If I believed in God or in some sort of divine Spirit, did I think that Spirit was good?

Through their questioning and my thinking, I had come to the conclusion that the coincidence/divine action controversy was a false controversy. Everything is somehow orderly, but there are mysteries we cannot understand. There is, I had decided then, a sort of wholeness to our world that was beyond my understanding.

Looking back, I thought afterwards that I might not have coped with the events of that night if I had not had that insight in the afternoon when I woke up, and that would perhaps not have happened if Job hadn't called round in the morning. Is this a coincidence, or the divine working of the Spirit? To be honest, I think the question is not relevant.

Despite my aches and pains I had made a proper meal that evening. The late afternoons and the time between six and eight o'clock were especially hard for me to deal with, because those had been the times when Tom came in and we discussed our days. We were coming up to the time when we changed the clocks, and each evening was darker than the one before. Mum had left some soya mince in the fridge and I used a variety of beans and a packet mix, and made a batch of chilli. It was the first cooking I had done in a while, and it felt good. I ate it with rice, and followed it up with an apple from our garden. Then I sat with a candle and an extra fleece in the conservatory, and waited in the Light, asking for strength to pay whatever price was needed to serve Truth.

★ ★ ★

I was deeply asleep when they came. It was pitch dark, after midnight, and the first I knew was a hammering on the door and some shouting. I was half out of bed, feeling woozy, when they broke down the door and stormed into the house, and I had hardly tied the cord of my dressing gown when they burst into my bedroom.

It was the ATTF. There were dozens of them it seemed, men and women, dressed in black from head to toe and wearing helmets. They had holsters on their hips and the woman in front was brandishing a taser gun.

"Stand still!" she demanded. "Hands in the air!"

It was like a cop show on a DeV.

I did as I was told.

"Search this room first," she commanded. "Take this one downstairs." Then, to me, "Who else lives here?"

"I'm on my own," I said, trying to stay calm.

"Husband?" she barked. "Tom, isn't it?"

"I… we… he isn't living here at the minute."

"Hmm. Take her downstairs then!"

I sat in the conservatory getting colder and colder as they searched the house. I could hear heavy feet stamping from room to room, drawers opening, things banging and bumping. They found my little DeV that had been beside the bed and I could see an officer in the kitchen scrolling through my documents, flicking from page to page, checking my phone history.

"Nothing here," he commented to the woman in charge and left the device on the counter.

They searched the kitchen last. They took every container out of the cupboards, stirring the sugar and rice with long wooden spills which they afterwards put in plastic bags, emptying the teabags onto the draining board, keeping one and replacing the others, and checking all the cleaning equipment under the sink. It would have been quite interesting if it hadn't felt so strange, as if I were a character in a book. It was getting light by the time they finished.

At last the woman came in to speak to me.

"Well, Mrs Walker," she said, sitting in the wicker armchair. "you'll be glad to know we haven't found anything."

I decided to be bold. "What were you looking for?" I asked.

She gave me a sharp look. She was a big woman, bulky in her bulletproof clothing and with all that equipment hanging from her belt. Her face was round, a bit grey looking in the dull light of the dawn. "I don't think you need to know that," she reprimanded me, "do you? Now perhaps you'll answer a few questions before we go?"

Then she questioned me about Tom, where he had gone and why, about Mum and the articles she had written, and about my health. She seemed to become a little more pleasant as I answered. She said, "I gather you are off work? How would you describe your attitude to our society? Do you plan to become a responsible citizen again?" and I heard myself answering, without thinking, "I have always been a responsible citizen and I hope I always will be!"

She raised her eyebrows, paused, then said, "Right, we'll leave you in peace. I would apologise for disturbing your night's sleep, but it isn't as if you have to go to work, is it?" Then they left.

When the front door closed I stood up, stiff with cold and tension, and wandered through the rooms, feeling disconnected. The house was quite tidy; they had been very efficient. If it weren't for the smell of men and uniforms, for odd things in the wrong places and for footprints and dead leaves in the porch you wouldn't know anyone had been there. All that seemed to be missing was the little red book with the inscription to the mysterious Karl, which had last been on the bed in Tom's room.

★ ★ ★

I made a pot of coffee and drank it looking out into the garden. It was a wild day. The wind was whistling round the house and the leaves were falling off the trees in showers of gold and brown and scudding across the lawn, back and forth, in crazy gusts. The sky was a dark, threatening blue, the blue of a storm, but as I watched, a streak of bright sunlight seemed to force the clouds apart and just for a moment it streamed down onto the river. Then the clouds closed and it was dark again, darker than it had been before.

Slowly, five steps at a time, then a rest, five more steps and another rest, I climbed back up to my bedroom. I went to the wardrobe and looked at my winter clothes. There was a red silky hoodie, one of those made from some new, fairtrade substance which comes from recycled nylon. I had bought it for our honeymoon, but hardly worn it since because the spring arrived so early. It reminded me of better days, and I lay it out on the bed ready to wear. My black jeans had red over-stitching, so I took them off the hanger too, and then I went into the bathroom and had a long, hot bath and a hair wash. I dried my hair carefully, tying a red bandana round it in the fashion of the day, and went back downstairs. I felt I was looking good. It did not matter that there was nobody there to see me. It was an act of rebellion against the ATTF, against their assumption that I was anti-social, a parasite on society. It was my way of saying I was prepared to pay the price.

I was very weary, and desperate to sleep, but before I lay down I knew I had some texts to send. First were my parents, then Tom, then the clerk of Meeting. I said the same thing to everyone: "Raided by the ATTF last night. All well. Don't worry. Plan to sleep now." Then I curled up under the throw on the sitting room settee and slept a deep and satisfying sleep.

For the second time I was woken by hammering on the door, but this time the knocking was followed by the turning of a key, and Tom burst in. His hair, which needed cutting, was windswept and his face was red. He rushed over to me.

"Carrie love!" he exclaimed. I stumbled to my feet to greet

him, and he threw his arms round me, holding me close. "Carrie, are you okay?" He drew back from me to look at my face, then hugged me close again. "Oh Carrie, I've been so worried. I couldn't get away. Ever since I got your text two hours ago I've been thinking of nothing else. Carrie, are you sure you're all right?"

His jacket was cold against my body but his arms around me had never felt better. I didn't say anything, just hugged him tight and burrowed my head into his shoulder. I could feel his heart beating even through his layers of autumn clothing.

We stood like that for a few minutes. I didn't think about anything, I just enjoyed standing there in Tom's arms.

After a while Tom stood back and held me away from him. I saw he had tears in his eyes, but he was smiling too. "Oh Carrie, I'm so pleased to see you. I thought... I wondered... I should have been here!"

"It's okay," I reassured Tom. "Honestly, it's all right. They searched the house. They weren't violent, they didn't threaten me. They didn't take anything as far as I can tell, except that booklet Ephraim lent you." Then I thought a bit more. "They did ask where you were."

"I should have been here!" said Tom again, and hugged me some more. He was kissing the top of my head, through my bandana. I hugged him even more fiercely.

After a few minutes we went into the kitchen. It was Tom's lunch hour and he was hungry. "I was supposed to be meeting Derek," he said. "But he'll understand. I should have sent him a text before I came but all I could think about was you." Then he looked at me again, noticing for the first time, I suppose, the clothes I was wearing. "Actually, Carrie," he said, "you look pretty good. Beautiful."

It was wonderful having Tom there, hugging me, paying me compliments. "Oh Tom," I said, "I have missed you."

He put down his sandwich and hugged me again, gently,

stroking my back, kissing my neck and then my lips. "Me too," he said, sounding sort of choked. "Carrie, shall we…"

"Yes please," I said, and we headed for the stairs.

★ ★ ★

My parents and the clerk of Meeting handled the news of our house raid with their usual calm. I had a phone call from Dad not long after Tom left, very late, for his afternoon's work. I was feeling sleepy and complete, my body tingling, my mind at peace. Dad must have been able to see my disordered hair, and the fact that I took the call in my dressing gown although it was well after two in the afternoon.

"Carrie love," he said, "we've been thinking of you. How are things?"

"Hi Dad," I answered, feeling like grinning. "I'm fine – really fine."

The picture on my little DeV is never good so it was mostly in my mind that I saw his eyes wrinkle up as he smiled. "Good lass!" he approved. "Have you seen Tom?"

"Yes," then I really did grin. "He came as soon as he could, at lunchtime."

"Good. That's good," said Dad. "Your mother is over at the food bank but she asked me to ask you whether it would be all right if we came up tomorrow?"

"That would be great," I said. "Thanks, Dad. Give Mum my love."

The clerk sent an email which I didn't read until later. She said simply, "Holding you in the Light. Are you up for visitors?"

Of course I emailed back that I was, then went into the conservatory for a period of quiet. The wind was still howling round the house and the rain beat on the glass roof. It was cold in there but I wore my old gardening fleece and enjoyed the wildness. I didn't know what would happen now. Would

Tom come home to me after work, or go back to Derek's? Was I under suspicion from the ATTF or was the raid just the tidying up of ends after Mum's arrest? Somehow, though, it no longer seemed to matter. Right here, right now all I could do was sit in the Light and wait for events to unfold.

★ ★ ★

Job and my parents arrived at the same time next morning. Tom had not returned after work, and I was disappointed. Disappointed, but not distraught. I had a feeling that I was walking a path that was leading somewhere, but I didn't know where. Anyhow, Tom had texted me several times. The first text said, *It was LOVELY seeing you again*. The second text said, *We need to talk*, and was followed by rows and rows of kisses. The last text, at ten in the evening, said, *Sleep well, my love*, with lots more kisses.

I had indeed slept well. Of course, I was very tired from my interrupted night, but there was more to it than that. My ankles and neck were still aching and I felt such weariness each time I tackled the stairs, but they no longer seemed like the most important things in my life. Those symptoms seemed, that day, no more important than a monthly stomach ache: something I noticed and then ignored, to get on with the more important matters of life.

I was up and dressed, and experimenting with a new hairstyle when they arrived. I had noticed on my rare sorties into town that more girls were wearing their hair plaited. My hair is long and dark, and I parted it in the middle and tried to plait it. It wasn't easy, but I had managed one side when they all arrived. Mum plaited the other side while Dad made coffee and Job regaled us with stories of terrible things he had done to little girls with plaits in his class when he was seven or eight, seventy-something years ago.

When I was a child we used to be far more open in our discussions at home. In those days there were no serious suggestions that the authorities would listen in on our conversations. Now we knew, or suspected, more. Our DeVs and our smartmeters were all, we were told, capable of picking up speech quite clearly. Tom and I tended to have our most private conversations outdoors or in our attic bedroom, with our DeVs left downstairs, but although the storm was over it was still wet, cool and blustery out there, we couldn't really go outside so we had to be rather guarded.

Mum, Dad and Job were sitting on the settee in a line, with Mum in the middle. I was curled up in the armchair. We all had coffee and Dad was dunking a biscuit in his. First I told them about the raid. I didn't need to be careful about that; obviously I couldn't tell my parents or Job anything the authorities didn't already know! I didn't mention the missing little red book, though. Then Dad asked me how Tom had reacted.

"He came as soon as he could," I reassured them. "And he's texted lots since."

Mum and Dad exchanged looks. "Is he still at Derek's?" Mum asked.

I looked down at my black jeans. "Yes," I said quietly.

Nobody said anything. After a couple of minutes Job said, "Would this conversation be easier if I left?"

Mum and Dad looked at me. "I don't think so," I said.

Job coughed, a clearing-the-throat sort of cough, then said, "Well, in that case I have a suggestion."

We all looked at him. "Job?" Dad asked.

"You still love Tom, don't you?" he asked me, giving me one of those kind but stern looks beloved of elderly members of our community.

"Very much," I said, and thought of Tom's visit the day before, and felt myself blushing.

"And does Tom love you?"

"Yes, I think he does. I'm sure he does."

I looked up. Mum and Dad were both smiling.

"Then I think you need to hold a Meeting for Clearness. You need to sit together with friends you know and trust, just two or at the most three, and you need to talk honestly, and you need to seek the right path for your marriage."

"Yes," said Mum. Dad nodded slowly.

"I'll talk to Tom," I said.

★ ★ ★

Of course we asked Job to be there. I wanted Ephraim to be invited, but Tom was adamant that he be left out of it, so we asked the clerk and Madge and Wolly, who had helped with the Young People's meetings and knew us both quite well. We met in the Children's Room, which is a separate log cabin in the garden of the Meeting House, where there are no meters, and we all left our DeVs in our coat pockets locked in the key cupboard. We had just changed the clocks back to Greenwich Mean Time, so at five thirty it was completely dark. The lights from the Children's Room streamed out across the black lawn, looking welcoming, when I arrived.

I knew about Meetings for Clearness, of course, but I had never been to one before. Job, Madge, Wally and the clerk were already there when I arrived, and Tom came in soon after, and winked at me as he took his seat. The room is small and there were only two seats left, so that Tom and I had to sit at right angles to each other, our knees almost touching. I was sure it was planned that way.

Job took the lead. First we had a silence. I felt nervous, and could not really settle. My mind was everywhere. What if it became clear that our marriage was indeed a mistake? What if these wise older leaders suggested we needed to spend time apart, move to another Meeting perhaps? I looked at Tom. He looked very still, with his eyes closed, but he was frowning.

After about ten minutes, Job said, "Thank you, Friends. Now, this is what I suggest. I am going to ask you both some questions. It is important that you think carefully and answer honestly. You will want to save each other's feelings, and that is natural and good, but there needs to be Truth if there is to be healing." Then he talked about privacy, about the fact that nothing we said must ever be repeated outside the room, except in the future if Tom and I agreed together that there was a testimony which needed to be given. "When we have finished," Job said, "we will ask for something – a picture or some words – to give you to hold on to. They will sum up for you all that will pass, we hope, this evening."

"So," said Job gently, "Carrie, would you say you love Tom?"

"Oh yes!" I said.

"Good." He paused. "Would you like to tell Tom what you love about him?"

I looked at Tom. "I love Tom because..." I started.

"No, tell Tom," prompted Job. "You are talking to him, not to us."

"Tom," I started again, "I love you because you are gentle and kind. I love you because you are creative. You are fun."

"Tom," asked Job, "do you love Carrie?"

"With all my heart," said Tom. He was looking down at the rag rug, but he reached out and took my hand. "Carrie," he went on, "I love you because you are full of life. I love you because you think about other people. When I look at you I can't believe you ever agreed to go out with me, never mind about marrying me. I think you are beautiful."

We were all quiet. Tom was holding my hand really tightly, and I squeezed his hand back.

A few minutes passed, then, "Carrie, do you want to be married to Tom?"

"Yes!"

"And Tom, do you want to be married to Carrie?"

"I want to be with her always," said Tom. "I want to have a family with her. I want to serve the Truth with her. I want to grow old with her."

"So why," asked Job with surprising bluntness, "are you living apart?"

There was a stunned silence. Tom muttered, "It's complicated."

"So let's unravel it. Tom, on the day or the night that you left, what triggered off your departure?"

Tom was quiet for a long time. Then, "I didn't feel wanted," he said.

"By Carrie?"

"Yes, by Carrie."

"Why did you feel that?"

Again Tom was quiet for a long time. "We had stopped making love," he said.

Again, the quietness. Then, "Whose decision was that?"

We both spoke together. I said, "Tom's." Tom said, "Carrie's."

I looked at Tom, surprised. "I didn't make that decision!" I exclaimed. "It was you. You wouldn't sleep in the same bed as me!"

"You kept coughing," Tom said. "I thought you didn't want me there. I thought…" He stopped mid-sentence.

"Tom," asked Job, "why would Carrie's coughing make you think she didn't want you in her bed?"

"It's just… I thought… someone told me that if a woman doesn't… isn't attracted to you any more, she will make up all sorts of reasons to get you to leave."

The clerk gave a little intake of breath, very loud in the quietness following Tom's comment.

Then, "Can you tell us where you heard that, Tom? Who told you such a thing?"

Tom let go of my hand and looked down again. He didn't answer.

"Tom, if this is to work we really need to know the truth," prompted Job. "Who told you that?"

Still looking at the rug, Tom said very quietly, "Derek."

"Derek!" I didn't plan to speak out of turn, but I was suddenly angry and indignant. "Have you been talking to Derek about our relationship? *Derek*?"

"Derek's my friend." For a moment Tom sounded sulky like a little boy. Then he looked straight at me. "Carrie, I didn't talk to him about our relationship. I told him I was worried about you. He kept asking about your health. Then he just sort of volunteered that stuff about women going off you, and making excuses. It just made sense."

Again we were quiet. Then, "But Tom, you knew Carrie was really ill, didn't you?"

"Yes. Well, I… No." Tom turned very red. "I'm sorry, Carrie," he muttered. "I thought perhaps it was like they said at the clinic. I thought it might be in your mind."

I looked across at him. I expected to feel angry, but I know Tom so well, I just felt sorry for him. "I know," I said. "I have thought about that too. But Tom, truly, truly I don't want to be ill."

Job took us back to the issue. "So you left because you thought Carrie might not be physically ill, and because you had stopped making love?"

Again Tom muttered, "Well, it wasn't just that."

We were all quiet. I asked, "So what else, Tom?"

"Alexis," said Tom.

For one awful moment I thought he was going to say that he had fallen in love with Alexis, but he added, "Her arrest."

"How could Alexis' arrest affect your marriage?" asked the clerk.

"Well, isn't it obvious? How did the ATTF know about

138

Alexis? About her being a failed asylum seeker? About her false papers?" Tom looked rather wildly around the circle of faces. "Nobody knew!" he said. "Derek and I knew, the warden knew," then, looking at the clerk, "you knew, and I told Carrie. Obviously Derek and I didn't say anything, and I'm sure you or the warden wouldn't. So that only left Carrie." Then, looking almost angrily at me, "And you talk to loads of people, Carrie. You could have said something at the clinic, you know you weren't always all that careful about what you said there, and Derek thinks…"

He stopped. *Caught out*, I thought.

"Derek thinks what?" Suddenly I felt really angry.

"Derek thinks you are too close to Ephraim. He is suspicious of Ephraim. He says we don't know anything about him."

He looked at everyone again, daring us to contradict him. "Think about it," he said. "What do any of us know? What did Ephraim do before he came here? How long has he been in our Society? What does he do all day? Who are his friends? I mean – nobody knows, do they? And Carrie, I think you'd tell him anything!"

The clerk and Madge exchanged looks. The clerk said, very mildly, "Just because you don't know someone, Tom, it doesn't mean none of us do."

Tom went very red. That was as near to a telling off as you are likely to get in our community.

"I know," he said. "I'm sorry, but it's just…"

Job said, "Wasn't Ephraim one of your visitors, when you asked to become a member?"

Tom looked surprised. "Yes, he was."

"And you trusted him then?"

"Yes, I suppose… Yes."

"So what changed?"

Tom was quiet, frowning. I waited, wondering. Would he see what I had seen? Would he be prepared to admit it to himself, or to us?

"It was when we started doing the food runs," admitted Tom at last. "Carrie was ill, so often it was just Derek and me. We talked a lot. Derek... I don't think Derek likes Ephraim."

"Derek has been a big influence in your life over the last few months," commented the clerk.

"Yes." Tom sounded subdued. Then he turned to me, "Oh, Carrie," he said, "I'm so sorry!"

Madge, Wally, the clerk and Job smiled. "Can you accept Tom's apology, Carrie?" Job asked. "I don't want you just to say yes, I want to know what you really feel."

"Of course I can," I said. "Yes!"

Madge said, "Good. Good. But it's never all on one side, is it? Tom," she asked, "is there anything that Carrie has done, however unintentionally, to hurt you, or which she needs to apologise to you about?"

Tom went pink again. "No, not really... well..."

"Out with it, man!" commanded Job. "We've got so far. Let's finish the job!"

I saw the clerk smiling. Tom held my hand hard, almost hurting me.

"You never seemed to trust me," he said. Then, "No, that's not right. You... I... I think... I thought you didn't trust my maturity. It seems as if all your family and all your friends have been trying to walk in the Light all their lives. Me, I'm still new to it. I think... I thought you are – were – always expecting me to do something unwise. You always wanted to talk to your Mum and Dad about everything..."

I gulped. As he was speaking I knew it was true. How could I be so uncertain about the man I had chosen – I had been led – to marry? "Tom," I almost gasped. "Oh Tom, I'm so sorry!"

"I really try, you know," said Tom, looking at me, his eyes pleading.

"Oh Tom!" I said again, full of remorse. "I'm so sorry!"

Tom had looked at the rug. Now he looked back up at me, and I saw that he was crying, tears streaming down his face. Without thinking, without any awareness of the others in that little cabin, I knelt in front of Tom and hugged him for all I was worth, my arms around his waist, his head resting on my head.

The room was quiet. We held each other, and the others sat in silence. At last Tom let go of me, and I of him. I sat back on my chair and Tom held my hand again. I looked at the others. Job and Madge were smiling; the clerk and Wally had tears in their eyes.

"Sorry!" muttered Tom, suddenly slightly embarrassed.

"Not at all!" said Madge.

The clerk said, "I think we've moved a long way tonight. Do you agree?"

I looked round the little circle. Everyone nodded. Job said, in the fashion of our community, "I hope so." Tom said, fervently, "So do I."

The clerk smiled. Thoughtfully she said, "There are always lessons to learn, of course. Tom and Carrie, do either of you know yet what you might learn from all this? It may take time; you may not see it yet."

I said at once, "To put Tom first – I mean his opinions, his thoughts – before my parents."

"Good." Looking at Tom she asked, "Tom?"

We were all quiet. Outside I could hear the fallen leaves blowing across the lawn, rustling in the darkness. Inside the room seemed very still. There was a clock standing on one of the shelves next to the children's books, ticking gently. Then Tom said, "I think I've learnt something really big. Or maybe re-learnt it. Rediscovered it."

There was another silence. The clerk prompted, "Tom?"

"One of the things that swayed me, when I joined this community," he said, speaking very quietly, as if he were talking to himself, "is the absolute truth of the idea, the discovery, that we can hear the Spirit – feel the Spirit – in our own lives. We don't need teachers or priests. We need silence, and openness, and we need to recognise the promptings of love and Truth."

"Yes," agreed the clerk. The others sort of grunted.

Tom gulped. "Somehow," he said, "I seem to have stopped listening to the Spirit. I've been listening to other people. I thought, I've got so much to learn, I could do worse than to learn from others. I've been listening to Derek."

"Ah …" The clerk looked thoughtful.

Job said, "We all fall into that trap, Tom, every now and again."

"It's good to listen to others," Madge encouraged. "But then we have to weigh it. You weren't so far off the right track – you just missed out the last stage."

"Yes," agreed Tom, tears in his eyes again. "But it is a pretty big stage!"

We were all quiet again, then Job spoke. "It can be helpful if we do one more thing, before we leave." He exchanged glances with the clerk, who nodded. "Sometimes," Job continued, "we understand situations or issues better if we have an image to hold on to."

"Like the image of Light for God," explained the clerk.

"Yes, so I want us all to keep silence for a little longer. Let's open our minds and see whether some words or an image come into our minds. It doesn't matter if nothing comes, but it can be surprising…"

Again a silence seemed to descend on the room. It was a deep, comfortable peace, like a hug from a parent, or like curling up under a duvet. It was like drinking a gin and tonic, or putting cold hands round a mug of hot tomato soup. I was very aware of Tom sitting so close to me. I felt a sort of peace. Then I started to think again about Dad's words all those months ago, the words I had almost forgotten until Job's visit after the ATTF raid: *But you must be prepared to pay the price* and *It is a little like sharing your life with a wild animal. You never know when it will pounce.* As soon as those words came into my mind I pictured a leopard, sleek and beautiful, and terrifying. I shivered. Tom turned to me and said, out of the silence, "What is it, Carrie?"

"I thought of a leopard," I gasped. "I could see it so clearly."

The clerk frowned. Madge looked taken aback, and Wolly looked confused, but Job smiled. "Interesting," he said. "Let's explore that."

Tom had grasped my hand again. He smiled at me. "Perhaps there's nothing to explore," he said.

We all looked at Tom, surprised. "Isn't it obvious?" he asked, looking round our circle. "It's just a warning. I let the leopard attack me when I listened to a person rather than the Spirit. We both let the leopard pounce on us when we started to think that maybe Carrie isn't ill at all. The leopard attacks when we don't put the Spirit first."

"Ah," said the clerk. "Like a roaring lion!"

Now it was the turn of the whole group to look at her in surprise.

She smiled at us. "It's in the Bible somewhere," she said. *"Be alert and of sober mind. Your enemy the devil prowls around like a roaring lion looking for someone to devour,"* she quoted. "If I were you, I'd concentrate on the first part, the alert and sober part. Roaring lions and pouncing leopards are a little alarming!"

We all laughed and bowed our heads again. I suppose about ten minutes passed, then the clerk stirred, crossed and uncrossed her legs, and smiled in a general way round the circle.

"Where will you go after this meeting, Tom?" asked Job.

Tom smiled, his big, wide smile, his natural smile. "I'll go home," he said. "With Carrie. To our home."

143

CHAPTER 5

The next few days were wonderful. Tom went in to work the following morning but came home at lunchtime with a bunch of red roses, a beautiful laminated picture of a resting leopard which he stuck on the kitchen wall ("to remind us" he explained) and the news that he had taken some leave until the History Society brochures needed printing – at least four working days. We spent a lot of time talking, and a lot of time in bed – in the same bed. I phoned Mum and asked that she and Dad skip their usual visit, explaining that Tom had time off work, and Mum sounded positively gleeful as she agreed. Tom phoned Derek and told him he was having at least a week off from doing the food runs, for personal reasons. One of those days was really rainy. The storm was one of the new type, with gale force winds and raindrops beating on the roof of the conservatory like a drum. We sat out there and watched the torrent of water pouring over the glass, washing dead leaves into the guttering and splashing onto the soggy lawn. The river was brown and swirling, with little waves from the gusts of wind, and we held hands, a still point in all that rampaging weather. The next day was bright and clear; I woke to sun streaming in through our attic window, and to Tom bringing me toast and coffee in bed. I stopped thinking about the past or the future, about being ill, about being transferred to Medical Assistance. When I looked at the picture of the resting leopard I realised that it was no threat to me. It could not attack me unless I invited it to. It felt as if we were living in a bubble of the present, in which Tom and I were never more than a few feet apart, and in our spirits we were never apart at all.

On the second day we started to keep silence together. It seemed the most natural thing, and indeed it was something we had done before, around the time we were thinking of marrying, and in those first few weeks of marriage. We would sit in the conservatory holding hands, or in the front room, or once propped up against our pillows in bed, and sink easily into a stillness which seemed timeless and whole.

We didn't go out at all until the Sunday, and then we knew that we wanted to go to Meeting together. We walked along the river path, not holding hands this time, but arm in arm, and arrived in good time for First Meeting. We sat on the window side and as soon as we had taken off our coats and settled ourselves, Tom reached for my hand again, and held it for the whole hour. Worship was easy but I hardly heard the spoken ministry.

I suppose it would have been totally unrealistic to expect that state of peaceful timelessness to last for any longer. On Monday Feany phoned and said that the History Society stuff had come in, and that it needed some cunning formatting, which is one of Tom's fortes, and also that as a result of some of Tom's earlier work they had a new client, and Feany wanted Tom to meet him. Tom said he would be in by ten o'clock (it was nine in the morning and we were both still in bed) and then, while he was dressing, the lights on my DeV flashed, and I took the call as voice only, because I wasn't decent.

"Hi Job," I said.

"Carrie, hello." It was good to hear his voice. "Have you got a moment?"

"Yes." I could hear the plumbing working in our bathroom, and Tom singing an American Country song about living in the back woods with a girl he loved. "What's up?"

Job said, "It was good to see you and Tom at Meeting yesterday. How are things?"

"Good," I said, then thinking about what had passed before Feany phoned that morning, "Excellent."

"As I hoped." I could hear Job smiling at the other end. "Carrie, I hope you don't think I'm interfering…"

"I'm sure you're not," I said, although my heart sank a little.

"No, well… the thing is, I wondered whether you would think of holding a small Healing Meeting in your house? Just two or three people you really trust, some silence and some ministry if anyone feels led to minister, but with a focus on your health."

I could feel, at the same time, a sort of resistance and a sort of attraction. "I don't know…" I said, then, "Can I talk to Tom and phone you back, tomorrow maybe?"

"That sounds good," said Job. "Give Tom my love," and he clicked off.

★ ★ ★

For a day or two I thought a new and comfortable normality was setting in. Tom went off to work in the morning whistling or humming, and came home with takeaway meals or simple ingredients for cooking. We went to bed early, and if I started coughing, Tom gave me drinks of water and cough medicine, and stayed beside me until I stopped and we both went back to sleep. After a few nights I noticed that I would wake up coughing and Tom would only stir and maybe murmur, "All right?" before sinking back into an apparently deep sleep. Even when I had a bad night Tom seemed to awaken fresh and optimistic. We were planning a monthly Healing Meeting to start the following week, on Wednesday evening, and while we both had huge reservations about the claims to miraculous healing made by some of the more extreme churches, we both believe that a human is a complicated and mysterious mixture of body, mind and spirit, and that there is no knowing what resting in the Light with a focus on health might achieve.

We went to First Meeting together again that Sunday, and again Tom started by holding my hand. It was a very still meeting, despite the sounds of the homeless people who come for breakfast and are often gathered outside the Meeting Room during worship. It is almost as if their talk deepens our sense of silence. Part way through the meeting Tom let go of my hand. I looked at him, surprised, but saw that he was sitting very still, breathing fast, clasping his hands together. After a few minutes he rose to his feet, ready to minister.

"Friends," he said, and then was silent for a moment. I looked at him. He was standing with his eyes shut, his face raised a little so that if he had opened his eyes he would have been looking at the ceiling lights. He started again. "Friends, in the last couple of weeks I have understood something all over again, and more deeply than I ever understood it before." Again he was silent for a moment or two, and then he said, "It is a great mystery and yet not mysterious at all. It is that the Spirit speaks to each one of us, that indeed if we listen we will all hear, because there is something of God within us all, and that something wants to hear, even hungers to hear." Again he was silent, then he started to say something else. "I..." He stopped, opened his eyes and looked at me, giving me a huge smile. He sat down.

They say your heart sings. I thought I knew that feeling before, but not the way I felt it that morning.

After Meeting, over coffee, Derek came up to us. He was smiling and friendly, he sort of thumped Tom on the back the way men do, and said, "Good to hear you, Tom."

"Thanks." Tom was looking happy. Already several people had said they appreciated his ministry, and the clerk had given the thumbs up sign to us as we all shook hands before the notices.

"So when do you start the food runs again?" asked Derek, and I thought he looked a little anxious.

"Oh," Tom looked at me. "I'm not sure. Give us a few days to talk about it."

I thought Derek looked, for a moment, almost angry, then he said, "Yes, sure. Phone me," and he walked away.

★ ★ ★

We did talk about it, but not in any great depth. Tom's comment was, "I don't think I'm ready to go back to that yet," and my comment was "Good," and that was that. Wednesday came, and with it the healing group, which was very undramatic. It was mid-November by then and in my childhood we would have needed heating in the house, but it was another exceptionally mild winter and we lit the fire for the first time that night. It was cosy and welcoming, and the sound of the wood crackling was the backdrop to our silence and our ministry. It was very like an ordinary Meeting except that at one point Madge and Wolly, Job and Tom, put their hands gently on my head while Job said, "We come into the Light asking for healing of body, mind and spirit." When they had gone Tom and I drank hot chocolate, sitting by the dying embers, and we didn't think to turn our DeVs back on until bedtime.

Tom had four messages from Derek. The first was a voicemail, sounding upbeat. "Hi Tom, have you decided when you're going to come back? We could really use your help." The next three were texts. The first said, *I've left you a voice mail. Answer as soon as you can, please.* The second said, *Tom, I really need an answer.* The third said, *Tom, I think we need to talk.*

"Bother!" said Tom, and left his DeV on the kitchen work surface where he wouldn't hear if another message arrived overnight.

I suppose we both knew that Derek wasn't going to let it go, and in a way I didn't blame him. He had no idea of what had been going on in the life Tom and I shared, since Tom had come home. I imagined that from his point of view one of his most reliable workers had just dropped out without explanation, and I guessed that he was hurt, and felt let down. Nevertheless, I didn't expect him to come storming round to our house the way he did the following evening.

I had lit another fire, although really it was not cool enough to warrant it, so we were both sitting in T-shirts and jeans, with takeaway Indian food on plates on our laps, and glasses of Indian lager at our feet. Our bell doesn't always work, so the first we knew was heavy, aggressive banging on the door. At once my heart was in my mouth. It was just like the ATTF raid.

Tom said, "Stay there," and put his plate on the stool as he got up to answer the door. The next minute, with a rush of cool air, Derek burst into the room.

"Oh, this is very cosy!" he said, taking in the scene. "Perfect! When there are people out there," he gestured a little wildly towards the window, "with nothing to eat and nobody to look out for them!"

"Derek!" Tom was obviously as taken aback as I was.

Derek looked furious. "It's all very well, saying 'Derek' like that," he said, standing in the middle of the room, making it suddenly seem very small. "I really thought I could rely on you, Tom. I really thought… But here you are, settled at home, enjoying all the pleasures of family life, without a thought for all those people we said we'd serve. Didn't our conversations mean anything, when we sat in my flat and talked about the need to put ourselves last?"

Tom had gone white. He was still standing too, looking

shocked. I felt angry. How dare Derek attack Tom in our home like this?

"Hey Derek," I said, not sounding as calm or as reasonable as someone who had grown up in our community ought to sound. "That's not fair! Tom's always putting other people before himself!"

Derek glared at me. "You could have fooled me!" he said. "And what have you got to do with all this, anyhow? You're the one who created this situation, with your illness and your demands on Tom. Don't think I don't know how you twist him around your little finger! You're just a manipulative…"

"Derek!" Tom stopped him just in time. "For goodness' sake!"

Derek stopped and looked first at Tom, then at me. He took a deep breath. "Oh, I'm so sorry!" he said, and without asking he sat on the settee, next to me.

Tom sat down too. "It isn't the right thing for me to be doing just now," said Tom, sounding amazingly controlled. "I have a wife to care for and a marriage to nurture. It isn't a good thing for me to be out every evening."

Derek clenched his fists. I could almost feel the tension in his body as he sat just a few inches away from me. He took a deep breath.

"But Tom," he said, sounding like someone struggling to be patient with someone who didn't deserve patience, "it isn't an either/or situation. You could spend some evenings on our project, and some at home, couldn't you?"

"Not just now, no." Tom's voice was firm, almost quiet. I had heard my dad use that tone of voice. I knew Derek didn't stand a chance of winning Tom over.

Derek gave Tom a long look. Then he turned to me, anger burning in his eyes. "Right," he said. "I see." He continued to look at me, scorn all over his face. "So you've succeeded.

You've wrecked our plans. I might have known you would."
He looked at Tom, "I told you she would!"

He turned back to me, and almost hissed his next words. "You don't know – you really don't know what you've done!" he said. "You think you're so wise, so full of integrity, so discerning, but I tell you now you've been taken in, well and truly! You're friends with all these people, with Job and his sort, with Ephraim, and not one of them is working for the good of our community. Job is just an old man, left behind in the last century, and Ephraim…" He took a deep breath. He glanced at Tom briefly, then turned his aggressive glare back on me. "I don't suppose you'll believe it," he went on, "but Ephraim is ATTF. I've thought so for a while, and now I know. The harm he's done to our community in the past, you wouldn't believe… and you tell him everything… everything!" His tone became even more angry. "You are doing so much damage!" he exclaimed. "You manipulate everyone around you. Everyone is oh-so-sorry about your illness. Illness! Huh! You're just an attention seeker. I don't usually agree with our government, but I tell you, Carrie, you are a leach on society and a leach on our community!"

"Derek!" Tom had leapt to his feet again. "Derek, I want you to leave NOW. Get out!"

"Oh, I'm going!" said Derek. "I would hate to disturb your domestic bliss further!" He stood, barged past Tom and left, slamming the door behind him.

Our Indian food was cold and the fire was too hot, and Tom and I looked across the room at each other, stunned and silent. Now what were we to do?

★ ★ ★

Of course we couldn't sleep. We lay in the dark talking and talking. Neither one of us had ever been spoken to like that before. At first we were just angry, and our anger was mixed with a little self-reproach. Had we somehow brought this upon ourselves? Tom said, a little mournfully, "I suppose when I stayed at his flat I must have given the impression that I would put our homeless projects before everything, before you. Perhaps it is my fault he feels so let down."

I could see what Tom meant, but I didn't agree. "He's a grown man," I said. "He knew you were married, he knew your first obligation was always going to be to me."

"I don't know…" I heard a note of uncertainty in Tom's voice. "I remember he had been reading a book about the founder members of our community. The first night I stayed at his flat he told me how they left their wives or husbands for months or years if they felt they were guided to be somewhere else."

I knew that was true, but I also suspected that such separations only occurred if the whole Meeting was clear about the rightness of such action.

"I think I did let him down," said Tom, but then added, "but I'm sure I've made the right decision now." He stroked my hair in the dark. "I love you too much to lose you, Carrie."

"There's something else," I said. "What he said about Ephraim. Do you believe it?"

Tom was quiet for a moment, his hand rhythmically stroking my hair, his breathing steady. Then, "Is it really true that you didn't tell Ephraim anything?"

I could have felt angry with Tom for doubting me, but I didn't. "I really didn't tell him anything," I said. "But Tom, I wouldn't need to, would I? I mean, isn't he involved in stuff with Derek? When we took that couple to Cambridgeshire, Ephraim was helping people to escape. Isn't that all part of the same activity? We feed them, we try to get them papers, we smuggle them into Europe – we do whatever we can to help people who've fallen foul of the government. I've always thought Ephraim knows far more than me about what is going on."

"You're right." Again Tom was quiet. His hand on my hair was still.

"Derek told me once," he continued, "that there is more going on than any one person might know. They just tell you the bits you need to know. That way, if they arrest you, you can't give too much away."

"Ephraim seems to know it all," I pointed out. "He came and rescued us when we had spent the night on the nature reserve. He drove us to Cambridgeshire…"

"Yes," agreed Tom. "But he wasn't supposed to know anything about Alexis. So how would he have found out about her?"

"Well, did he?" I asked.

Tom paused. "Oh, I see," he said. "Derek and I both thought it was Ephraim who betrayed Alexis to the ATTF, but we don't actually know that, do we?"

It was my turn to be thoughtful. "We don't actually know very much at all, do we?" I said.

Tom laughed. "I know one thing," he said, turning to me. "I love you, Carrie Walker!"

★ ★ ★

Tom left me sleeping the next morning, so I was only just up and dressed at ten when I heard a knock on the door. I almost ran down the two flights of stairs and only dimly realised how energetic I felt, before I was opening the front door to Ephraim. Neither of us had seen Ephraim for a couple of weeks, not even at Meeting, so I was surprised, but pleased.

"Hi Friend!" I said. "You're just in time for coffee!"

For a moment I thought Ephraim was going to hug me, as Job certainly would have done but as Ephraim never did, then he just smiled and shrugged his shoulders.

"That would be good. You're looking well, Carrie."

"Yes," I smiled. "I'm surprised really, I had quite a bad night, but I'm feeling well this morning."

"It's a beautiful day," said Ephraim as he followed me through to the kitchen and leaned against a cupboard, watching while I filled the kettle and spooned coffee into the pot. I saw him glance around, taking in the two plates still left on the work surface from last night's dinner, the two mugs and the one cereal bowl from Tom's breakfast. Indeed, it was a lovely day: bright sunshine highlighting the bare branches of trees, the grass glinting with moisture, the river dappled.

We sat in the conservatory – ridiculous at the end of November, but comfortable because it was so warm. I looked at Ephraim properly for the first time. I found myself thinking, *he's getting old*! I had never noticed that slight stoop before, or realised how lined was his forehead.

"You've been away?" I asked.

He seemed to relax, and smiled. "I have!" he agreed. "Will and Mia send their love. They'd really like it if you were to go and visit them again sometime, maybe take Tom. The twins are back, of course. Really, those kids!" He looked out at the river, still smiling. Then he turned to me, and said a little cautiously, "And how are you and Tom?"

"We're good," I said, feeling a blush creep across my face. "Very good, actually."

Ephraim seemed to relax, as if that was the answer he hoped for but wasn't sure he would hear. "Tom's home then?" he queried, a little tentatively.

"Living at home, yes," I agreed. "He's at work right now."

"Excellent!" Ephraim drank his coffee in peaceful silence while the robin pecked around on the grass right outside the conservatory and two swans glided downstream.

"Actually," he said, when his mug was empty, "there's something I'd like you and Tom to think about."

I waited. When he didn't say more I prompted him, "What, Ephraim?"

"I wondered…" for someone who always seemed so much in control he was strangely hesitant. He paused, then looked very directly at me. "Carrie, would you and Tom consider putting up someone in your home for a few days? In secret?"

"Oh!" I realised at once he must mean a refugee or someone in trouble. I gulped. "The thing is, Ephraim, we've already been raided by the ATTF once. We're obviously under suspicion."

"Well, yes and no," said Ephraim. "Of course they know all about you – about your upbringing, your membership of our community, your refusal to take the Oath and your inability to graduate from university as a result. Like all of us, you are not considered ideal citizens, you and Tom."

"Thank you!" I said, laughing. I had grown up with that knowledge.

"The thing is," Ephraim went on, "they have already raided your house. They didn't find anything, did they? No secret hiding places, no incriminating terrorist-related documents, no subversive stuff on your DeVs? I heard nothing was removed from the house and you weren't arrested."

"Mm," I said, wishing Tom were there.

"I thought," said Ephraim, ploughing on, "that in a way you've already been checked out and been found innocent. It makes your home an ideal refuge. Don't you see?"

I did see, but once again I had that strong feeling that I was dealing with more than I understood, that I was playing some sort of game in the dark.

"I'll talk to Tom," I said.

★ ★ ★

It was a difficult conversation because Tom felt as uncertain as I did about what we might be getting into.

155

"The thing is," said Tom, "you trust Ephraim, and I used to until Derek…"

"I know." I thought for a while. "I do sort of trust Ephraim," I said. "But I don't totally trust myself any more. I can't help thinking what Derek said, that Ephraim was ATTF."

"Yeah," agreed Tom. "But Derek is a prick… sorry, Carrie, a fool."

"Well, he's certainly got a temper," I said. I had been thinking about it all day. "But you know, Tom, he's only been in our community a few years and before that I don't know what he was into. It takes time to change."

Tom looked thoughtful. "Let's think about it logically," he said. "Suppose Ephraim was ATTF, does that mean he still is?"

"Well, no, maybe not, but do you really think they'd let someone change sides like that? I mean, they must know where he is and what he's into."

"So if he was ATTF, why would he be helping refugees now? And why would he want to involve us?"

"Of course," I said, "Ephraim might not have been ATTF. Derek says he was but he's never told us how he knows. And if it were really true, wouldn't he have gone to the clerk or the elders? What if it's all in Derek's head?"

"Derek really doesn't like Ephraim," Tom said. "He was seriously critical of him when I was staying at his place."

"Tom," I suggested, "what if it's all one of those alpha male issues? You know, Derek and Ephraim both wanting to be top, in control, and getting in each other's way?"

Tom looked thoughtful again. "You know, I could believe that of Derek, but not of Ephraim. Ephraim just seems too – oh, I don't know, too grown up!"

"Yes."

"The other thing," said Tom, "is that obviously there are people who need shelter – secret shelter. And Ephraim has got a point. Now that they've searched the house once and found nothing, this might be the ideal place to hide someone. Leaving aside all our unanswered questions, how would you feel about putting someone in the back bedroom? After all, you'd be the one who had to live with her – or him – all day, while I'm out at work."

At once I saw that Tom was on the right track. There were hundreds of things we just did not know about Ephraim and Derek, and no doubt it would always be like that. In fact, if we were going to be useful it had to be like that. Otherwise, if we were arrested, we might give too much away. I thought of the bruise on the warden's face the day she was freed after her arrest. "Perhaps we should have some silence?" I suggested.

★ ★ ★

Since we were married, and mostly I think because of my illness, I didn't really have many friends of my own age. A lot of my gang had left the area. In fact, several had gone to Dublin or cities in Scotland when travel into Europe was easier, because they could get university places there after the rule about taking the Oath came into effect here, and before the borders were closed. Few of them had ever returned to England and none to our home city. Zophia would have been a natural friend if I had been well, but she was happily pregnant and our lives seemed miles apart.

When we agreed to take a lodger it never occurred to me that I might personally benefit. I prepared the back bedroom with care, removing some junk that had accumulated there and emptying the wardrobe of old shoe boxes and Christmas decorations. Ephraim was to bring our guest round after dark, at about five o'clock, when there were still a lot of people in the street and they would attract no attention, and Tom came home early with ingredients for his chicken and mango speciality.

Billy was as skinny as a rake and had a smile that flashed

like lightening. She wore her dark hair unfashionably short and she had black eye make-up which emphasised her brown eyes and her very white skin. She was wearing tight black jeans, a black hooded top and a fashionable black silky waistcoat with shiny green stitching. Her outfit was topped off with the old-fashioned black bin liner she was carrying, containing, I supposed, her worldly possessions.

The first thing I noticed was the overwhelming blackness of her person and that stark, white face and the second thing was the life in that face. I don't really know how to explain this. For one thing, her eyes seemed to dart everywhere, taking everything in, flashing from my face to Tom's and back again, and expressions seem to flicker in quick succession over her face as if I were watching her in fast-forward. Her features were very fine. Novelists of a certain ilk would probably call them elfin. I thought that evening, when I first saw her, that we were about the same age but I discovered later that she was older, closer to thirty, and she had packed an enormous amount into her life so far.

Ephraim didn't stay for dinner which was just as well. We had agreed, Tom and I, that Tom ought not to start buying larger portions of food, because although our city is quite large the centre is small and personal. Tom usually shopped in the same places and recognised the same shop assistants. No doubt they would recognise him too. Everything needed to go on exactly as normal.

Since it was dark and all the curtains were drawn, Billy could move around the house freely at night, without the fear of being seen. We ate our chicken and mango with rice, sitting in the front room and chatting, after carefully putting our handheld DeVs in the kitchen. Actually our electricity meter is in the sitting room and they say the authorities can listen in through meters nowadays, but Tom had stuffed a cushion in the meter cupboard before the Healing Meeting, and it was still there.

With some people it might have been a little awkward. We knew nothing about Billy and we had no idea what she knew about us. Somehow, though, it was easy from the very beginning. She loved the food and asked Tom about the recipe. It seemed she liked to cook too. She commented on the wall hanging my Mum had made, which hung above the fireplace, and talked about rail journeys she had made. Billy was well travelled. She had been to a lot of European countries, which is unusual for people of our generation but normal among older people. By the end of the dessert (bought by Tom, *an ultimate chocolate treat*, it claimed on the pot) we had begun to realise that at least some of her travelling had been with our Society. We didn't ask her any personal questions, nor did she question us, but as we approached ten o'clock she said, showing a little shyness for the first time since her arrival, "I like to have a short silence before I sleep. Would you like to join me, or shall I go to my room?"

Tom glanced at me, smiled, and said, "Let's do it here."

★ ★ ★

Billy was a joy to have around. In her black bin liner, she had a Bible and a handbook for the Society to which our community belongs. She studied both often, but there seemed to be nothing of the religious fanatic about her. She also had several books of poetry, and one day I found her writing in a little exercise book and realised that she was a poet too. From things she said it soon appeared that she had grown up in a family like mine, except that she had had several brothers. She knew all about the caution with which children from our communities need to talk about their home lives at school, and one morning when we were watching the news and there was an article about bullying, she wondered aloud whether it might be kinder to educate our kids apart, in schools of our own, as the original founders had done. She was good at remaining hidden, spending a lot of time in her room and never making much noise, although once I heard her singing rather loudly and had to ask her to quieten down. Our house is terraced, after all, and you can hear quite a lot through the walls.

When she had been there about a week Billy found me late one afternoon, asleep on the settee. She had helped me with some housework in the morning and after eating cheese sandwiches together at lunchtime I had told her I needed to rest and she had headed back to her room. I was a little disappointed that after that first flush of renewed energy following the Meeting for Healing, I found myself once again bone-weary and desperate to sleep at all sorts of times of the day. Usually I only slept for about an hour after lunch but when Billy came down it was four o'clock and already dusk. She came in and drew the curtains, then turned on one of the table lamps.

"Are you okay, Carrie?" she said, perching on the settee next to me.

I surfaced slowly, feeling groggy. "I think so," I said, and stretched. "What time is it?"

"Just after four," said Billy, checking the clock on the big DeV in the corner. "You mustn't let me tire you out," she added.

I sat up. "It isn't you," I said. "It's this illness. I've been like this for months."

"I knew someone who had an illness like yours," said Billy, looking suddenly very sad. "She was… she was my partner."

"Oh Billy," I said. "I'm sorry." Then I asked, wondering if I should, "*Was* your partner?"

"Yes." Billy was sitting on the hearth rug now, resting her chin on her knees, looking about twelve years old. "She died. Three years ago."

I didn't know what to say. I tried to think how I would feel if Tom were to die. "What happened?" I asked.

"She was a reporter," said Billy. "She was part French, part Palestinian. She reported on English news stories for a French magazine. She could do that even though she was ill, because we lived in London and she really just had to keep her eyes and ears open."

"But they let her work here?" I was surprised. The Alliance has become very sensitive to reporting from England in the last few years.

"Well, Khadi wasn't in our Society," explained Billy. "And she was an accredited French journalist, so they might not have liked it, but there wasn't much they could do really."

"So how... she didn't die from her illness, did she?" For a moment I felt real alarm, although I have always known mine is not usually a progressive disease.

"No! Oh Carrie, no, not at all. We thought she was getting better. We had all these plans..."

"So?" I prompted.

"She had a road accident," said Billy, looking at the rug. "Outside Marylebone Station. A hit and run."

"That's awful!" I said.

"Of course, it wasn't really a hit and run," added Billy. "We all knew that. They just got her out of the way."

"Oh Billy..." What could I say?

She understood. "I know," she said. "It was tough. It's still tough. So I started sending stories to her editor instead. I was really careful. I kept it up for two years. I knew how to get them out of the country, you see, through other French citizens, through her mates. But then a few months ago... well, obviously I need to get out now."

★ ★ ★

161

At first I thought that Billy might only stay with us for a few days, but as Christmas approached Ephraim explained that border crossings were being more strictly regulated than ever. So many English people have relatives in Europe that it is a headache for the authorities to stop disaffected people from leaving or subversives from arriving. Tom and I had told no one about Billy. When my parents came she stayed upstairs, and she kept out of the way if Job called round, and when we had the second Healing Meeting. She only came down to meet a visitor once, when Ephraim came home with Tom after work, and we sat in the dining room and drank sherry from a bottle given to Tom by a happy client.

We told my parents that we wanted to spend Christmas in our own home, and asked if they would mind us not being together that year. Far from it, they seemed quite pleased, I dare say because it was proof that all was well between Tom and me, but also because the Meeting in their town was working with the Sikhs to put on a huge festive meal on Christmas Day (the Sikhs are amazing at catering for large numbers) and my parents really wanted to be involved.

I was looking forward to Christmas. Strictly speaking our community does not place any special emphasis on one day over another, since the Spirit is with us and within us every day and wherever we are, but we do like a celebration. When we were children this was a time of year for being especially generous to the poor and to those suffering social injustice, but I also remember gifts and carol singing, and huge teas consisting of exactly those sorts of goodies our parents usually rationed, or banned altogether. Tom wanted to cook a traditional English Christmas dinner such as he had when he was a boy, although Billy and I vetoed Christmas pudding because of potential weight gain, and we agreed that we would give one gift each to the other two people in the house. There would be a short Meeting for Worship to which Tom and I would go, but otherwise we would stay home and just enjoy the peace, the good food and each other's company.

The only thing to mar the day, however, was a new anxiety which was growing in my mind about my health. Well, not exactly about my health… The thing was, I had missed a period. It should have come just after the second Healing Meeting but so far, nothing. It was hard to know whether I was feeling more nauseous because, on and off ever since the illness had started, I tended to feel a bit sick and dizzy first thing in the morning, but it did seem to be getting worse.

It was a measure of our friendship that I spoke to Billy about it first.

It was two days before Christmas. Tom was at work and Billy had been hoovering the house in the dull grey light of an overcast December day, unable to turn on the lights because then prying eyes would have been able to see in. I had only wanted toast and water for breakfast, but even then I felt sick and for the first time it was more than just a feeling. I came downstairs feeling woebegone and with a foul taste in my mouth and turned on the kitchen light. Billy, who was putting the furniture straight in the safe shadows of the dining room, took one look at me and said, "Carrie, what's up?"

I was so glad she was there. I just blurted it out. "I think I'm pregnant!"

"Hey Carrie, that's great!" The expressions of pleasure and surprise flashed in quick succession across her face, followed rapidly by concern as she took in my unhappiness. "What's the matter?" she demanded. Then, more quietly, "Don't you and Tom want children?"

"It's not that," I said. "Of course we want children, it's just… the fecklessness."

"What do you mean?" Billy looked confused. "You're married, you've got a nice house, it isn't feckless to have a family! It's great!"

"No, you don't understand." So I explained it to her: how I needed to be back at work nine months after my diagnosis, at the latest, if I wanted to avoid going onto Medical Assistance. How if I became pregnant it would be treated as a further act of malingering. How Tom and I could not afford for me to lose my benefits, or to raise a child who would not be eligible for any state aid, not even free education. How we could not afford for Tom's reputation to be tainted by association with a malingerer.

Billy looked stunned. "Of course," she said, "I half knew about some of that but in gay circles… Goodness, Carrie, what are you supposed to do, then?"

"From the point of view of the Health Service?" I asked, and I couldn't keep the bitterness out of my voice. "I'm supposed to have an abortion – at my own expense."

★ ★ ★

I couldn't have managed Christmas if I had tried to keep the secret from Tom, but speaking to Billy in the daytime made it easier to tell Tom in the evening, in the dark, when I was cuddled up to him.

"You were quiet this evening, Carrie," commented Tom. He shifted one leg so that his foot was touching mine. "Has it been a bad day?"

It was the perfect opportunity and so I told him, trying to keep the emotion out of my voice, the fear and the longing and the terrible regret about what we would have to do.

Tom was quiet for ages, then he gave a big sigh and rolled over from his back to his side to hold me tight. "Oh Carrie," he said, rather breathlessly. "A baby! Our baby!"

"Yes." I was slightly smothered in Tom's cotton T-shirt. "But we can't keep it, can we? They'll say…"

Tom stiffened. "No baby of mine is going to be aborted!" he said with suppressed rage.

164

I was quiet. Mum once told me that in her childhood abortion was a right women fought for, that our community had refused to condemn women who had abortions when other churches were treating the act as a terrible sin. Just at that time there was a small influx of new babies in our Meeting, and I can remember looking at them and not understanding why anyone might want to get rid of a little one. I was only young then, ten or eleven I suppose, past playing with dolls but more into puppies and kittens than babies, but there was this one little chap who used to be brought into Meeting looking as alert and as bright as anything. I could not imagine then wanting to kill such an amazing creature. Of course, that was before Meeting organised a small group of us to visit the Rape Crisis Centre to talk to that woman police officer. After that I understood a bit better, but really only with my head, not with my heart.

"I don't want an abortion," I said. "I really don't."

Tom said with surprising firmness, "Good! Because you're not going to have one!" Then, a little tentatively, "Have you mentioned it to anyone other than Billy?"

"No." I thought about it. "Do you think we should?" I asked. "My parents, or yours?"

"Not mine!" Tom managed a chuckle. "They will certainly agree that we are feckless. They more or less invented the word!" He paused for a few minutes. "How sure are you?"

"Well, I'm not. My period is only five days late and I've been sick once, although… well, I do sort of feel different."

Tom eased up on his hugging and rolled onto his back again. He sounded worried but also quite decisive. "Right, then how about this? We wait until after Christmas and buy a pregnancy test. If you are pregnant, we tell your parents and maybe someone at Meeting, and together we make a plan of action. Would you be happy with that?"

"I suppose so," I said, feeling sad. "Do you think we might

end up having to abort? I mean, they make things pretty difficult for people who have babies irresponsibly."

Tom sat up. "Let's have a glass of wine," he said. "To help us to sleep. And because it's nearly Christmas." He put the light on by his bed, looked at me and suddenly gave a sort of sad grin. "On second thoughts," he said, "perhaps not! Shall I make a pot of tea?"

Tom took longer than I expected, and when he finally came up he was smiling again, and he had tears in his eyes. He put the tray down on the floor (the bedside tables are always too cluttered to put a tray on) and handed me a piece of paper. "I found this by the kettle. Billy must have put it there."

It was a small square torn out of an exercise book, and one verse from the Bible was written neatly in the middle. *For I know the plans I have for you, says the Lord, plans for welfare and not for evil, to give you a future and a hope.*

"Oh!" I exclaimed. I looked at Tom and then looked at it again. They were just words on a piece of paper, but there seemed to be Truth in them, like the Truth I sometimes feel when someone ministers. As I held the piece of paper it was as if some of the words soaked into me. That sounds freaky, and it is hard to explain, but it was a bit like when you bathe in scented water and you know that the smell, the lavender or whatever, will still be on your skin even when you have dried yourself and dressed. The words which had somehow transferred themselves into my... my what? My heart, I suppose... the words which seemed so powerful were *welfare*, *hope* and *future*.

Tom poured the tea and handed me a mug, put his own mug on his side, on a rather precarious pile of books and magazines, then climbed back into bed. He rearranged the pillows carefully to prop himself up, put an arm round me and picked up his mug with his left hand. He took a sip, then, "You know what, Carrie?"

"What?" I prompted.

"Being married to you is turning out to be much more of an adventure than I could possibly have guessed!"

★ ★ ★

My heart sank when Derek arrived on Boxing Day. We thought that if we sat in the dining room, which is rather dark at the best of times because it has a small window, and if Billy sat with her back to the bookcase, no prying eyes looking in would be able to spot her. We were playing a really old, pre-digital game that Tom had brought with him when we married, a board game he had been given as a small boy, involving dice and little plastic objects, and artificial money in pounds and pence rather than dollars and cents such as we use now, and the buying of houses and the acquiring of property. "Very capitalist!" declared Billy, but she turned out to be really cunning, and was building hotels in expensive locations amidst much mirth.

Tom went to the door while Billy dived for the stairs and I did my best to disguise the fact that there had been three of us playing. I heard Tom stalling on the doorstep, then he called out rather stiffly, "Carrie, put the kettle on! It's Derek."

I tucked Billy's chair back under the table and went through to the kitchen. I really didn't want to see Derek after the last time he had called round, but in our community we are supposed to be loving and forgiving, and Tom was right to invite him in.

They came through to the dining room. I said, "Sit in the sitting room, you two, I'll bring the coffee through. Mince pies?"

Derek was sitting on the edge of the armchair by the window, looking awkward, and holding a beautiful flower arrangement of white roses, holly and some other greenery, wrapped in green and red paper with a red bow.

"I've come to apologise," he said as I put the coffee pot on the hearth. "I was way out of line last time I came round. I'm sorry. I can't tell you how sorry I am…"

I wasn't going to say, "That's all right," because really it wasn't, and there's no point in lying. I said, "Thank you, Derek. I appreciate you coming round."

Tom said, "You were so angry, Derek. Was there more to it than we know? Had something happened?"

Derek looked gratefully at Tom. "Well yes," he said, and I thought he was choosing his words carefully. "I was… I am worried about you two. I thought… I think you've got in too far, too soon."

Tom sighed. "Well, really," he said, a little impatiently. "If you're right, who is responsible? We wouldn't have known much at all about the food runs if you hadn't talked to us, and as for the other business…"

"Yes, I know, I do understand," said Derek. "But you see, I knew what I was doing." He put the flowers on the window sill, unzipped his green jacket and sat back in the armchair. I thought, *He's taking control!* and I glanced sideways at Tom. I couldn't tell what he was thinking.

"You see…" Derek paused, a frown on his face. Was it just because I already mistrusted him that I thought it was a calculated frown? I thought he was acting. "You see," he started again, "I was trying to involve you one step at a time, when you were ready. I wanted you to do things that didn't touch your home life. I thought Tom could help us but go back to you, Carrie, leaving behind whatever he had been doing. I thought I had sorted it so that if they got suspicious the ATTF could raid your house and find absolutely nothing." He had an apparently open and honest expression, sitting slightly forward now, concerned that we should understand. *What is he up to?* I wondered.

"It would have worked, too," Derek went on, "but I didn't take into account any other influences."

"What do you mean?" It was Tom, looking, I thought, a bit confused.

Derek looked down at his hands, with that apparently concerned frown furrowing his brow again. "I almost don't like to say…"

"I think you'd better say!" I demanded, and my voice sounded harsh to my ears.

Derek hesitated. "Derek?" Tom prompted.

Derek sighed. "That weekend," he looked at Tom, "the weekend we sorted Alexis' papers…"

"What about it?" Tom was sounding somehow stiff.

Derek turned to me, "Where were you that weekend, Carrie? Tom just said you were away, but you weren't with your parents, were you?"

When I didn't answer he turned to Tom. "Tom?"

"Is it any of your business?" asked Tom.

Derek paused. He tried to smile at us, sitting side by side on the settee. His face looked shadowy against the dim December light of the window behind him. "I wish it wasn't," he said. "I wish I could just let you both get on with it, but I can't, can I? It wouldn't be responsible. And anyhow, you could be putting other people at risk too."

"Derek!" exclaimed Tom, sounding impatient. "For goodness' sake! What are you trying to say?"

"Okay," said Derek, sitting back in the armchair again, as if he had reluctantly come to a conclusion. "Okay, this is what I mean. I need helpers, the community needs helpers if we are going to serve people in need, but I'm careful. I introduce volunteers to only one aspect of the programme at a time, when I think they're ready. I look after people, I protect them. I was trying to protect you. But there was another player, wasn't there? Someone else got involved, and sucked you in, and didn't protect you at all. That's true, isn't it? Someone with a completely different agenda."

Tom and I were quiet for a moment, then I asked, "Are you talking about Ephraim?"

"Yes," Derek sounded disgruntled. "If that's what you want to call him."

Tom sighed. "Derek," he said, "honestly… you've got this thing about Ephraim. He's fine. He's been in our community for ages, the clerk and the elders trust him. He's one of the good guys."

"Oh no he isn't!" Derek sounded angry again. "He isn't! He's ATTF. He was ATTF all his life, until a few years ago, then – oh miracle! – he suddenly became convinced of the Truth and swapped sides. He was called Karl. He *is* called Karl still. And he's still working for them. He's undercover, and he's skilled – oh yes! Very skilled!" Derek was glaring at the empty hearth. Then his expression changed to one almost of sadness. "And there's nothing I can do to stop him," he added. "All my life I've come across people like Ephraim. They're charming. They're friendly. You can't help but trust them. They're always popular, they are quickly promoted, they are wherever things are happening. And me? I turn people off. People are suspicious of me. When I was a kid parents didn't want their kids to play with me. I wanted to work in fashion but my face didn't fit, and I ended up managing a dollar shop. A *dollar* shop!" He paused again. "And he's sucked you in well and good." He looked at Tom again. No, he glared at him. "He's infiltrated the Overground completely. There are people who trust him at every stage now. I think you've got someone here. You have, haven't you?"

Neither of us answered. Tom held my hand.

"Right," said Derek. "And you trust him more than you trust me, so you won't even tell me that, but I know. Oh yes! Because people don't think I'm as intelligent as him but I've got his number!"

Still neither of us said anything. Then he stood angrily,

zipping up his jacket again, making for the door. As he opened it, he turned to us again. "I'll tell you what," he said, "you need to get out of here, the sooner the better – you and that girl hidden in your spare bedroom. Believe me, you aren't safe. You've been raided once and they'll raid you again, and I really don't want to tell you what they'll do to you, you really don't want to know! So it's time you left!" He slammed the door behind him.

★ ★ ★

Billy came down at once. "I heard that," she said, standing in the doorway of the sitting room, unable to come in further in case she was seen from the pavement. "Who is he?"

"Derek," we said in unison, then Tom added, "He's a member of our Meeting."

"Wo!" exclaimed Billy. "He sounds pretty messed up. Aggressive."

"He is," I agreed, and we went back to the safety of the dining room. "Could you hear what he said?"

"Not all of it." So we told her.

Billy was quiet. "Is it possible?" she asked. "I mean about Ephraim being ATTF?"

Tom sighed. He explained about the little red book which Ephraim had lent Tom as he was applying for membership, how it had said, *To Karl from all in Aylesbury Meeting.*

"Hey, I've been to Aylesbury Meeting!" said Billy. "Several times. When I was in that drama group. But I didn't see Ephraim there. I only met him for the first time when he arrived at the Salvation Army shelter in Kensington where I was hiding, to bring me down here." Then she said, "May I see that booklet?"

Tom and I looked at each other. "We haven't got it any more," Tom said.

"Where is it then?"

I was feeling uncomfortable. "It was the only thing the ATTF took when they raided the house."

We all looked at each other, minds ticking over, trying to make sense of it all.

"If Ephraim is ATTF," Tom said, "why would they need to take that booklet? Surely they'd already know we had it? Wouldn't he have to report in?"

Billy was sitting at the table with her elbows on her piles of fake money and her head in her hands. She looked up. "What if they wanted to remove any evidence that Ephraim had ever had another name?"

I could see what she meant, but I had spent a lot of time with Ephraim by then and I just didn't believe it. I said, "Or what if they're on Ephraim's trail, looking for evidence against him?"

"But surely they know where we are, all of us?" said Tom. Again we all looked at each other. "We're really no further forward, are we?" Tom asked.

Billy was looking thoughtful, expressions passing across her face, short black hair standing on end where she had put her fingers through it. "There is one thing, though," she said. "I think Derek was right when he said we needed to leave. Me of course, but you as well. This is all a big mess and I just don't think we can be sure we're safe here."

Tom said, "Well, we need to be as informed as we can be, and there's one thing we can find out, for sure. Carrie, I'm going down to the chemist to buy a pregnancy test!"

So the one fact we did have in front of us by the time we tucked into turkey sandwiches an hour later, was that there was a little Walker on the way.

★ ★ ★

Of course, I wanted to tell Mum and Dad. So did Tom, he was as proud as can be, with a huge grin he seemed unable to wipe off his face. We both knew we couldn't tell anyone, though. Instead we talked about names. Tom wanted to call the child Che if it turned out to be a boy. He said it is the ultimate name for a revolutionary and any son of his was going to be in revolt against the authorities, for sure. I said that if it were a girl I would like to call her Mutlu. I had a friend called Mutlu at school, a Turkish girl who went back to her home country after college to marry the man she loved. The name means *happiness* or *laughter*, and I said that my great hope for any child of ours was that she or he should be happy. Then Billy said, "Perhaps you should call the baby Stewart or Jean, or maybe Sean or Sinead, because surely you'll be bringing your family up in Scotland or Ireland?"

That brought a moment of sudden, down-to-earth realism into the conversation. We looked at each other.

"Sorry," said Billy, looking down at the tumbled heaps of fake money. "I didn't mean to spoil the fun."

Tom stood up, picked up the empty sandwich plates and went into the kitchen. I heard him put the kettle on, then he came back into the dining room.

"No, Billy," he said, "you're right. The one thing Derek said which was absolutely, unmistakably true is that we're going to have to leave."

Instinctively I looked around to see if either of us had left our DeVs lying around, but we had developed cautious approaches and we routinely exiled our electronic devices to places where they couldn't hear us. Before Billy came down Tom had put them in the conservatory.

"How do we do that?" I asked. Suddenly I realised what a huge undertaking it would be, to leave all this, to leave Mum and Dad, to leave our community and to go to another country, to claim refugee status... Of course we had talked about it many times, especially me, growing up as I did, but never as something I might actually find myself doing, the next important action in my life.

Tom said, without conviction, "It was Derek who suggested it, perhaps we should ask him for help."

Billy looked surprised. "Would you do that?" she asked. "Do you really trust him?"

Tom and I looked at each other, then "No!" we said, in unison.

"Then you have to ask Ephraim," said Billy, matter-of-factly.

"But do we trust him?" Tom asked. "All those things Derek said… And really, we know nothing about him."

We were all quiet, then Billy said, "Actually, we do know a few things about him."

"Like what?" In my opinion he was quite a mysterious person.

"Well," said Billy, counting the points out on her fingers, "we know that the people at the Salvation Army place where I was hiding trusted him. We know that your clerk trusts him, or anyhow that whoever was clerk when he was accepted into membership trusted him. We know that your Meeting as a whole trusted him enough for him to be asked to visit you, when you were considering membership. That's right, isn't it, Tom? That's quite a lot of weighty and wise people who trust him. And in your heart of hearts, don't you two trust him?"

We looked at each other. "Yes," I said.

Ye– s," said Tom hesitantly. "Well, when I was coming into membership I trusted him entirely, but now it's hard, after what Derek has said. Derek is so sure."

We were all quiet. Then Billy asked, "So is it down to who you trust, Ephraim or Derek? Whoever you trust most, that's the person you talk to, about escaping?"

Again we were quiet. It seemed like a pretty bleak choice. "It looks like it," said Tom.

"I don't think I can help," said Billy. "I don't think I should even try. It's such a big thing." She turned, smiled a little sadly, and went upstairs.

We didn't speak. Tom cleared up all the debris from the board game, carefully sorting the money into different denominations and putting the little green houses and the little red hotels into different cardboard compartments in the box, then sliding the packed box under the bookcase again. When he had finished he sat down at the table and reached across to hold my hand. "We need some silence," he said. "If ever we needed guidance, it's now." He closed his eyes but continued holding my hand, stroking it gently with his thumb. I closed my eyes too, and felt a deep stillness descend on our dining room, and on my heart.

★ ★ ★

The decision was made and we told Billy, who seemed really pleased. When Tom went out to buy a takeaway, Billy and I sat in her room, and talked.

"It's strange," I said. "When Tom and I agreed to marry I felt this sort of calm excitement. I don't know… as if something was complete in my heart. I thought it was just how people felt when they knew they were going to marry the man they loved. But I feel the same now – excited but really peaceful."

"Oh!" Billy was excited. "I was reading about that. There's something in the Old Testament. Wait a minute…"

She picked up her shabby Bible and started leafing through it. "Those old guys knew a thing or two!" she grinned. "It's somewhere round here…" She ran her finger down a page, turned to the next page and I saw a couple of lines of print had been underlined. "Here it is! *Your ears will hear a word behind you, This is the way, walk in it, whenever you turn to the right or to the left.* She kept her finger on the print and looked at me, her eyes sparkling. "I didn't know what it meant when I read it. I mean, it seems back to front. We need the guidance before we make a decision, otherwise how can we be sure we're doing the right thing? This verse seems to ask so much of us – that we make a decision and then we're told it's right or wrong. But now I get it! This is what has happened to you! You've made the right choice and the Spirit is telling you as much! And they knew about this – well, way back, whenever Isaiah was written! Isn't that incredible?"

I thought about all the sages who had written wise words hundreds or thousands of years ago, and how little I knew about them. That was when I first started to think that if Tom and I ever lived in a country which was free enough, I would study those old writings. Really study them, in depth. Right at that moment, though, my main feeling was of reassurance.

★ ★ ★

After that, because the decision had been made, it was hard waiting to see Ephraim again. He wasn't at Meeting the following Sunday, although we waited until after Second Meeting had started just in case he was late, which to be honest was pretty unlikely. I asked Job casually whether he had seen Ephraim recently and Job said comfortably, "Oh, I dare say he's off on his travels." Job was wearing his Christmas pullover, given to him by his great-grandchildren, and I noticed that he was developing a bit of a paunch. He looked jolly and happy, the way a great grandfather ought to look.

We didn't see Derek at all. At least, he was at First Meeting with us, but was sitting across the circle in the back row, and after Meeting he seemed to be in serious conversation with a couple who had just started to come on Sundays. They were an older couple, perhaps the same sort of age as my parents, and I had heard someone say that they had been worshipping with one of the more traditional churches until recently. It is a brave thing to follow your conscience and to explore a community like ours with things as they are. Derek didn't look in our direction and of course we didn't weave our way between the chairs to see him, as we might have done once.

Tom went back to work and we settled into our routine, so that from the outside everything would have looked entirely normal. Tom worked a couple of Saturdays they had another big job from the university and Tom's expertise was essential. They paid him extra for working anti-social hours, which was new. Feany said it was because Tom was bringing in so much business.

It was helpful having Billy around. It was not just that she was company for me, it was Billy who stopped me from cancelling my monthly shop of sanitary products. "You don't know who is watching," she warned. "And you don't want to alert anyone that you might be pregnant, especially because if they are watching they will know that Tom bought that pregnancy testing kit. If they think you're fecklessly pregnant they'll watch you even more closely, because people in your situation have every reason to try to leave."

She was right, of course, so we spent hard-earned money buying products which I flushed down the loo, simply for cover. Well, it was better safe than sorry, and I was glad Billy was there to keep an eye on us.

When Ephraim did turn up, just after the beginning of February, he looked fit and well, and perhaps a little suntanned. Or was he wind weathered? Anyhow, it was good to see him. He knocked on the door around six o'clock, when there was a good chance Tom would be home, and came in wafting the smell of cold February air with him. Frosts are unusual nowadays of course, but it was going to be frosty that night, and Ephraim had a plaid scarf wound fashionably round his neck. He looked like someone from one of those clothes outlets that manage to defy spam blocking and appear periodically on DeVs.

Ephraim kissed me on the cheek and gave Billy a huge hug. He thumped Tom on the back, looked between the three of us and said, "Well, you all look great! How's it going?"

It was really good to sit down in the sitting room, the fire lit because of the rare treat of a frost, and mugs of hot chocolate in our hands. "Actually," said Ephraim, fishing a bottle out from the deep pocket of his long, black coat, "I brought something to celebrate the New Year – rather belatedly, I'm afraid."

Tom looked at me. I looked at Ephraim. "I'm not drinking alcohol just now," I said.

For a moment Ephraim's expression was blank, then slowly a smile spread across his face. "Oh ho!" he said. "Am I guessing correctly?"

"We think it's due around about August," said Tom, grinning proudly. "Although we can't know for sure. Carrie hasn't seen a doctor."

"Mm." Ephraim was thoughtful. "Well, a toast is definitely in order," he said, "but certainly it needs to be in chocolate!" Then he looked more serious. "Who knows?" he asked.

"Just us three," I said. "And now you."

"Not your parents?" checked Ephraim.

"No, nobody else," confirmed Tom. "It's a big deal, with Carrie off work anyhow."

"Yes, I see that." Ephraim was staring into the fire, a slight frown on his face. "You're in a bit of a fix," he added.

"They need to get away," said Billy. "Don't you think so, Ephraim?"

Ephraim remained quiet. The fire crackled and a piece of wood flared up with a bright orange flame. I thought he wasn't going to answer, but at last he looked at Tom.

"What do you think, Tom – you and Carrie?"

"We've got to go," said Tom. "They'll call this pregnancy feckless. There'll be no help with the baby because Carrie'll be on Medical Assistance. They'll want us to abort, and if we don't we'll be on our own. So there's not much of a choice really, is there?"

"No," Ephraim agreed, but didn't say anything further.

Again we were all quiet. Then Tom said, I thought a little breathlessly, "We need your help, Ephraim."

"My help?" Why was he questioning us like this, wasn't it obvious?

"To get away," I said. "We need to get into the European Union, to Scotland or Ireland."

"Or anywhere safe," added Billy.

Again Ephraim was quiet. It might have been a bit weird under other circumstances, but these thoughtful moments of stillness are part of the way we do things, so I felt more reassured than anything else. Then Ephraim sat up, he stretched as if he had been asleep, and sat back with his hands behind his head.

"You've thought about this," he said. "And kept silence? You know what you're risking?" He looked from one to the other of us, and smiled. "Of course you know," he said. His eyes moved from Tom to Billy, from Billy to me, and then back to the glowing fire. "I'll be honest," he said, "I wasn't expecting this… I need to give it some thought." He started sipping his hot chocolate with that slight frown creasing his forehead again. We all stayed quiet. Then, "Right!" he announced. "I need to go away and do some thinking and planning. I was hoping to move you, Billy, in the next couple of days." He smiled at us, the frown fading. "Although I see no sign that you've overstayed your welcome!" He paused, then added, "It might take me three weeks to plan all this. Try to behave as normal. Don't tell anyone." He looked approvingly at me.

179

"Carrie, you've done well deciding not to tell your parents. Both of you, keep acting as if nothing is happening – nothing at all. Can you do that?"

Tom looked relieved. It was good to have Ephraim on our side. "Of course," said Tom, at the same time as I said, "Yes."

"Billy," checked Ephraim, "are you willing to risk three or four more weeks here?"

Billy grinned. "Absolutely," she said, "if Tom and Carrie are willing to have me!"

So we finished our hot chocolate, which had become lukewarm chocolate, and Tom and I saw Ephraim out into the frosty night.

★ ★ ★

One surprising result of our decision to leave, however that might be managed, was that I no longer felt entirely comfortable with the little healing group. It didn't seem quite right, that they were there holding me in the Light, and all the time I had secrets: the secret of my pregnancy and the secret of our hope to escape. I felt I was deceiving them. At our next meeting Job asked questions about my energy levels, and I answered honestly that I was quite weary still, and didn't always feel good, but in my heart I no longer knew what was illness and what were the normal symptoms of pregnancy. Nor was it possible to find out. I couldn't search for information on a DeV because the authorities might see and draw their own conclusions, and of course I couldn't ask anyone. In the healing group I actually had to try to put them off the scent.

There was one aspect of my situation, however, with which the group was able to help. It was just at the beginning of February, just after Ephraim's visit and a day before the healing group was due to meet, when I had a letter from the Medical Assistance Board. Our post was delivered late in the morning, and this very official letter arrived with the usual unsolicited mailings about pizza deliveries and gym memberships. Billy was upstairs doing whatever she was doing in her room and Tom was at work. I sat in the armchair, feeling a bit wobbly, to open the letter.

It was, I suppose, simple and straight to the point. It noted that I had been off work for ten months and that an official diagnosis of CFS had been recorded on the 1st June. It noted that I had attended a clinic and completed the course satisfactorily, but that according to their records I had made no further steps towards returning to work. My contract at the school was terminated at the end of the last academic year, and they had no record of me applying for work anywhere else. Throughout this period the state had paid me full benefits. Then it went on to say that, according to National Health legislation, my benefits would end in March, my last monthly payment would be deposited in my bank account on the second working Friday of February. A leaflet was enclosed which the letter recommended I read carefully, as my circumstances were due to change significantly in March and neither the Health Service nor any other organisation funded by the tax payer would be able to offer me assistance from that point.

Of course I knew something like this was going to happen, but still it was a shock to read it all in black and white. With my heart beating fast I turned to the leaflet. It was called, optimistically, *Getting Back on Your Feet*, and the cover showed a very healthy-looking couple smiling happily as they left a job centre, in the doorway of which stood a suited older man, waving, obviously happy to see the two people setting off for their new jobs. Inside it was more realistic. There was a short list of websites for charities to which a person might go for emergency support, and a paragraph about how to cope in areas where feeding stations had been closed down. I was glad to see that our Society was listed among those organisations to whom a person might go for help. There were several pages about the difference it would make when transferred from the Health Service to Medical Assistance, with a warning against buying medicines illegally on the black market immediately following the page about now having to pay in cash for doctors' appointments and for legal prescriptions.

The second part of the leaflet was a little more helpful. There were two pages called, as was the leaflet, *Getting Back on Your Feet*, in which they recommended steps to take: apply for every job you might possibly be able to do, be prepared to work for minimum wage and on zero hours contracts, take on voluntary work to demonstrate you are not workshy, apply for apprenticeships in areas where we had a national shortage because of the exodus of Eastern Europeans from the country, or appeal to one of the special Boards if I felt the move to Medical Assistance was unjust. The last page, *Towards Responsible Citizenship*, suggested a counselling service which offered one-to-one and group help to overcome inner resistance to the culture of work. Nowhere in the whole colourful leaflet, illustrated with cheerful cartoon characters, was there any acknowledgement that there might be factors such as poor health making a return to work impossible. I am sure some people, reading the leaflet, would just want to throw themselves off the nearest railway bridge.

Tom and I showed the letter and the leaflet to the group. Madge and Wolly seemed to be quite familiar with this type of communication. Apparently I was not the first person they knew to have received a letter like this. Job was really interested in the leaflet. He said it ought to be sent to the Scottish branch of our organisation and on to Amnesty International, and asked if he could have it when we had finished with it. Feeling a bit hypocritical I told the group how anxious it made me feel, that in such a short time I was to lose so many of my citizenship rights. Even as I told them this, which was true as far as it went, I felt bad. My situation was so much worse than I could tell them, because of my pregnancy.

Wolly, however, was really helpful. We kept silence for about ten minutes, then he looked up and said, "Carrie and Tom, this is not ministry, but I have some advice to give you. Would you like to hear it?"

We looked at each other. "Of course," said Tom. "Fire away!"

"Right," said Wolly, and looked down at his hands. Then, after a pause he said, "The first thing you need to understand is that this whole Medical Assistance scheme is not aimed at people like you."

"You could have fooled me!" I said.

"No, well, listen," suggested Wolly. "This government, the whole Alliance approach to work, taxation, loss of citizenship rights… all the stuff you're having to deal with now, it's really all geared at saving productive people from having to support those who are not productive. It's capitalism in action, or what the ordinary person calls Darwinism, the survival of the fittest."

"Yes," agreed Tom. "But Carrie isn't fit!"

"No… yes, I know," said Wolly. "But she is the sort of person who *should* be fit! I mean," he looked at me and smiled, "you're middle class and reasonably well educated. You read books. You're married. You and Tom are buying your own home. You really belong with those young couples the state so loves, whose children join the Little League and whose teenagers go to camp in the States, who worry about the new High School Diploma that is replacing A levels and who vote Centre Right because they believe only the Right can manage the economy."

"I don't see that," said Tom. "Carrie doesn't fit at all. She's mixed race, she was brought up in a suspect organisation, she refused to take the Oath, and she's considered to be a malingerer."

Everyone smiled at Tom's rather unflattering description of me, but Wolly continued seriously.

"That's true. But look at it another way. If too many people like Carrie go onto Medical Assistance it will only be a matter of time before someone starts organising, because you are the sort of people who organise, aren't you? And then the government is faced with protests and demonstrations, with social media coverage and interest from the foreign press. No, the people they really want on Medical Assistance are the semi-literate, the believers in conspiracy theories and alternative medicines, the obviously inadequate and the badly spoken. If they are interviewed by the foreign press, or if they try to organise demonstrations, they just make themselves look silly."

"There's another thing," said Madge. "You went to school round here, didn't you?"

"South of here," I said. "Blackberry Academy."

"Exactly," said Madge. "A good school with lots of other middle-class children, who you were friends with."

"Yes," I agreed.

"And you went back to their homes, and some of them came round to your house?"

"Yes," I agreed again.

"So they know you, and they half know your family. And if they hear that you are on Medical Assistance, some of those you were at school with will be shocked and will despise you, but not all. Some will be bound to say, 'Carrie! That can't be right! Carrie isn't feckless or work shy!' And then they'll start to question the system. And believe me, the authorities absolutely do not want the system questioned!"

"But I don't see how this helps," asked Tom. "I mean, Carrie's got the letter. They are going to transfer her to Medical Assistance."

Job had been following the conversation in silence. Now he asked, "So what are you saying? That there's a way out?"

"Perhaps," said Wolly.

There was a short, silent pause, then Madge said, "There's a game to be played here. We've seen others play it."

"Go on," prompted Job.

Wolly continued. "Let's assume we're right, and they don't really want to put people like you onto Medical Assistance? Right, so they need a face-saving device, so that they can let you off, without seeming to break or even bend their own rules."

I couldn't see it. I thought Madge and Wolly were missing the main point. "But I'm ill!" I reminded them. "I honestly can't work, and that's why I'm losing my citizenship rights. And I really *am* ill!"

"Carrie," said Madge, reaching out and taking my hand, "of course you're ill! But do you think you're the only one with an illness like yours? Don't you think the wives or children of government officials catch viruses? Do you think the families of high-ranking ATTF officers are immune from disease? And honestly, do you believe they are put onto Medical Assistance? You can bet your bottom dollar they're not!"

Tom was looking thoughtful. "So what do we do?" he asked.

"Right!" said Wolly, sounding almost triumphant. "So this is where we get to my advice! I think you two need to start thinking about playing the game."

"How do they play?" asked Job, looking worried. "What are the rules?"

"Okay," said Wolly. "Let's think of everything that is against you. I don't honestly think being mixed race is a problem. Remember that the United States has a mixed race vice-president and he is the darling of their extreme Right. Your inability to go out to work is a big problem, but how would it be if you worked from home?"

I thought about that. "I don't have any skills," I said.

"No craft skills? No needlework?" suggested Madge.

"None."

"Oh, but I do!" said Tom. "I have all these computing skills."

We all looked at Tom. I couldn't see how that helped, until Tom said, "So how about I start my own business and employ Carrie?"

Job was still looking worried, but Madge and Wolly looked pleased. "That's good," said Wolly. "But of course, on its own it won't solve the problem."

"What do you mean?" Tom asked.

Job sighed. "I thought we were moving in this direction," he said.

Wolly looked sad, exchanging a glance with Madge and then speaking to Job. "It might be for the best, you know," he said.

"What might be for the best! What are you talking about?" I felt threatened and uncomfortable, as if I were missing something obvious.

Job turned to me. "A lot of suspicion would be removed from you – from you and Tom – if you left the Society. If, maybe, you started to worship somewhere else."

"No!" Tom stood up, his face suddenly very red. "We can't do that!"

"Can't you?" asked Wolly. "Not even for your wife's well-being, and for any family you might have in the future?" Then, more gently, "There are good people in those churches you know. And you could still keep silence together here." He was quiet for a short time. Tom sat down slowly, still looking shocked.

"You wouldn't be the first people to do that," said Madge. "Our own daughter and son-in-law…"

"And are they happy?" asked Job. "Really happy?"

Madge looked a little taken aback. "Well, of course… life isn't easy for anyone nowadays. I wouldn't say they were always happy, but there's food on the table. Our grandchildren see doctors when they need to. Peter has been promoted… of course it isn't ideal but we honour their decision…" Madge seemed a little deflated, even sad.

Tom said, "I think this meeting has ended, don't you?" And on that rather unhappy note the others left.

★ ★ ★

Tom stayed talking to Job, who was the last to leave, for several minutes while I was in the kitchen putting on the kettle and clearing up the mugs and plates we had used. When he came in I turned, expecting to see a grim-faced husband, but instead he gave me a huge grin, and a hug. "Hey Carrie," he said almost jubilantly, "I can see our next step now, thanks to Madge and Wolly!"

"You can?" I was stunned. Five or ten minutes earlier he had been dead set against leaving the Society. Could he have changed his mind that quickly and that completely?

"As he was leaving," said Tom, "Job said something to me. He said, *Don't forget, appearances can be deceptive.* Don't you see, he was telling us to act a part! We don't need actually to leave the Society at all, but we could act as if we were thinking about it!"

I felt dubious. "But it will become clear…" I said.

Tom hugged me again, enthusiastically. "No it won't!" he said, "Because we've asked Ephraim to help us to leave! Remember, Madge and Wolly were assuming we are staying. They were thinking in the long term. All we have to do is to pull the wool over the eyes of the officials for a few weeks!" He beamed at me.

"But… what's the point," I asked, "if we're going anyhow?"

Tom grinned again, looking at my worried face. "It's just a ploy," he said, "to cover our tracks. Ephraim is doing his bit, whatever it is, and we can do ours."

I went into the dining room and sat down on the nearest chair. I swallowed, and tried to think. "Do you think it's necessary?" I asked.

"Well..." Tom sat down too. "Maybe not strictly necessary. But sensible. Don't you think so?"

"So what do we do?" I asked slowly, not fully convinced. "What is our next step?"

Tom was quiet for a minute or two. "Okay," he said, "I think on Sunday we go to one of the other churches, for a start."

"But..."

"I think we really have to," said Tom, gently.

I stayed quiet. Billy appeared on the stairs. "Sorry," she said, "I couldn't help hearing. And tomorrow, Carrie, you contact those counsellor people from the leaflet, and you arrange to see them, saying you really want to get back into work."

"So you think we should do this too?" I asked Billy. "Pretend?"

"I pretended for more than two years," said Billy, and I thought she sounded sad. "It won't last forever."

"Or even better," said Tom, going back to his plan, "tell the counsellors that we are thinking of setting up our own business, that will employ us both, and asking for their advice."

I looked from Tom to Billy, and thought about it. Looking at the issue from the point of view of any officials who might be interested in my case, the tactics Tom had suggested would seem like an entirely reasonable response to the letter they would know I had just received, and so acting like this could put them off the track. They would hardly expect us to be talking about setting up a new business or changing our worshipping community if we were planning to go in three weeks.

"Yes," I agreed, feeling uncomfortable. "Okay. We'll do it."

★ ★ ★

I would have liked to have spoken to Ephraim about our ideas, and rather hoped he would call by next day, but he didn't. I hadn't slept well. Our community believes in plain dealing, and I was still worried in case our subterfuge went against our commitment to integrity. Shouldn't Tom and I simply stand by what we believed and take the consequences, trusting the Spirit to provide what the State would not? I was shocked too by Madge and Wolly's revelation that their daughter and son-in-law had left the Society in order to avoid Medical Assistance, or some other state-imposed sanctions I didn't know about. When I was growing up us Young People used to talk about people who left under pressure with real scorn. Understanding, as I now did, how tough the decision could be, I was ashamed of my naivety. Then, of course, in the early hours of the morning when frightening thoughts are most likely to emerge, I started worrying about my pregnancy, about having to go through it without the help of a doctor. What if the baby was sick or deformed? What if I miscarried?

I finally went to sleep after the clock at the shopping centre chimed it's tinny three o'clock, and woke to Tom, dressed for work, putting a cup of tea by my bed and leaning over to kiss me. "Okay, Carrie?" he asked gently, and ruffled my hair.

"Mm." I rolled over onto my back and stretched. "Good morning, what's the time?"

"Eight fifteen," said Tom. "I'm just off. What are you planning to do today?"

I sat up slowly. "I think… I think I'll contact that counsellor and start researching other churches."

Tom didn't say anything further, he just kissed the top of my head and smiled a little sadly, then he was thumping down the two sets of stairs and I heard the front door slam.

★ ★ ★

The harder task was contacting the counsellor, so I did that first. There was a phone number and a website. I went on the website and read the information I found. The counselling service had been started some years ago by a local charity, but was now funded by a grant from central government. Their local office and counselling rooms were in the old library. They had another office and more counselling rooms in the city where Mum and Dad lived, and they were prepared to do home visits where such visits are imperative. I filled in an online application form for an appointment. I needed a reference number, which I found on the letter from the Medical Assistance people. I tried to fill the form in as I thought an official might like it completed, so I called my condition a *syndrome* and named it CFS, instead of saying I had an illness called ME. When I had filled in the form I sat in silence, offering all my worries from last night and my uncertainties to the Light. I remembered that quotation from the Bible which Billy had left by the kettle: *I know the plans I have for you, plans for welfare and not for evil, to give you a future and a hope.* I clicked on *send* and watched the screen on my DeV blink, then a tab appeared on the bottom right-hand corner: *Form MA27745 sent.*

I checked my emails. There was a long, newsy letter from Mum, who sometimes couldn't sleep and emailed people in the middle of the night. I decided to phone her later. While I was reading an email from the clerk of Meeting about an evening course on meditation which was due to start soon, an out-of-office reply arrived from the counselling service, saying that my application for help would be reviewed and I would receive a reply within twenty-four hours.

Billy came down at that point. I was working at the dining room table. She glanced at me, sitting there with our large old DeV, mimed drinking something so I guessed she was saying 'coffee?' and went through to the kitchen. Obviously she couldn't talk to me while I had my DeV switched on, in case someone was listening in.

I put in a search for churches in our city, and clicked on a site which said it was sponsored by some ecumenical body, and a surprisingly long list of churches appeared. I decided to start at the top. The first church was called All Souls, and the website had last been updated months ago. It was still advertising Christmas services. That didn't seem very promising. There was a church called Andover Road Pentecostal and Holiness Community. I like the word *community* and clicked on that link, and brought up a bright and colourful site with a silent video showing people worshipping with their arms in the air, children holding up and waving worship banners, and crowds of people pouring into a windowless auditorium. It was all very attractive and happy, and the banner along the top of the home page read *Everyone Welcome!* and glittered in a heavenly light. However, the smaller text was less encouraging. It told how the church had grown in recent years because here the gospel was preached without excuse and the Bible was followed to every jot and tittle. It also said that the church especially welcomed our first cousins and close friends from across the Atlantic who have brought such a wealth of Christian understanding to our fellowship. I knew that neither Tom nor I would be able to tolerate a community like that.

Billy brought the coffee in and stood looking over my shoulder. There were a few churches in the surrounding villages, then the Christian Scientists and the First Church of Latter Day Saints. I knew from conversations at home when I was a teenager that there are good people in both these groups, but that they tended not to reciprocate that opinion. There were a couple of Methodist Churches and a Central Baptist Church. There were loads of churches named after saints, and some from groups I knew nothing about: two Reapers' Churches, a Church of Hidden Treasure and some churches which simply called themselves *evangelical*. I took a piece of paper and drew a question mark on it. *Where do I start?* I meant.

Billy sat down at the end of the table, took a sip of her coffee and a bite of her toast and marmalade and wrote with a rather sticky hand, *Saints*.

I drew another question mark.

She swallowed her mouthful, wiped her hand and took the pen from me again. This time she wrote, *The churches with 'Saint' at the beginning are usually Episcopalian – what we used to call 'Anglican'. They tend to be more moderate. Some, anyhow.*

I nodded and clicked on the first Saint church on the list. St Anthony's was in a residential part of the city; it would probably be within walking distance for me. The site, though, when it came up, was remarkably similar to the Andover Road church. There were the same crowds of cheerful worshippers flocking into a bright, airy church, although this time the building was more traditional, with stained glass windows and an altar at the front. There were more clean, attractive children, this time singing in a choir and swaying to the music. There was a picture of a noticeboard highlighting first one and then another activity: youth work, young mothers' groups, outreach in the city.

I shook my head negatively to Billy.

She looked thoughtful. *What about the cathedral?* she wrote.

At once I liked it. I scrolled down to the cathedral, which was right at the bottom of the list. The picture at the top of the page showed the building lit up at night. On the right was a list of services (up to date). There was a button to click on for more information about times and types of worship, and further links to The Choir, Worship and The Diocese. The most recent evensong sermon was available, and it was all about different sorts of love. Apart from the frequent references to the Bible, it would almost be possible to believe someone from my community had said those words, except that we never preach sermons! There was some stuff about the Eucharist, which worried me less than it might have done before I went to communion at Will's church. There was nothing about evangelism, miracles, abiding by the Revealed Word or making a choice between heaven and hell.

As with most of the sites, there was a contact form for more information, but the cathedral is close to our home and I thought we could just turn up. I spent a bit longer surfing around the site, in case my activities were being watched, then just for good measure I texted Tom and said, *I like the look of the cathedral. How about the 9.45am service?*

Then I turned off the DeV, put it back in the conservatory where it lives next to the red wine, and followed Billy upstairs for a chat.

CHAPTER 6

Mum came up to visit the following Monday. She was wearing a knitted poncho made from recycled wool, and carrying a big bag with a casserole in a plastic container, for dinner that night. She seemed cheerful and relaxed.

"Your father's playing golf!" she announced.

"What!" It seemed such a strange thing for Dad to be doing, right out of character.

"He's become quite friendly with Kamal," she said. "After we all worked together on the Christmas meal. And Kamal does love his golf!"

"He'll be way out of his depth in a golf club, Mum!" I giggled at the thought.

She smiled too. "Oh, it'll be good for him to be outdoors for a bit, and Kamal's sense of humour appeals to your father. So what have you been up to? Were you well enough to go to Meeting yesterday? You look well."

"Um…" This was going to be difficult, but it had to be done. "Actually, Mum, we went to the cathedral instead."

"You did what?" Mum looked as if I had said something in a foreign language, as if she just didn't understand. "What do you mean?"

"Sit down, Mum," I suggested. "We… Tom and I… we thought we would go to the cathedral, just to see…"

Mum took a long breath, sighed, and asked in a rather tight voice, "What brought this on, Carrie?"

Tom and I had agreed we wouldn't tell anyone else about the pregnancy, about our planned escape or about our attempt to deceive the authorities. I suddenly realised how hard this was going to be.

"We got this letter," I said, taking the Medical Assistance letter and leaflet from the sideboard, and passing them to Mum. "I told you. We thought… going to the cathedral is much more respectable than worshipping at our Meeting House."

Mum looked really sad. In fact, her eyes suddenly looked moist.

"Carrie love," she said, "this just isn't the answer. They won't let you off just because you leave the Society. It's all gone too far for that."

I took a deep breath, and told her the rest. "It's not just the cathedral, Mum," I said. "We are thinking of Tom setting up in business on his own, and employing me, so I'll be a contributing member of society again."

Mum was quiet. "Well, that's not altogether a bad idea," she mused, "if you can raise the money to get started… But Carrie love… are you really sure this is the way you are being guided? You're taking some big decisions, you and Tom. Have you talked to the elders or to someone you trust? It's easy to think you've heard the Spirit, when you're under stress, but really it's just your mind, trying to find a way out."

Of course I couldn't tell Mum what was really going on. I felt sick when I thought how much I was deceiving my parents, and so many others to whom I owed so much. What had happened to my belief in integrity, in truth-telling? It was a relief when Mum, distressed and not knowing what to say, left to catch the midday bus. When the door was closed behind her I checked my DeV. It was on, left casually on the bookcase. For once I really hoped the authorities were listening in.

★ ★ ★

My self-referral to the counselling service was accepted in principle within twenty-four hours, as the site promised, and I received an email that Monday afternoon with a choice of dates, all about two weeks ahead. The email was friendly enough, and told me I could bring Tom too, since I had explained in my application that we were thinking about setting up a business. I texted Tom at work and he answered about an hour later, saying which day was best for him, and I filled in the reply form and sent it at once.

It upset me more than I had realised it would, that I had not been honest with Mum. Billy was reassuring. Of course she had grown up in a community very similar to ours, and she had also gone through a heartbreaking experience when she had realised she needed to escape. "I didn't have to lie to them," she told me. "Not directly. But I couldn't tell them the truth either. One weekend I was there for Sunday lunch, reassuring them that I was getting back on my feet after Khadi's death, and telling them about things planned in my Meeting for later in the year. The next Sunday they expected me to come mid-afternoon for tea and to stay the night, and I just didn't turn up. They have no idea where I am, or what I'm doing." She looked very sad. "I suppose, given what happened to Khadi, they think I'm in the hands of the ATTF. Or maybe in prison in the States by now." We were both quiet, thinking about our grieving parents, then Billy cheered up. "But Ephraim says they'll get a message to Mum and Dad when I'm safely out of the country, so it's only for a little while."

It was almost as hard talking to Job when he came round, as it had been talking to Mum. His comment to Tom had shown us a way forward, but he hadn't explained what he meant when he said, "Don't forget, appearances can be deceptive." He could have meant anything. I even wondered whether he might be talking about someone in Meeting – Ephraim perhaps, or Derek. Job didn't know about our planned escape, so he couldn't know that our first visit to the cathedral was all for show.

"You weren't at Meeting on Sunday," he queried when he called in on me.

"We went to the cathedral," I explained.

"Ah!" I thought he looked sad. "So you're taking Madge and Wolly's advice?"

I couldn't bring myself to say, "Yes," so I said instead, "It was a nice service. Quite reflective."

"Yes." Job looked at me searchingly for a few seconds. "I've heard they do some good things there. Our Ellie's class went to a children's festival at the cathedral last summer. She had a whale of a time."

Suddenly I felt a great need to be honest. My relationships seemed so full of half-truths and I hated it. Since I couldn't be honest about the big things I blurted out something small. "They say the creed there," I said. "In every service. They say it together. Job, I don't know if I can do that!" And I found myself starting to cry.

Job came over to me and put an arm round me. "This is all so hard for you," he said softly, into my hair. "But all will be well, and all will be well, and all manner of things will be well."

★ ★ ★

It was a huge relief when Ephraim called round at the end of that week. He arrived after dark, and presented me with a bar of chocolate priced in Euros. "Since you can't drink wine," he said, "I thought Belgian chocolate might serve instead. We're celebrating."

"Are we?" asked Tom, who was feeling the stress of our situation at least as much as me, and who had been working long hours too.

197

"We are!" Ephraim promised. "Where's Billy?"

"I'll get her, she's upstairs," said Tom.

While Tom's feet went thumping up the stairs Ephraim said to me, "So how are you feeling, Carrie?"

"Okay," I said. "You know…"

"Up to travelling?" he asked. "By car?"

"Oh yes, I think so. As long as we don't leave too early." I had been sick several times first thing in the morning, but it never lasted.

When Tom appeared with Billy in tow, and Ephraim and Billy had exchanged greetings, Ephraim told us the plan.

"I've been to Cambridgeshire," he said. "To Will and Mia's. I had to be over that way anyhow. Tom and Carrie, they would love you to visit, say in a couple of weeks?"

"Oh great!" I was happy to think we might go first to people I knew.

"Billy too," said Ephraim. "But after that your paths will divide. Of course I can't tell you much but there's a small group of French students who have been taking a language course in Cambridge, and who will travel back to Normandy by coach. There'll be a place for you. But you two," and Ephraim smiled at Tom, then me, "you need to bring some warm clothes."

Scotland, I thought, and smiled back.

★ ★ ★

It was odd, but once we knew when we would be leaving everything seemed easier. We went to the cathedral again the following Sunday, and I didn't wear jeans this time. They were definitely more formal than our Meeting. There were even men and women scattered in the congregation in uniform, some ATTF people and a couple of uniforms I didn't recognise. Of course that never happened in our Meetings but it didn't really bother me because I had a new sense of distance from everything, now that we knew we were going. After the service that Sunday we had quite a long chat with one of the clergy, a kindly woman with a large, ornate cross on a chain round her neck. We talked about impersonal things: the excellent choir, the problems during the short holidays when the choir school is closed, or when the choir is on tour, the scaffolding in the south transept and the problem of badly behaved tourists talking during services. "See you next week!" she said as we left and I thought, *Yes, but not the week after!*

When Mum came over I found I wanted to be especially caring towards her. She would find out what our apparent defection was all about one day, but in the meantime at least I could show her how much I loved her. Of course she asked about the cathedral and I told her we had been there again, but then we changed the subject as if by mutual consent, and talked instead about things that were going on in their Meeting. We talked about Dad's attempt at playing golf, which had apparently been disastrous, and about a film we had both seen on our DeVs, and which Tom and I had really enjoyed. We kept silence together and Mum gave me a big hug as she left. "Tell Dad to come too, next week," I suggested casually on the doorstep. "I haven't seen him for ages."

"I'll do that," agreed Mum.

I checked through our clothes and looked out our warmer winter items. Our southern counties have been warming up all my life and neither Tom nor I owned much that as a child I would have considered to be proper winter clothes. We both still had old-fashioned fleecy hoodies from our time with the Young People, though, when we used to take part in lots of night-time activities, and Tom had good warm socks from his hiking days before I knew him, which fitted me as well. While I was sorting through my wardrobe I also gave some clothes to Billy. We both thought she needed to dress less dramatically if she was going to merge in with a group of returning French students. I went online and did a search on French fashions. I thought that if my internet footfall was being monitored, as I thought it probably was, a new interest in fashion might seem, to those watching my online preferences, to fit entirely with a young woman leaving a community considered by some to be austere. I was sad to pass some of my more glittery clothes and my best waistcoat to Billy, but they were light garments, not suitable for a cooler climate.

★ ★ ★

We had one really difficult thing which Tom and I had to do before our departure. When we had got down to detailed planning we realised that the day Ephraim had initially hoped to drive the three of us to Cambridgeshire was in fact the day before our scheduled appointment with the counselling service. Obviously our failure to appear might trigger all sorts of interest in us, which was just what we would not need. Ephraim thought we should put off our departure by two days, go to our counselling session and then leave, having satisfied officialdom that I really was set on becoming a responsible citizen at last.

Ephraim wanted us to talk to Madge and Wolly, for a little private coaching about how to deal with the interview. He seemed interested in the moves we had made, our responses to the letter, but he hadn't expressed any strong opinions one way or the other about whether we had done the right thing in seeming to leave our community and appearing to want to start up our own business. His attitude, if anything, seemed to be, "Well, it can't do any harm."

However, both Tom and I felt a bit uncomfortable with Madge and Wolly now. I think in our heart of hearts we felt that they had given us advice that did not really fit with Truth, and although we were giving the impression that we had taken that advice, in reality we had not and would not. We tried to explain this to Ephraim, and he listened sympathetically. When we had finished he said, "Yes, I have always admired people who truly stick by their principles, but the cost can be huge." He sighed, then agreed to help us to prepare.

As a result, we arrived at the old library smartly dressed, with a file containing an outline business plan. We were ushered into a small office and invited to sit on plastic chairs on one side of a large wooden desk. On the other side was the man who I suppose was to be our counsellor. His name badge announced that he was Rob Deacon.

He had a pile of papers in front of him, which he was reading as we were shown in. He looked up after a minute or two and smiled rather distractedly.

"Right, Mr and Mrs Walker?" he checked.

We agreed, and waited. He looked back at his papers, then addressed me. "You have been claiming benefits for Chronic Fatigue?" he checked.

"Yes," I agreed.

"And are you fatigued today?" he asked. "You look remarkably healthy to me."

If we hadn't prepared for the interview, or perhaps if we really were hoping to get me off the Medical Assistance register, I think this line of questioning would have frightened me, but I knew I was just acting in a play.

"Thank you," I said politely and smiled. "I'm definitely getting better. The advice they gave me at the clinic has been very helpful."

"Good…" He looked down at his papers again. "But you haven't applied for any work. That could give the impression that you quite enjoy a life of leisure."

"It's been a bit lonely," I said, without a shred of truth. "It'll be good to have Tom around and to be doing something useful at last."

The man looked down at his papers. He had dandruff in

his hair and on the jacket of his suit, and I saw a little snowdrift of white flakes drift down as he scratched his head. "Well, as to that… Mr Walker, you are suggesting, I understand, that you start your own business working from home, and employ your wife?"

"Yes." Tom was prepared too. "I've brought my initial plans." He opened the folder he had placed on the desk, and pushed it across so that the counsellor could see it.

"I'll have a look at this," agreed Mr Deacon, "but I don't want you trying to play the system here. You wouldn't be the first person to put a malingerer on the books in order to cheat hard-working tax payers, you know. We will expect Mrs Walker to put in at least twenty hours a week and to pay her taxes, and your business will be subject to the usual checks. *If* we think it is a viable plan and *if* you can raise the capital you need."

Tom said, "Yes, we understand that."

"So how do you plan to raise the capital?" Mr Deacon asked, rather aggressively I thought.

"We'll start with family," Tom said. "My father has run a business all his life." It was true, but Tom's father hardly spoke to us. The thought of him lending us money was ridiculous.

The man leaned back on his chair, tipping it so that it rested on the back two legs and he was leaning against the wall behind him. "But my information, Mr Walker, is that you may not be on very good terms with your family."

That did take us by surprise, but I was impressed by how Tom coped. He swallowed hard and said, "I'm afraid I let them down rather badly."

"So I understand," agreed Mr Deacon, glancing at his paperwork. "Do you want to tell me about it? It's always best to be honest in these interviews, you know. We always find out, anyhow."

Tom hesitated, then, "I joined an extremist organisation," he said, as if confessing to a dirty secret.

"And stayed in it for several years, and married within it," prompted the man, curling his top lip a little in disdain.

"Yes, and I'm so angry with myself for being taken in," said Tom. "But I was young, and new to religion…"

"And now?"

"I… We… Carrie and I are looking for somewhere else to worship now, somewhere more…" Tom stopped. I butted in. "More moderate," I said. "We want to worship in a more moderate community."

"Mm…" Mr Deacon scratched his head and another little flurry of white descended. "And is this change of heart real, or manufactured for this interview? What have you actually done about it?"

"We've started worshipping at the cathedral," I said.

The man leaned forward sharply, the front two legs of his chair banging as they landed back on the floor. "Now that is interesting," he said. "The cathedral. Of course, there are a few extremists there too, I understand, but basically the clergy have their feet on the ground. So what do you think of it?"

Tom said, "The first time we went, Canon McAllister preached. We thought she was really good."

"Yes, yes," said Mr Deacon. "I know Julie McAllister. I don't much like women preaching, myself, but I think she's rather popular. Well now, you know we'll check all this, don't you?"

"Of course," said Tom, calmly.

"Good, good." The man glanced out of his window. An electric vehicle had stopped just outside and the orange roof of the truck was level with the window sill. He looked back at us. "Right, so this is how it will work. Mrs Walker, we have only ten days before you are moved to Medical Assistance. I don't think we can do anything in that time, so," and he gave his first smile of the morning, "I advise you to avoid needing medical care for a few weeks! But I'll start checking your plans and the story you've told me, and if it seems above board I have the authority to restore your citizenship rights completely for six months when there will be another review. You've left it rather late but it does seem to me that you are on the right track now."

He stood, and we stood too. He reached out and shook Tom's hand. He didn't shake mine. "Well done, young man," he said. "It isn't easy to get back on the right path after you've got in with these extremist groups, but I like to see it when it happens. Mrs Walker, I wish you good health."

★ ★ ★

Tom went back to work and I went home to finish packing. It was a good thing Tom had been working a lot of overtime, because Feany had agreed to a long weekend so that we could go and visit family. That meant nobody would start asking questions at work for several days. Mum and Dad came over that evening and it was good to see them, but I was uncomfortable about keeping such huge secrets from them and because I couldn't say a proper goodbye.

The cover story for our journey this time was different. When I had just gone along for the ride the last time Ephraim took me to Will and Mia's, the story had been that Naomi and I were Mia's nieces. This time we were to travel in one of those white hybrid vehicles that are made in China, with two rows of seats in the front and a space like the back of a van behind, and the story was that we were taking furniture to Cambridge where Billy was going to study, and Tom and I were taking the opportunity to hitch a lift to visit my aunt. Sure enough, when Ephraim called for us next morning there was furniture in the back: a bookcase (rather battered), a small table, and some boxes. I could see a desk lamp and an iron with the cord wrapped round its base, and one cardboard box which seemed to be filled with books. When we put our stuff in the back too it looked entirely natural: a blue suitcase and a backpack. What else would you expect a student to have?

The journey was quite different too. We were stopped three times at different checkpoints, once by an ATTF spot-check team and twice by ordinary British police in marked cars, pulling vehicles over apparently randomly at laybys. Each time we all had to climb out of the van and show our identity cards, and Ephraim had to hand over the van registration and hire documents. The ATTF took just about everything out of the back of the van and checked under the eco-plastic flooring, but the police were less interested in us; one team even seemed rather sympathetic. Ephraim, in his usual polite manner, had said, "Not the most exciting duty on the station roster, I imagine?" and the older officer had answered, "No, and not what I thought I was signing up to when I joined the force, either." I wasn't worried about Tom's ID or mine standing up to inspection since I knew both were the genuine article, and I assumed Ephraim's was too, but Billy was carrying fake ID and false papers purporting to be from the college where she was going to study, and I was a bit worried in case someone saw through them.

Travel was slower in the van than last time, when we had been in that rather smart car, so it seemed to take forever to get to Cambridgeshire. It was a dull, grey day, with moisture on the roads although it wasn't actually raining, and the traffic around us seemed mostly mud-splattered or grimy. We stopped for lunch at a motorway service station and watched the pictures from the news on a giant screen without any sound, while we ate cheese waffles with apricot jam, and drank sweet, sticky carbonated drinks out of cans. I asked Ephraim whether we should buy something for Will and Mia, as a thank you for having us. Last time we had given them that chocolate cake. Ephraim thought it was a good idea, but there was nothing suitable in the shop and Ephraim didn't want to leave the motorway. He said our van would look odd driving down country lanes and it wouldn't fit in with our story. I thought Ephraim seemed a little distracted, even worried, and that in turn made me feel less confident. Nevertheless, when we set off again after we had eaten I fell fast asleep with my head on Tom's shoulder while Billy sat in the front seat and made quiet conversation with Ephraim.

★ ★ ★

It was lovely to see Will and Mia again. They were both there when we arrived, Mia wearing an apron and obviously in the middle of baking, and Will just seeing a visitor out.

"Ah, good, you've arrived!" he said, then to his visitor, "Patrick, meet my niece Carrie and her husband Tom. You might have met Carrie before?"

"I – no, I don't think so," said an embarrassed-looking Patrick, going very red for no reason I could think of. Then, "Thank you, vicar, for your help!" he gasped and nearly ran down the short drive to where a bike was leaning up against the hedge.

Will's eyes followed his fleeing visitor, then he murmured under his breath, "Poor lad!" before turning to give me a big hug and to shake Tom's hand.

Mia, meanwhile, was being introduced to Billy by Ephraim, and with a general babble of greetings and talk about a long journey to take in a van, and dull winter weather, and increased numbers of roadside checkpoints, we all went inside.

It hadn't occurred to me when Ephraim had told us we were to go to Will and Mia's that last time I had been there it had been the summer and the twins had been away on summer camp. They were in their last year at High School, so presumably as it was half way through February they would be at home. I saw no sign of them, though, and when Billy was told, as I had been last time, to excuse the pinkness of the room where she was to sleep, because it had been decorated for Charlie, I asked Mia, "So where are the twins? Will we meet them?"

"Ah, no." It was Will who answered this time. "They know, of course, that their parents are… engaged, shall we say… in some… rather unofficial activities, but we do our best not to involve them at all. This week worked for us because Charlie is on a field trip and Harry is staying over at his friend Jason's, so that they can get in some good band practice, and then do their first gig at the Ely Chapter House this Saturday."

"It's all very exciting," said Mia, bustling in and out of the kitchen with mugs and a plate of biscuits. "Their first proper gig! We'll eat at seven, so this is just to tide you over. Tom, don't just take one cookie! You look like a young man who needs feeding up. Carrie, would you like to go and rest until we eat? Billy, just put your mug on the table. We're way past worrying about rings on the wood now. We've had children in the house for seventeen years!"

Dinner was fun. Billy was entirely in her element, and while I had rested in the big double bedroom where Naomi and Joshua had slept on my last visit, Tom, Ephraim and Will had been to the local pub down by the church for a pint of beer and, as Will said, "To check on my parishioners." Mia had made a steak and kidney pie and served it with green beans and mashed potato, and Billy had obviously been helping in the kitchen because she and Mia were getting on as if they had known each other for years. It was difficult to tell, with Billy contributing so much to the lively conversation, but once again I thought Ephraim was quieter than usual, maybe a bit worried.

Afterwards, when the dishes were removed and the mats wiped and put back in a drawer, Will said, "Okay. Let's discuss where we go from here. And as Mia and I are in the minority in this esteemed company, would you like to start with a little silence?"

Then Ephraim took over. "Right," he said, and exchanged a glance with Will. "This is the situation. Billy, I'll drive you into Cambridge tomorrow and hand you over to Ruth, who will see you safely through the Tunnel on the student coach, and take you to our contact in Calais. You'll need new ID and I don't have that. If all goes according to plan Ruth will give you your papers tomorrow. Make sure you mug up on your new identity, in case you're checked at emigration – but that's unlikely, we think." For the first time that day he began to look a little more relaxed. He smiled at Billy, and added, "As soon as I know you're safe we can get a message through to your parents."

Ephraim turned to us. "It's a little more complicated in your case," he said, and I thought perhaps the complications, whatever they were, had been the cause of his apparent ill ease. "We hoped to pass you on to our next friends, either tomorrow or Saturday, but there's been a hitch. You might have to stay until Sunday afternoon, but if the worst comes to the worst you've got an excellent cover story, since Carrie, you met people from the village last time you were here."

Mia said, encouragingly, "I'd rather like having Carrie and Tom here for the whole weekend. It makes up for the twins being away!"

★ ★ ★

I went downstairs late on Friday morning. I had slept well, curled up against Tom who was snoring, which I had not noticed him do before. When I went into the kitchen wearing my warm pyjamas and the fleecy hoodie because I didn't have a dressing gown, Tom was leaning against some kitchen units while Mia unpacked the dishwasher. As I walked in Tom was saying, "... so I studied computing as an artistic expression as well, which has turned out to be a really good choice."

"Ah, Carrie!" Mia beamed at me. "Cooked breakfast? Cereal? Toast? Tea or coffee?"

Suddenly the thought of all that food hit me, as it sometimes did first thing in the morning, and I turned and rushed into the downstairs cloakroom, just making it in time to be sick into the loo.

Mia was standing behind me when I had finished. "Goodness," she said cheerfully, "my cooking isn't that bad!" Then she looked more serious. "I used to find dry toast and tea helpful. Why don't you sit in the other room with Tom and I'll sort something out?"

She seemed so certain that I was pregnant that I assumed Ephraim must have told her, but it turned out not to be the case. "Ephraim tells us as little as possible," she explained as she put a plate of brown toast in front of me and poured the tea from a brown teapot like the one my mum has. "But I see now why it's so urgent that you leave." She smiled at me. "The Europeans have had a bit of a chequered history with refugees over the last thirty years, but they seem to be good with people who make it out of the Alliance, and their medical care is as good as ours." She looked at me, then corrected herself. "As good as the care we receive if we're not on Medical Assistance."

Once I had chewed on the dry toast and drunk the tea, which was wonderful, and showered in our en-suite bathroom, and dressed, I felt fine. Really well, in fact. Mia suggested we take a walk round the village. She wanted to ask shopkeepers to put up notices about a barn dance the church people were organising for Easter bank holiday Monday, and it was a much brighter day than the day before. Ephraim and Billy, it seemed, had left early, which meant that I hadn't said goodbye, although Tom had been up to see them off. "I dare say you'll see her again," commented Mia in her usual encouraging way.

I saw more of the village this time than when I had visited before. There was a bakery, a butcher and a grocer. "Although we buy as much as we can from the farm shop," said Mia. There was a small Co-op, a Chinese takeaway and the pharmacy we had been into before. Mia seemed to know everyone, and introduced us happily to all and sundry as we walked around. Several people said they remembered me, and one woman in a lavender-coloured jacket and matching boots asked how my cousin was getting on. Had she had the baby yet? It would have floored me, but Mia stepped in easily, "A little boy!" she said. "Eight pounds two ounces! Perhaps I'll bring them all to church one of these days."

When the lavender lady had gone I asked, "Is that true? About Naomi's baby?"

"I have no idea!" She smiled cheerfully at me. "But I had to say something. We rarely hear, Will and I, want happens to people when they move on." Then she added, as we turned into the lane leading to the rectory, "I like to imagine them living in a little flat in some friendly town, like Dublin maybe, with a little one in a highchair throwing bread onto the floor and a Mums' and Tots' group for Naomi to make friends."

Will was out for lunch, but came back mid-afternoon just after my rest, on his bike, whistling a hymn and carrying two boxes of eggs which had been in a pannier. He kissed Mia on the cheek, smiled at us, and asked over his shoulder as he went into the kitchen to put the eggs away, "Is Ephraim back yet? I didn't see the van. Oh, and Mia, the Willerbies asked me to thank you for the pasties. The children loved them."

"Ephraim's not back yet," said Mia comfortably, putting down some knitting and going into the kitchen, where we could hear her filling up the kettle. "If they were a success I can make more pasties for next week. Do you remember how Harry used to love them?"

"Mm, before he became so concerned about eating beef, and climate change," said Will. "I dare say Ephraim will be home later."

"I hope so," said Mia. "Tea, everyone? I'm making fish and chips for dinner."

★ ★ ★

In fact, Ephraim wasn't home in time to eat, he was not even back when Tom and I went to bed. "I hope he's okay," I ventured, feeling anxious, as we put our hot chocolate mugs in the dishwasher at about ten o'clock that evening.

"Oh, I'm sure he is," said Will. "He's probably just catching up with friends. Ephraim knows people everywhere!"

He still had not returned by breakfast the following day. It was another bright, warm day. We ate toast and marmalade with the French windows open, watching birds hopping around on the feeder and the lawn in the back garden. Tom said, rather nervously, "Has Ephraim done this before, just gone away and not come back when you expected him?"

Will patted Tom on the shoulder. "That's the sort of question you don't ask," he said, but I saw him exchange a glance with Mia, and I realised it wasn't just Tom and me who were worried.

Mia had various errands to do that morning, so she wheeled a bike out of the garage, put on a red cape and set off in one direction, while Will set off on his bike in the other. Tom and I were left holding the fort, with instructions not to answer the phone. "There's a perfectly good answer machine," said Will. We were to tell any parishioners who might call by that they would be back by lunchtime. Mia showed me where there was a store of crisps and a tin of sausage rolls. "If anyone comes knocking asking for food," she said, "give them two sausage rolls, a packet of crisps and an apple, and tell them there'll be hot soup in the church hall at six, as usual. Don't ask them any questions."

Tom overheard. "But what if they're not really in need?" he asked.

"Well, if they come begging for food they're in need of something, even if it isn't food!" explained Mia. "Would you go begging at doors? So maybe they want attention, or they like to feel they've got one over on us, for some reason. It doesn't matter. Just give them the food!"

It was odd to be in someone else's house on our own and we spent a few minutes wandering around downstairs feeling a bit lost. We didn't like to use any of their DeVs and of course we had left our own at home. In the end we settled down with books from the living room shelves and spent a quiet morning reading. Tom looked up once and said, "You know, I quite liked drawing up that business plan. When we get to... wherever we're going, I would really like to set up on my own." I was reading an old detective novel set in the Shetland Isles. I wondered if refugees ever found themselves in such remote communities, and how we would cope if we were sent somewhere like that.

At about midday we heard a car approaching, a little too fast for a country village, and then stopping in front of the house. Tom stood up to see over the hedge, and turned white.

"Carrie!" he said, then nothing further.

I stood to join him and to see what he had seen. It was Derek, climbing out of an old red Citroen, slamming the door and marching – there is no other word for it – purposely up the drive to the front door. He hammered hard, rang the bell, and called out angrily, "Are you there, Tom and Carrie? For God's sake, what have you done now? You'd better let me in!"

Tom and I looked at each other, shocked and confused.

Tom said, "We can't leave him on the doorstep, making that racket," and walked through the porch to open the door.

Derek marched into the living room, followed by Tom. He glared round the room, fury all over his face. "Honestly, you two..." he stormed. "You really know how to stir up trouble, don't you?"

I was proud of Tom. He sat down and said quietly, "Calm down, Derek, and tell us what on the earth you are talking about."

Derek was still standing in the middle of the room. I went to sit by Tom on the settee, and held his hand. Derek gave us both a long, scornful look, then sat opposite, his green jacket falling open on his dollar shop uniform shirt.

"Well," he said, "I really didn't think you'd go this far or be so utterly stupid!"

I didn't know what to say, and Tom didn't answer either.

Derek went on, "You really don't know what you've done, do you?" he stormed. "You with your selfish small concerns!"

Tom took a deep breath. "Derek," he asked, sounding a little fraught himself, "for goodness' sake tell us what is going on. What are you doing here? How did you know where to find us?"

I had a quick thought: what might Mia or my mother do in such a situation? "Derek," I asked, "since you're here, would you like a cup of coffee?"

Both Derek and Tom looked surprised. The question seemed to take the wind out of Derek's sails. "Well, yes I would, actually," he said in a much more normal voice. "I've been driving since eight this morning, non-stop."

They were both completely quiet while I filled the cafetiere, heated some milk and put three mugs and Mia's pottery sugar bowl on a tray. I added a plate of biscuits and brought it all through. Tom followed my lead, pouring the coffee, adding milk and a spoonful of sugar and passing the

213

mug to Derek. He took three big gulps, took a biscuit, then sat back in his chair.

"I thought you would be here," he said, sounding much less confrontational.

"Do you know Will and Mia?" Derek seemed out of place in the rectory. It was hard to imagine him sitting down to dinner there, as Ephraim did.

"You ask altogether too many questions." Derek scowled at me again. Then he seemed to make a big effort. He took a deep breath, finished his coffee in one gulp, and put the mug at his feet.

"Look, you two," he said, leaning forward, "I tried to warn you earlier. You're in far too deep. You don't know what you're messing with."

"Then tell us." Tom sounded a little angry himself. "If we've done something wrong, you'd better explain it to us." He looked at me, "Because I don't think we have."

Derek sighed. "Okay, okay." He paused. "I really hate giving away too much information," he said. "But you two won't trust me, so I'd better explain." He looked out of the window as if gathering his thoughts. "Right," he said. "Some of this, just the tip of the iceberg, you already know. A group of us, not all from our community, help people get away, escape to another region, usually the European Union but sometimes further afield. Well, Tom, you know about that because of the papers we created, and Carrie, you've been here before. Am I right?"

When I didn't answer Derek went on. "We've had problems for a year or more. We haven't been able to work out what was going on. Someone seems to be feeding information to the ATTF. You know about the arrest of the warden, and in fact, your house was raided once, wasn't it? But whoever is betraying us seems to be giving away just snippets of information. A few people have been detained, but only Alexis has been really damaged by these raids, and she was a rather unusual case. Finally, a few months ago, we realised that whoever is betraying us is playing the long game. He really isn't interested in the small fry, people like you or your parents, Carrie. We think now he's been slowly, carefully infiltrating the whole Overground. Sooner or later the ATTF will arrest the lot of us."

Tom and I looked at each other. As always, Tom was more inclined to believe Derek than I was. "So how do we fit in?" asked Tom.

Derek sat back in his chair again. "I think you're bait," he said. "You and whoever you had staying in your back bedroom. I think the final raid could be any time now."

He looked out of the window again, then back at us, a weary expression on his face. "Where's Ephraim?" he asked bluntly.

"I don't know," I said. "We don't know."

Derek looked fiercely at me again. "Don't speak for Tom!" he exclaimed. "Your husband has more sense in his little finger than you'll ever have!"

"Derek!" warned Tom. Then, more quietly, "He went out yesterday morning, and hasn't come back." Tom looked at my surprised face. "Carrie," he explained, "there's no point in pretending to Derek. He obviously knows Ephraim was here."

"He's setting you up," said Derek. "He's setting us all up."

★ ★ ★

When Will and Mia came home, cycling together and talking, Derek had taken his coat off and was looking more relaxed. Will looked a little surprised to see that they had a guest but Mia's face was entirely and impressively passive. I suppose if you're a vicar's wife you get used to anything. Tom introduced Derek as a friend from our home Meeting, and Will reached out and shook hands.

"I'll make lunch," said Mia. Then, politely to Derek, "Can you stay and eat with us? Carrie, come and help me, will you?"

In the kitchen Mia turned on the radio. "Let's get the news," she said, and then, when an American voice started describing conditions on the Caribbean islands and our voices were partly drowned, she said, "So who is he, Carrie? Were you expecting him?"

"No, not at all," I hissed back.

In a perfectly normal voice Mia said, "I hate to think of those children in Barbados, being deprived of an education for so long. Carrie, if I cut the bread, will you butter it?" Then, much more quietly, "What does he want? How did he know you were here? What's going on?"

"Shall I slice these tomatoes?" I asked in my normal voice, then quietly, "I don't know what's going on. We didn't tell him we were coming here and I can't think Ephraim would have done." Then still quietly, "He thinks Ephraim is a traitor."

Mia called through, "Chicken and tomato sandwiches, everyone? Or are you vegetarian, Derek?"

"Chicken's fine, thank you," Derek called back.

"Do you trust him? Derek, I mean," asked Mia quietly, then, "Put the kettle on, will you?" in her normal tone.

"No, I don't," I answered. "But he's been sure for ages that Ephraim is really ATTF, and now he thinks there's going to be this massive raid, to catch the key players of the Overground."

"Oh dear!" said Mia, softly. "It all gets so complicated!" Then speaking loudly and turning off the radio, "Okay, everyone. Lunch is ready."

★ ★ ★

It was a strange afternoon. Neither Will nor Mia asked Derek to stay but he showed no sign of leaving. I went upstairs for my rest and Will sat in the living room with a pocket DeV, saying he needed to read over his sermon. Since I knew he had an office I assumed that in fact he was keeping an eye on his uninvited guest. Derek talked of being weary after his long drive, and vaguely said he would head home later. He picked up the *East Anglian News* and appeared to be engrossed in it. Tom went out for a walk. When I woke up nothing seemed to have changed. Ephraim hadn't come back and Derek hadn't left. Tom was sitting by the window in our room, staring out and looking worried.

Mia brought us up cups of tea, and hissed in an unchristian way, "I don't like that Derek of yours!"

"He's not ours!" I hissed back.

"What does he want?" asked Tom, rhetorically. "I wish I knew what was going on."

"So do we," whispered Mia. "He told Will the same story he told you, about a traitor and the Overground being cracked wide open, but he doesn't seem to be doing anything about it. It's as if he's waiting for something." Then, "Come down when you're ready," she said sounding perfectly normal. "We'll play Scrabble!"

★ ★ ★

Things became rather strained as the afternoon progressed. Mia and I played Scrabble and I won, mostly because I had a seven letter word: *theatres* built on Mia's *t* and extending to a triple word score. When we started to clear up, and Mia's mind seemed to turn to dinner, Derek was still sitting there. I heard murmurs in the kitchen as Will and Mia cleared up the afternoon tea cups, then Will came through and said, "Are you off now, Derek? It's going to be a wet night, I don't think the drive back to Hampshire will be much fun in the dark."

I thought Derek looked really shifty. It was weird, him sitting there. "Would you mind," he asked, "if I left it to the morning? I'm really tired."

It was obvious to us all that he was waiting for something – or for someone – but we were all acting, pretending the situation was entirely normal, so Will said, "I'm sure that can be arranged." He looked at Mia. "The futon in my study?" he suggested, and Mia nodded.

"Sausage casserole tonight," she added. "Will that suit everyone?"

I thought Derek had the grace to look a little ashamed. "That's fine by me," he said. "Thank you. Thank you for everything. I… thank you."

★ ★ ★

While Mia and I had been playing Scrabble Tom had been out for another walk. Will had told us about the windmill on the edge of the village, and about a circular route that would take him close by. He came in as it was getting dark. I was on the bottom stair, about to rest a little before dinner, and because I wanted to get away from Derek. "I think I need a shower," announced Tom cheerfully (he did!) and he followed me upstairs.

"What's going on?" Tom asked, once our bedroom door was closed. "What does he want? And where's Ephraim?"

"I've no idea."

We stood looking at each other.

"Do you think Mia and Will know what's going on?" Tom asked.

"If they do, they're not letting on." I thought about Will trying to suggest that Derek should drive back to Hampshire before it got too late. "They don't want Derek here any more than we do," I added.

"He's waiting for something, isn't he? Derek, I mean." Tom was standing by the window now, staring out.

"I think he's waiting for Ephraim to come back," I said.

Tom was talking with his back to me, his voice low. "He might be here to protect us, you know," he said, hesitantly.

I felt myself getting angry. "Oh, I don't think so!" I retorted. "You know what he thinks of me. Protecting me would be the last thing on his mind!"

Tom turned to look at me, but it was dusk and we had not turned on any lights. I couldn't see his face. "You know what he said," Tom went on, "that time at our house? How he's the sort of guy nobody trusts and Ephraim's the sort of guy everyone likes and believes in?"

"Yes, I remember."

"Well, what if he's right? What if we've trusted the wrong person? You must admit, it is odd, Ephraim going away like this."

I just couldn't see it. "Don't do this, Tom," I hissed. "Don't start letting Derek get between you and me again! We chose to trust Ephraim. We decided together!"

Tom sighed. "Well, you rest," he said, "I'm going to have my shower." He turned the bathroom light on as he went in, making the bedroom seem even darker by contrast. "Try to sleep," he said.

I lay on the bed. The curtains weren't yet drawn, and there was a street light just down the road from the vicarage. I could see light traces of raindrops on the window. I wished Ephraim would come back. I felt in a sort of limbo, so that it was hard to rest for wondering what on the earth was happening.

Then I heard a sound. It was just a quiet sound, a sort of click, like a door being closed very quietly. I climbed off the bed and walked across the room to the window, and looked out. For a moment all I could see were the shadows of the front garden and the trees across the road, then out of the corner of my eye I saw movement. Keeping myself shielded behind the open bedroom curtain I peered out, and saw Derek standing in the driveway. As I watched he walked over to his parked car and opened it. The interior light lit him up as he reached across to the glove compartment on the front passenger's side, and took out a little DeV. I saw the familiar rainbow lights as he turned it on. One of my DeVs does that.

He's going to make a call, I thought.

Suddenly I felt determined to find out what was going on. I found my shoes in the half light and grabbed my jacket. The landing and the stairs seemed suddenly very bright as I crept downstairs, but the light was on in Will's study and I could hear pots and pans clattering in the kitchen, and the sound of music. I went downstairs and out through the side door, the door from the cloakroom that Derek must have used.

Derek was still up by his car. There are three large wheelie bins by the vicarage back door, and I crept behind them in the shadows, closing the back door with the same gentle click that had first alerted me to Derek creeping out.

At once I realised that I might have been unwise. If Derek stayed by his car and spoke quietly on his DeV I probably wouldn't be able to hear. If he sent a text or an email I certainly wouldn't be able to read it. There was too much light from the street light lighting up the drive, so although I was well hidden where I was, I couldn't get any closer.

Who would Derek be contacting, I wondered. Then I thought that was a silly question. It was Saturday evening. Probably Derek had commitments at Meeting on Sunday. He could be welcoming at the door, or helping the warden with refreshments, or any of a host of things. But why didn't he just go home? If he really believed the Overground was going to be blown wide open, how did his being here, doing nothing, help?

Then Derek played right into my hands. Because his DeV was the same as the little one I sometimes kept by my bed, I knew what the different lights meant. At one time DeVs made little bleeps when you pressed the number keys, but the DeV 10X is a piece of novelty equipment and each number flashes

220

a different colour. I knew that Derek was calling a number that was not saved on his phone. He held the phone up in the air. I thought he must have a poor signal. Then he walked down the drive towards the house. For a moment I thought he would see me, but he stopped in the shadow of the porch, less than a metre from where I was hidden, with his back to me.

Obviously someone answered, because Derek started to speak.

"No developments," he said, without any preamble. Then, after a short pause, "He's not here… No, I don't think they know where he is…. Well, it's quite awkward… They're not asking any questions, but of course they are wondering. No. Yes, I think so." There was a longer pause, then Derek said, "Yes, that's good." He ended the call. I felt none the wiser. Was he talking to some member of the Overground, concerned as he said that we had somehow affected their plans? Was he involved in damage limitation? I was sure that the person who was not there was Ephraim, but why did that matter? Unless, of course, the things that Derek had told us all along, the things that even now Tom was half inclined to believe about Ephraim not being trustworthy, were true. It was odd that he seemed just to have vanished.

Then came the green flashing light, which on a DeV 10X means you have an incoming call. Derek clicked on something, and spoke at once. "Commander!" he said, sounding as if he were standing to attention. Then, "Yes, sir!" There was a pause, then "I was sure he would be back by now… I don't think they know what to make of it… no, they can't stay here after tomorrow because the children are coming back, and I've never know them to traffic when the kids are around. Yes, sir. Well, I think he's bound to return tonight or tomorrow. Well, I don't see how there could have been a leak… No, they're as trusting and as naive as the rest of their community, they still don't know whether to trust me or him… Of course this is all true, sir. No, I am not wasting your time! Yes, I think we'll have to do that. Yes, sir. Your direct line? Yes, sir, as soon as there's a development."

He clicked his phone off and stood staring up at the black sky. Then Derek sighed, and suddenly he seemed so human and somehow alone. While he walked back to his car and replaced his phone in the glove compartment with his back to me, I crept back into the house and fled upstairs.

One thing I was convinced of: there was no way that people involved with the Overground would refer to someone as *Commander*, or say, *Yes, sir, no, sir!*

★ ★ ★

When I got upstairs Tom was out of the shower and towelling his hair. The bedroom lights were on and the curtains drawn. "Couldn't sleep?" he asked, looking flushed from the hot water, and cheerful. Then, looking at my face, "Hey Carrie, what's up?"

I sat on the bed. "It's Derek," I said. "I just overheard him on his DeV. He was talking to someone he called Commander."

"Oh ho." Tom sat on the bed. "Are you sure?"

"Absolutely."

We both sat in silence for a moment.

"How did you come to overhear him, Carrie?" Tom asked. "I mean… are you sure?"

"Yes." I explained how I had followed Derek outside, and what I had heard.

"We need to tell Will and Mia," said Tom.

"How can we? Derek is back in the living room."

"We'll find a way," said Tom, sounding a little desperate. "We've got to."

Just then, "Dinner in five minutes!" called Mia. Tom pulled on his jeans and jumper and we went back downstairs.

★ ★ ★

Dinner was about as stressed a meal as I have had since the time Tom took me to meet his parents, and things did not turn out well on that occasion either. Derek seemed to be working hard at being relaxed and sociable. He complimented Mia on the sausage casserole and insisted to Will that he loved to drink iced water rather than wine with his meal. Mia and Will, however, seemed to be acting strangely. For one thing, it was odd, in my brief experience of their hospitality, for there to be no alcohol with the evening meal. It occurred to me that perhaps they wanted to keep clear heads. For another thing, the general conviviality of the occasion seemed false compared to a couple of nights ago when Billy and Ephraim had been there, and it had been such fun. It was hard to put my finger on it. Will talked sympathetically about one of his parishioners, an elderly lady who was struggling with the fact that she could no longer manage her own garden, and who did not like the way the newly employed gardener was caring for her pride and joy, and Mia told us a funny story about the twins when they were little and they tried to convince everyone they were identical, despite one being a boy and the other a girl. Somehow, though, I thought the stories seemed rehearsed, Will looked more worried than usual, and Mia more impassive. Tom and I, of course, had to act as if all were well when all we really wanted to do was to discuss what I had overheard with each other, and talk to Will and Mia.

At about the point when the main course plates were taken away and Mia brought through the apple crumble and custard, a horrible thought occurred to me. I was sure Derek was just waiting for Ephraim to come back. What would happen if he walked through the door now? I felt slightly panicky. I had no idea what I thought Derek was going to do, or what there really was to worry about, but I was frightened. Several times as I toyed with the pudding I could no longer swallow, I thought I heard cars driving past the vicarage, and each time I held my breath, hoping the vehicle did not stop. I was a nervous wreck by the time Derek had finished his second helping of crumble and Will was helping Mia to stack the dishwasher and make the coffee.

I was impressed with Tom. I had not particularly thought of him as a good actor, but when we left the table and moved to the settees, Tom said, "Hey Derek, have you ever driven one of these?" and pointed to one of the new hydrogen cars featured in an article in *The Cambridgeshire Weekly*. Derek took the paper and had a look. "Oh yes," he said, "My area boss has one…" and they started to discuss the performance of the car. Tom gave me a quick look and I got up and said, "I'll help Mia," and went into the kitchen.

As I put mugs on the tray I whispered to Mia, "We've got to talk," then took the tray through before Derek could get suspicious. Mia followed me through almost at once with the coffee pot and asked if we'd mind if she watched the news. As when I visited last time, I was surprised that she watched such a right-wing, pro-Alliance channel. My parents had subscribed to the BBC when it lost its public funding, but perhaps Will and Mia had to be careful, as we all did, not to be seen as extremists. Then I said, genuinely weary, "I need to go to bed now. Goodnight everyone."

As I stood to leave the room Mia said, "Oh Carrie, would you mind if I just get something out of the wardrobe in your room?" Then, smiling at us all, "We're using the glove puppets with the little ones in Sunday School tomorrow." She followed me upstairs.

★ ★ ★

There really were glove puppets in the bottom of the wardrobe and Mia stayed only a few seconds in the room, but just long enough to say, "We'll come and talk later," before she left.

It must have been two hours later when at last there was the quietest knock on our door and Will and Mia came in. They were both still dressed, but the landing light was off and we didn't turn on any lights in our room either. Tom and I were in bed, and Mia and Will perched on the bed too. "I thought Derek was never going to go to sleep," whispered Will. "But he's snoring like a hurricane now!" chuckled Mia.

I explained what I had overheard, keeping my whispers as quiet as I could. When I had finished there was a long silence. Mia tiptoed to the door and opened it, listening for sounds. "Still snoring," she whispered when she was back in her place by my feet.

"I don't really know what's going on," whispered Will, thoughtfully. "We've known Ephraim for several years but he's never gone off like this before... and this Derek guy... it's not easy to warm to him, is it?"

Mia was more direct. "If he's talking to someone he calls Commander," she hissed, "then I don't trust him at all. Sounds like the ATTF to me."

"That's what I thought," I agreed.

Tom said cautiously, "But Derek thinks Ephraim is ATTF."

"So I understand," whispered Will. "Well, that would be a turn up for the books."

We could not see each other's faces because we were sitting in the dark, but when she spoke next I could hear an unusual vulnerability in Mia's voice. "I'm so glad the twins aren't here," she said.

Will moved and put his arm round Mia. "We'll manage this," he whispered reassuringly.

We were all quiet for a few moments. Then, "First things first," whispered Will. "If either of these two gentlemen are ATTF, and we are raided, they need to find a perfectly ordinary vicarage with nothing unusual going on. I'm sorry, Carrie and Tom, but I think we need to get you out of here."

"Where can they go?" hissed Mia. "Carrie's in no state…"

I thought I could hear a smile in Will's voice. "I've got the perfect solution," he whispered. "Tom and Carrie, you need to dress and pack. Be careful not to leave anything at all behind. Mia love, do we have the kids' sleeping bags anywhere handy?"

★ ★ ★

Creeping out twenty minutes later, without turning on any lights, reminded me of antics when I was younger: a midnight feast with my cousins, or the time when we teenagers had a silence on the hill one Sunday morning as the sun rose. I could hear Derek's steady snoring and, once again, the click of the back door opening. Will had an old-fashioned battery torch to light our way, and we stopped to put our shoes on, and followed him.

It was late, there were few lights on in the houses on the village side of the vicarage or in the windows in the tree-lined estate of larger houses opposite, but it was not yet midnight; the street lights were still on. Will whispered something to Mia, who gave us both a hug and then crept back inside, and Will beckoned to us to follow him. We walked softly to the dark building on the other side of the vicarage, the old volunteer fire station, and walked round to the side of it.

Will stopped at a door, just like an ordinary house door, and took out some keys. It was very dark there. The hedge on the edge of the vicarage property was quite high and we were in total shadow. It was a very dark night. Will fumbled a little then unlocked the door and let us in. He followed after us and closed the door behind him.

"The fire station?" I could not tell whether Tom was surprised or impressed.

"Volunteer fire station," agreed Will, talking in a normal voice which for a moment seemed dangerous, so that I wanted to hiss, "Sh!"

"The vicar traditionally always has a spare key," explained Will. "Common sense when we live next door. To be sure the first of the crew can get in if he doesn't have his key with him. Or her, of course."

He waved his torch around. There was one rather old-fashioned-looking fire engine, the sort with a ladder on it, and various bits and pieces of equipment. There was another ladder leading up to a sort of mezzanine floor at the back.

"The office," indicated Will. "Such as it is. I think you should sleep up there." He started to climb the ladder, waving the torch ahead of him and leaving Tom and me in the dark. Half way up he said over his shoulder, "There's electric light here, but there are three small windows upstairs. If people saw lights on in the fire station it really would cause a stir, so we're stuck with my torch, I'm afraid!" Then, after a bit of scrambling around on Will's part, "Okay, throw the sleeping bags up," then, "Right, up you come. It could be much worse."

With Will holding the torch we explored our new bedroom. There was a table and six plastic chairs, stacked in one corner. There was a sink and a kettle. Will tried the tap, "The water's still on," he said, "and I can't see why you shouldn't use the kettle." He opened and closed a couple of cupboards fixed to the wall. "There's nothing to make a drink with, though," he added. "So you have the great choice of hot or cold water!"

Tom started to unroll the first of the sleeping bags. "No sleeping mats, I'm afraid," commented Will.

"That's okay," said Tom. "We'll manage."

"Then I'm off," said Will. "Don't come out until we tell you it's safe."

"What if there's a fire?" asked Tom. "Won't the fire crew find us?"

"Better just keep your fingers crossed," said Will as he started to climb down the ladder. Then, when only his head showed, looking a bit strange by the light of the torch, "Or you could pray," he added.

So when the door had closed behind Will and the other sleeping bag was unrolled, we climbed into our makeshift beds, still clothed because it was so cold, and held hands, and kept a long, deep silence together.

★ ★ ★

I don't know if Tom slept, but I went into a sort of drifting, half-waking, half-sleeping state in which I think I knew where I was but ideas and images just flickered through my mind in no particular order. I was not cold in the sleeping bag, curled up against Tom with my head on his arm, and it was incredibly quiet. When we first settled down we could still see the vague glow from the street light through the high office windows, but next time I opened my eyes it was pitch dark. When I opened them again there was a greyish light outside, and I could feel the tension in Tom's body.

I started to stretch but Tom squeezed my shoulder and breathed into my ear, "Sh, Carrie! Someone's coming in!"

I held my breath, and I heard it too: the gentle sound of a door opening slowly and the crunch of something under a shoe. We froze, and my heart pounded.

Then, "Tom? Carrie?" It was the voice of Ephraim.

Tom said, quite quietly, "We're up here, Ephraim."

We heard him walking across the floor downstairs, and the creek of the ladder, then his head and shoulders appeared, and there was Ephraim, smiling in the dim light and climbing nimbly into the office.

He was carrying a backpack, which he swung onto the floor and started to open. "Well, Friends," he said cheerfully, "this is turning into rather more of an adventure for you than I had anticipated. Here, have some breakfast!" He took out a flask and poured coffee into the lid and a spare mug, then passed us each a bread roll wrapped in plastic film.

As we ate Ephraim stood up and prowled around the little mezzanine area. "This was a good idea of Will's," he commented. "They send their love."

"Thanks," said Tom through his egg and bacon sandwich.

"Ephraim, what's happening?" I asked. "Everything is so weird!"

Ephraim sat down again. "It is, isn't it?" he agreed, and now that the light was brightening I saw that he had a real sparkle in his eyes, as if he were playing a big joke on somebody. Then he added, "Oh, and before we talk about anything else, I need to tell you that Billy is safely in Europe. You don't need to know more now, but later, when you're safe too, I'll tell you how you can contact her."

It might have been partly the hot coffee and the breakfast roll, but I was feeling happily and deeply reassured. It was so good to have Ephraim back. When I was in the same room as Derek I felt ill at ease and confused. With Ephraim sitting there smiling at us I felt as if everything was under control.

"So what happens now?" asked Tom.

"Ah, yes..." answered Ephraim. "Well now a rather tricky game begins..."

We both waited. "I arrived back a couple of hours ago," he went on. "We had some... let us say some issues... in getting Billy out, and there were a couple of other things that came up unexpectedly. Mia has explained what's been happening here while I was away."

"Why do you think Derek is here?" I asked. "He was talking to someone he called Commander."

"So I'm told." Ephraim looked away, staring up, out of one of the high windows at the dull, grey morning sky. Then he looked back at us. "This is rather complicated," he said, "and if I can, I want to keep you right out of it."

"Well, we seem to be in the middle of it!" pointed out Tom.

"Actually," Ephraim's eyes were sparkling again, "to all intents and purposes you seem to have vanished!"

"What do you mean?" Tom queried.

"Well," and this time Ephraim grinned at us both, "look at it from Derek's point of view. He is waking up about now in a vicarage. There seem to be just two people living there at the moment. The vicar has gone off to the little church in the next village to take early morning communion, the vicar's wife is preparing to cook him a hearty breakfast when he returns. The spare room is neat and clean, with fresh sheets on the bed, in case they have visitors. The children are expected back later and their rooms look just the way they will have left them a couple of days ago. The only unusual thing about the vicarage this morning is that a stranger turned up yesterday and seems reluctant to leave."

"Oh!" We both spoke together. Tom added, "Ephraim, does Derek know you're back? He was waiting for you."

"I dare say." Ephraim paused, then said, "It's very sad when someone is so deluded. He needs help, really."

"What do you mean?"

At first, when Ephraim answered, I didn't follow his reasoning. "Will and Mia have a very special ministry," he said. "Will especially is the sort of man who inspires confidence in people who have deep trust issues, and even quite serious neuroses."

"Yes, but…"

Ephraim smiled at my interruption but just kept talking. "Mostly he has counselling sessions in his office. You might have come across a young man called Patrick on one of your visits? And there is a dear old woman who cleans the church, who is an elective mute apart from when she talks to Will." He paused again, and I finished my coffee while we waited.

"Occasionally," Ephraim continued, "someone turns up

out of the blue with nowhere to go. They are good people, Will and Mia. They demonstrate that this country, now we are in the Alliance, is a more caring and compassionate society." Tom gave a little gasp but Ephraim gave him a sort of direct look, and kept going. "They won't turn such people away," he went on. "They try to help them."

Tom interrupted, "But, Ephraim..."

Ephraim just kept going. "They offer these people a bed for the night, and try to sort out a way forward for them. But of course, they have kids, so they never put strangers up in the spare room. They let them sleep on the futon in Will's office, away from the main part of the house. And if the kids are home, they lock their doors at night."

Tom's frown had gone and he was beginning to smile a little. "What do two such good people do if they can't help a stranger?" he asked.

Ephraim gave Tom a broad and approving smile. "Ah, in that case," he said, "they will call the Mental Health people. It is better for someone to be where he or she can get professional help."

"So?" Tom prompted.

Ephraim stood and took one of the chairs from the pile in the corner. He put it by the wall below one of the high windows and said, "Will returns from St George's around 8.45am – any time now. St Mary's has a family service at half past ten today, complete with a play about the Prodigal Son, performed with glove puppets I believe. So if Will and Mia decide they need the Mental Health people to come, I expect they will arrange it for some time within the next hour or so." He stood on the chair, looked out of the window, then stood down again. "You should be able to see the whole thing from here."

"What about you?" Tom asked. "Where's your car? Or do you just keep out of the way, like us?"

Ephraim smiled again. "Oh, I arrive back from my friend's

in Grantchester any time now, hoping to have breakfast with Will and Mia before going to church with them." He stood again. "In fact," he added, "I'd better be gone. It would blow the whole story if I were to be seen leaving the fire station!" With that he headed for the ladder, climbed down out of sight and left the building.

★ ★ ★

I have read whole books in which none of the characters ever seem to need the bathroom, but the uncomfortable truth was that the coffee, welcome though it had been, had left me desperate for the loo. There was nothing on the mezzanine floor, but when Tom explored downstairs he found a cubicle with a stained toilet and a roll of toilet paper with Father Christmases and holly printed on it in green and red, so that we both started giggling. We didn't dare flush the toilet so after we had both used it we just put the lid down and went back upstairs, feeling a little awkward about this lack of hygiene.

We had only just rolled up our sleeping bags when we heard sounds from outside. Tom grabbed another chair and placed it next to the one Ephraim had moved, but even standing on it I wasn't tall enough to see out, and I was feeling a bit queasy too, so Tom stood and peered out, and told me what he could see.

"Will's home," he said, first of all. "His bike is propped up against the wheelie bins. Mia's come out to give him a hug. They're talking about something." Then, "Oh, this is what Ephraim was talking about. An ambulance has arrived!"

I heard the electric hum of the vehicle, then the banging of the doors. "Two medics have got out," Tom told me. "They're shaking hands with Will and Mia. They're going into the vicarage."

For a few minutes there was nothing else to see, and I commented, "I wish we knew what was going on in there!"

Tom said, "I can see a couple of people standing in the drive. Oh, I think one might just be the papergirl. Mia's come out again… she's talking to them… they're going away. Mia's gone back inside."

There was another pause, then we could hear a second vehicle approaching, driving fast. "What!" Tom suddenly sounded alarmed. "Carrie!" he exclaimed, "I think it's… it is! It's the ATTF! They've parked in front of the drive. There are four of them." I could hear car doors slamming. "Carrie, they're armed!"

I felt a sort of tightness in my chest and a feeling of panic. "Oh Tom!"

But Tom just went on with his running commentary. I could hear the noise of someone pounding on a door as Tom said, "They're at the front door. It looks like a raid!"

There was some shouting, then a quiet voice. Will had answered the door.

"He's letting them in," said Tom, standing on tiptoes and peering sideways because the angle was bad for watching that part of the vicarage. "Oh, Mia's there too!" he added. "She's shaking their hands!"

"Tom," I gasped, "do you think Derek was right? Do you think we have done something to get the vicarage raided?"

"I don't… Oh, now what?" exclaimed Tom. "Ephraim's just arrived. He hasn't got the van; he's got that metallic blue hybrid."

"What's he doing? What's happening?" I was desperate to see for myself, but I felt sick too.

"I'm not sure… Oh, the medics are coming out. They've got Derek. Carrie, they've got him in some sort of handlock." As Tom said that I could hear shouting. It was Derek, sounding angry and frightened. He was yelling, "I called the ATTF. It was me! You need to listen to me! I know what's going on here!"

There was a babble of voices. I thought I could hear Will and Mia, and then the quiet, controlled murmur of Ephraim. From the fire station we could only hear properly when someone raised his or her voice, so the next words we heard clearly were Derek's again.

"But they're people smugglers! They're traffickers!" he was yelling, sounding more and more frantic. "They had a young couple here, I can tell you all about them!"

We heard the quiet, soothing voice of Mia, but not her words, then, "Hold still!" commanded a different voice. "Don't worry, we'll check it all out. Keep still!"

Tom looked down at me. "They're restraining Derek," he said. "They're putting him in the ambulance."

"Now what?" I prompted, as Tom stood on tiptoes again to peer down the drive.

For a couple of minutes Tom didn't answer, then I heard the sound of several engines being turned on. "The ATTF are moving their car," explained Tom. "They were blocking the drive... The ambulance is reversing out. They're leaving. Hey Carrie, they've turned on their blue light!" He was quiet a moment. "Oh, I see," he said next. "The ATTF and Ephraim have parked alongside each other. Everyone's going inside." He was quiet again, then he climbed off the chair. "There's nothing else to see," he said. "They've all gone inside. I wish I knew what was happening!"

We sat quietly, waiting for the next development. Tom said, "Shall we have some silence?" We sat and held hands, but to be honest I couldn't concentrate. I was listening for any sounds from outside our refuge, wondering what would happen next, trying to work it all out.

★ ★ ★

It was Mia who came to give us the all clear, after church. The ATTF car had left at the same time as Mia and Ephraim, and after Will had cycled off to prepare for the family service. Tom watched them go and told me about the shaking of hands and one of the officers slapping Ephraim on the back. "You know," said Tom, "I'm sure those guys know Ephraim. It's obvious." The church bells were ringing and when they stopped there was a Sunday morning quietness over the village. We were cold, and put the sleeping bags round us like blankets. I started coughing and Tom rooted around among the stuff we had packed so hurriedly the night before, and found my cough medicine, and also the warm fleeces I had put in the bottom of the bag. For some reason I was feeling uncomfortable about Derek. "I wonder what's happening to him now?" I asked. "You know, perhaps he was right about Ephraim being ATTF."

"Hmm. He'll be okay," Tom reassured me, "I think."

There were five of us for lunch, and it was wonderfully warm in the vicarage. Mia served us French onion soup with fried bread croutons. "I'm saving the chicken for the evening," she explained, "when the twins are back."

"So what happened," I asked, "about the ATTF?"

Ephraim looked down at his soup bowl. Will and Mia looked at each other. Mia reached out and put a kind hand on my arm. "It's really better for you not think about that," she said. "Your lift will arrive in about an hour, with new papers for you both. Try not to think about everything that's happened here."

CHAPTER 7

It is not as cold in Scotland as I expected. Tom says that my pregnancy kept me warm through those first few months, but the flat is snug and south facing, so I think I would have been comfortable anyhow. It was surprisingly difficult to get used to not having to watch what we said, and to not putting our DeVs in cupboards or smothered by cushions to protect our privacy. There is some bad feeling about the number of refugees arriving from south of the border, but we are protected from most of that by the warmth shown to us by the members of our new Meeting. Anyhow, now that Tom's business is taking off and he is employing a local school leaver as his apprentice, it is easier to feel that we are giving back a little, to this country which is already so good to us.

There was an international conference for our Society in Berlin at the end of May and we were able to send a message to Mum and Dad via the Scottish delegates, and later we heard back, although we don't know how that message reached us. I miss them, but they sound very upbeat.

When the baby was born the names we had first thought of around Christmas didn't seem right. I wanted to call him Ephraim, but Tom pointed out that we still didn't know for sure what the original Ephraim's relationship was with the ATTF. It is true, there are unanswered questions. In the end we have called him Will. Will Thomas is a cheerful, messy little chap and we adore him. When our papers are through and we can travel freely around Europe we plan to go to France for a little while to visit Billy, although my energy levels are still poor.

Tom is full of plans for the future. He wants the business to grow, he wants a baby brother or sister for our little Will, and he wants to get involved with the group at Meeting which helps new arrivals. I am content to be part of the Meeting, to do what I can do and to rest when I need to rest. I understand now that we all have to live with something: a bad experience in the past, a medical condition, a separation or an unfulfilled dream. South of the border they have to live with the ATTF. These things might feel like wild animals, things in our lives which we can't control or predict. If we let them, they might spring up and attack us, but if we depend on the Spirit we will know peace. They make us more dependent on the Light. I am not alone in living with a leopard.